UMA'S
HEAD

UMA'S HEAD

A NOVEL

KRISTIN KELLY

STICKS ON FIRE BOOKS

Published by Sticks on Fire Books, La Jolla, CA

Edited and designed by Girl Friday Productions
www.girlfridayproductions.com

Cover design: David Fassett
Project management: Kristin Duran
Image credits: cover © Adobe Stock/Vitou CG Art,
Shutterstock/d_odin, Adobe Stock/Noppasinw

ISBN (paperback): 979-8-9990718-0-4
ISBN (ebook): 979-8-9990718-1-1

Library of Congress Control Number: 2025912430

First edition

To the three generations of the family:
Carolyn, David, Justin, Corinne, Van, and Kelly

Where, for a start, is Uma's Head?
—*The Economist,* June 7, 2007

Shiva and Uma. Temple of Banteay Srei, second half of the tenth century CE. Sandstone, ca. 25 × 20 × 17 in. Collection of the National Museum of Cambodia. Photograph © John McDermott.

PROLOGUE

Phnom Penh, Cambodia
April 12, 1975

The Americans were departing from Landing Zone Hotel.

The military had named the evacuation Operation Eagle Pull, and for those few who remained in the city, the order to leave had come yesterday. They had been told to report to a soccer field a little over half a mile northeast of the United States embassy, now designated as LZ Hotel.

He had gone to the national museum that afternoon to say good-bye to the staff, with whom he had worked sporadically over the past couple of years. Many had become his friends. He doubted that most of them would survive more than a few months after the arrival of the Khmer Rouge. As he and his colleagues at the embassy abandoned Phnom Penh to its fate, none doubted that a bloodbath was coming.

Feeling as if he were sleepwalking through the eerie early morning calm of Phnom Penh, he headed south, paralleling the Tonle Sap River for the last time. It had rained a couple of days before, the first indicator of an early monsoon. Today was hot and bright.

The city had changed a great deal since his arrival in 1973 as the war's impact on Cambodia had increased. Over half a million refugees had fled the countryside, overwhelming the capital city's infrastructure and inhabitants. The Khmer Rouge had been within artillery range of the city for almost two years now, and the swollen population was on constant edge.

During his time there, Phnom Penh had rapidly deteriorated from the formerly graceful and prosperous city that, for years, had been able to defy the war swirling around it. Once called the Pearl of Asia, it was now a paranoid place governed by incompetent and corrupt officials.

Still, he would miss this city. Under the garbage and deterioration, glimpses of the old elegance still remained, and the morning markets, though poorly stocked these days, retained some of their vibrancy. Most of all, though, he would miss the lovely Buddhist people of Cambodia, and particularly the staff at the museum.

As many of them were initially suspected by US intelligence of being Khmer Rouge sympathizers, he had been assigned the task of investigating them. When it became clear they were not, he was reassigned to other embassy duties, but his connection to the museum did not falter. Its collection and dedicated staff had deeply moved him, and he had immersed himself in the art and culture of this extraordinary country. Even though his job responsibilities changed, he continued to spend his free time there, working with some of the staff. It sickened him to think that much of the collection might be destroyed by the incoming zealots after hearing rumors of the Khmer Rouge mining the temples at Angkor, even using them for target practice. He believed those rumors were true.

It had been especially difficult saying goodbye to his friends given that they didn't have access to the same information he did. Many of them seemed to believe the Khmer Rouge were true liberators and their imminent arrival in the capital city would mean better times for all of Cambodia. He had tried to encourage the museum staff, including his friend Sokha, to leave the city with their families, but Sokha and most of the others were determined to stay.

As he walked through the galleries of the museum building toward the exit, an overpowering urge for a memento of his time in Cambodia hit him. He stopped before a tenth-century sculpture from the temple of Banteay Srei, northeast of the main Angkor site. The small sculpture, one of the most beloved in the museum, was only about twenty-six inches high and seventeen inches wide, and it depicted the Hindu god Shiva, the destroyer and creator and also the loving spirit of light and wisdom, with Uma, goddess of beauty and divine wisdom, seated on his left knee. In a tender gesture uncommon in Khmer art, Shiva and Uma had their arms entwined around one another's backs. The sculpture was one of his favorite pieces, and its temple of origin was one of his favorite destinations, though it had been too dangerous for him to visit for years. Uma's head had broken off the sculpture during an attempted theft the previous year, and the museum had recovered the head. His friend Sokha, after giving it a basic cleaning, had attempted to reattach the goddess's head to the body.

But the join Sokha created was not solid, and with a forceful yank, the head now separated from the rest of the sculpture. He placed it in the bag he had been carrying and headed for the museum doors. Although it couldn't have weighed more than fifteen pounds, the head did weigh down the bag, but not as much as the guilt weighed on him. He rationalized, albeit sadly, that this small piece of Cambodia's heritage probably didn't matter much at this juncture. Lost in thought, memories, and worry about the fate of his friends and the museum's collection, as well as the fate of the country itself, he failed to see a figure watching him from an adjacent gallery.

Once at the LZ Hotel, he found a helicopter waiting for him and hoisted himself, with the bag slung over his shoulder, on board. The chopper ascended quickly and swung sharply to the southwest toward waiting ships in the Gulf of Thailand. He sat with the bag at his feet and peered out the window at the poor, war-torn countryside of Cambodia. He would be back someday. He would be back.

CHAPTER 1

Bangkok, Thailand
Early Tuesday morning

"Don't fuck this up." Nigel paused for effect before going on, murmuring into the burner phone. "I cannot stress enough how important it is that this operation go smoothly and without any problems. No one sees anything. No harm done."

He still didn't know how the team was going to pull this off. They were more accustomed to working at remote archaeological sites, and he didn't think that any of them were as sharp as the tools they were experts at using. But he trusted his field team leader, to whom he was speaking. Nigel also realized that he had to let go. He had no choice. But could they actually do this successfully? He knew his team leader would never tell him that he couldn't do something even if he was worried about accomplishing it. It was the Thai way to try to figure out the situation and make it work.

The voice on the other end of the phone replied, "Yes, there's no problem. Everything is OK. We have a plan. We have walked through it twice since yesterday morning. It works. The guys are ready."

"See that they are. No screwups. Text me when you're done and we'll move on to the next steps. And please, I cannot emphasize enough, no harm!"

"OK, no problem, no problem. Talk soon."

Nigel tapped the phone with his finger to cut off the call and stood staring out the window for a moment. "Our last operation," he muttered, "and this complication surfaces." It might be just a small complication. He had only learned of it in the last few days. He had confidence. But this was also something new, something they had never done before. He sighed and shook his head, telling himself it would be fine. It always had been.

Still, Nigel was worried.

CHAPTER 2

Phnom Penh
Tuesday morning

Sam Heng was preoccupied and lost in thought as he walked early Tuesday morning along the quay on the bank of the Tonle Sap River. There was a lot to cover on the Zoom call to which he was headed. He planned to take it at the National Museum of Cambodia rather than back at home so he would have access to files and other information. He looked forward to seeing his friends and colleagues Sarah Burroughs and Nigel Sanderson, if only on a computer screen, and to working through the current issues they faced. There were many complications with the massive exhibition they were organizing, though the issues were gradually being resolved.

Heng's wife, Som Jorani, often remarked how completely devoted he was to his work and his friends. She was right, but he was just as devoted to her and her career as a rising Phnom Penh–based artist. Heng was also—according to Jorani—brilliant, charming, obsessive, and an occasional goofball who had surprisingly come home from graduate school at Berkeley looking like an American. She often ribbed him about his wardrobe of jeans or khakis, polos or long-sleeved shirts, and sneakers or sandals. But he knew she adored his warm brown eyes and quick smile, and she also loved to give him those frequent reminders to get a haircut. The one thing she didn't often comment about, but which he knew to be absolutely true regardless of what she thought or said, was that he was a star in the field of Khmer art history.

Heng was not generally given to introspection. But in the past weeks he had been forced to drastically rethink who he was and what he was doing, and he was beginning to feel the strain of trying to cope with all of it. He knew he could be too sensitive about his personal relationships, but it seemed to him that two of the most important people in his life—his best friend, Anada Srisawat, and Nigel, his mentor and benefactor—had not been themselves recently. Coupled with the discovery he had just made at the museum, he found himself unsure about a lot of things that he'd thought he knew. But he had tried to compartmentalize all this because, after years of preparation, he had become involved in a once-in-a-lifetime exhibition with Sarah, an American curator of Asian art, and Nigel, another renowned expert on Khmer art. The project had been approved and funded, and it promised to be spectacular.

Still, he couldn't quite shake the reservations he had been having. Walking along the river past Wat Ounalom Monastery, he thought more about Anada, whom he had seen a few times on his latest visit to Bangkok. He and Anada had known each other for what seemed like forever, and they could frequently finish each other's sentences. They had studied art history together at Chulalongkorn University in Bangkok, spent long days visiting sites and museums, and passionately discussed the art that so mesmerized them both. Anada was Thai, and Heng was Cambodian, though he had been raised in Bangkok, and although their respective governments sometimes had disputes, the two friends never did. His relationship with Anada was rock solid. Or at least he'd thought it was, until this last trip to Bangkok.

On the surface, everything had been fine, like old times, as they barhopped and ate dinner over the course of a couple of nights and chatted about everything under the sun. But Heng had thought his friend seemed preoccupied, and he'd tried, unsuccessfully, to draw him out. In the end, Heng decided to let it go. He knew that Anada always had ongoing concerns about his family: His father was dead, his mother old and sick, and his sister permanently disabled. Anada had always been the glue holding the family together. Maybe there was something more going on with that part of his life? Anada had not offered anything, and although there had been a few moments when Anada looked as if he wanted to open up, he had pulled back and said nothing. So Heng had decided not to ask.

While in Bangkok, Heng had stayed, as he normally did, in a guest room of Nigel's spectacular apartment. Heng normally loved the break from his hectic life in Phnom Penh and was able to accomplish a great deal whenever he went to Thailand. Not many would consider frantic Bangkok to be a respite from slower Phnom Penh, but he had fewer responsibilities when he was there, and his phone rang less frequently.

Now, however, in addition to his observations about Anada, Heng was troubled by his discovery several weeks ago and Nigel's reaction to it. As part of his research for the exhibition, which would open in San Diego and then move to Phnom Penh, Heng had been searching through the archives of Cambodia's national museum. In a cabinet, shoved at the back of a jammed drawer, he had found a box containing a diary that had changed everything for him. Ever since, he had not been able to completely process the improbable information contained in it, and he became preoccupied, finding it hard to concentrate on anything else. He had even been short with Jorani, which had never happened in the past.

He hadn't seen much of Nigel since the discovery, though he had spoken to him a little about it, mentioning it in passing on the phone soon after he had found it. Heng had not told him much about the contents or that he was deeply troubled by what he had read. Nigel had expressed some interest in seeing it. He'd also made it clear that the diary probably could not be incorporated into the exhibition and therefore was not a topic for major discussion. But then Nigel had seemed to lose interest altogether when he'd realized Heng had not brought the diary with him on that last trip to Bangkok.

After turning right onto Street 178, away from the river quay and toward the national museum, which had formed one of the axes of his life, Heng walked along the edge of the park toward the gate. Just then, a bulky figure emerged from between two buildings across the street and grabbed him. The last things he remembered, before losing consciousness, were a jab in his arm, being thrown into the back of a car, the door slamming shut, and the car speeding off. They drove a short distance before turning left. As Heng began to pass out, his last thought was that he was pretty sure they were heading south on Monivong Boulevard.

CHAPTER 3

Bangkok
Tuesday morning

"Heng, answer your damn phone," Sarah muttered to herself while waiting for Heng's voicemail to pick up for the fourth time. She started in on another cup of strong black coffee as she stood at the window of her room on the tenth floor of the Shangri-La Hotel, looking out over the fast-moving muddy waters of the Chao Phraya. The vast chaos and freneticism of Bangkok never failed to enthrall her. She once again thought about how lucky she was to be here organizing the exhibition of a lifetime with her favorite colleagues.

Sarah was a product of California sun, sport, and surf. With the exception of the years she had spent in graduate school in New York City, she had lived her entire life in California. But she had periodically spent long stretches of time in libraries, museums, and research centers across Southeast Asia, Europe, and the United States. At almost fifty, she still had the blond hair that had been one of her best features since she was a little girl, though these days some of the color came from the salon. She was also tall and still relatively athletic. No one would ever have called her beautiful, but there was an intelligence and liveliness about her that attracted people. There had been a number of men in her life over the years, but she always joked that Mr. Right had never appeared. Or at least he hadn't wanted to stay. She was single and happy to not have the complications she often saw in the lives of so many of her friends and colleagues.

This freedom had allowed her to choose to be a workaholic in her current position as curator of Southeast Asian art at the Asian art museum in San Diego. The hours were long. The pay wasn't great. The rewards, however, were immeasurable—working alongside smart, committed, perfectionist colleagues and knowing she could make a difference in the world by introducing people to a magnificent cultural heritage completely different from their own. Perhaps best of all, she felt she had a role, albeit a small one, in helping a culturally rich but economically struggling country like Cambodia continue to emerge from an unspeakable past into a brighter future.

She had arrived in Bangkok late the previous night so she could show up on time to a meeting the next morning at the apartment of one of her collaborators, Nigel. Their colleague Heng would Zoom in from Phnom Penh. When she'd arrived, the streets had been full of people eating and chatting.

After just a few hours of sleep, she had showered and eaten breakfast by herself at a riverside table in the hotel restaurant, watching the catfish and carp jump out of the river and resubmerge. Now back in her room, Sarah waited for Heng to return her call. She had yet another cup of coffee and thought about her upcoming meeting at Nigel's.

Almost every Western scholar of Southeast Asian art thought of Nigel as their leader. He had been a mentor to Sarah, and especially to Heng, for many years. Though they'd had disagreements, in part about the murky provenance of many of the objects that filled Nigel's magnificent apartment in Bangkok, no major exhibition of Khmer art was possible without his assistance, and he had generously offered both his collection and expertise to the upcoming show. Sarah was grateful to him for what he had done for her career and for the field. She loved him for his crotchety but straightforward approach, both to scholarship and to other experts in the field, whom he regarded as overly intellectualized eggheads who didn't understand the realities of the culture and background of the art about which they spoke.

Recently, when he had announced that upon his death, his estate would return all the objects in his collection to their country of origin, she had been irrationally proud of him. There was a part of her that wondered why he didn't return the objects now, but she had said nothing about his choice. She was deeply grateful to him for everything. At eighty, he worked harder than anyone else she knew, and he still ran circles around most people, including her.

Sarah thought again about the enormous responsibility she had been given with the organization of this show. She could never clearly explain to her friends who were not in the museum world how important major exhibitions like this were for her and other curators, and how high the stakes were. And the stakes *were* high, particularly for this exhibition. Careers, including hers, were on the line due to the revolutionary concepts underpinning the whole thing. The investment of resources—human, technological, and financial—was staggering. And, in addition to the novel approach to the installation, she and her fellow curators planned to highlight the problem of how so many objects had been illicitly taken from sites around Cambodia, with special attention given to the French exports taken from Cambodia and shipped home to fill the Musée Guimet in Paris. It was a potentially risky approach to a fraught topic. But the time had come to confront these issues clearly and directly in a major exhibition, and the three of them wanted to be the ones to take on the challenge. Nigel had led the efforts on this front. Having made the decision to disperse his collection, he wanted others to do so as well. *There is no zealot like a convert,* Sarah had thought when Nigel had told her of his decision.

Sarah tried Heng's phone one more time before heading down to the lobby in the hotel elevator. While there was still no answer, she wasn't worried. Heng had an annoying habit of either turning his phone off or forgetting to charge it, especially if he was working intently or in the field. He would surface. He always did. She was sure he would appear on-screen, ready to work, during her meeting later that morning with Nigel.

She checked her reflection in the mirror. Having learned over the years to dress for Bangkok's heat and humidity, today was no exception, and she had chosen a loose-fitting, short-sleeved blue linen dress that came to her knees and flat sandals. It didn't matter what she wore, though. She knew she would be dripping by the time she arrived at Nigel's apartment.

Exiting the elevator moments later, she waved at the lobby staff who had been on duty when she arrived just a few hours ago. They were still there. They returned her wave with a wai, the charming Thai gesture of bowing the head over hands held, palms together and chest high, as if in prayer. Sarah had long ago realized she would never master the social niceties of how low to bow and how high to raise her hands. She had decided to stop trying and, depending on the situation, to shake hands, or to nod and smile, and let loose with a "Sawasdee ka," the standard Thai greeting.

Exiting the air-conditioning of the hotel lobby into the steam of a Bangkok morning felt like being hit in the face with a warm, wet towel, which was a curiously comforting feeling. Her glasses fogged up almost instantly. She covered the couple of blocks to the Saphan Taksin BTS station quickly, and by the time she arrived on the platform, she was—as predicted—already melting.

But this was no problem. She was here. She was working. She would soon be with her friends and colleagues. This was her place. All of that made her intensely grateful that life had worked out the way it had.

CHAPTER 4

Bangkok
Tuesday morning

Nigel stood behind his massive teak desk, an antique from the office of a European trading company of a century ago. He looked out over his art-filled and paper-strewn home office, thinking about the agenda for the day with Sarah and Heng. He chuckled to himself: He really was getting too old to be working this hard, not only on an exhibition but in general. He had to admit, though, that it had been exhilarating. He viewed it as a kind of culmination of his career before he truly retired and began to make the arrangements to return the art objects from his considerable collection to their respective countries of origin. Nigel loved his collection and had come to view some of the objects in his apartment almost as members of his family. He knew everything about the stories and mythology of each of the objects and could recite the history of most of them as well, though he admitted that the provenance and more recent history of some of the pieces in his collection were murky.

Though Nigel was a thoroughly American person, he had been

saddled—as he thought of it—with a British first name, which had automatically made people think he was something he was not. In Thailand, though, that didn't matter. Moreover, he had been in Southeast Asia for so long that the thought of returning to the United States, even for a visit, was stressful. He didn't even like to think about it. As the family members of his generation had died over the years, he had returned less and less frequently. He hadn't been back for five years now, and the exhibition opening in San Diego was likely to be his last trip to the land of his birth. His life was in Bangkok, where he was respected locally and could live a life that he could never have dreamed of in the US.

He had access to excellent medical care and to libraries and information and experts. He had a wide circle of friends from all over the world in this city. He had his collection, at least for now. His life in Bangkok was good. It was all he needed or wanted, for the most part—although lately, he had to admit, he was more concerned about his finances, as medical bills had been rising and his income stream would soon be ending. He hoped this concern would dissipate within a few days.

Today, he was focused on this extraordinary exhibition that he, Heng, and Sarah were trying to pull off. It would launch both Sarah's and Heng's careers into the stratosphere. He already knew they were both ambitious, but the rest of the world would soon see this as well, and they could both have their choice of positions after the exhibition opened. That is, if they decided to move on from where they were, though he wasn't sure that either of them was interested in moving.

The logistics surrounding an exhibition of this magnitude, which involved dozens of museums and private collectors, had been formidable. He was glad he wasn't the one who needed to worry about shipping sculptures of such extreme size and weight or deal with all the technology that would be used throughout the galleries. Also, as more of a consultant than curator, he wouldn't have to take full responsibility for the idea Sarah and Heng had fabricated to end the exhibition with not one but two galleries devoted to the continued illicit trafficking of antiquities out of Cambodia. He had acquiesced and even acted enthusiastic, though he admitted to himself that he felt a little uncomfortable about it.

He had one other small concern that had triggered a nagging uneasiness after Heng's visit the week before. Nigel had never had children—at least, he often thought to himself, none that he knew about. But his relationship with Heng was as strong as it might have been with a son, perhaps even more so. He had known the minute he had seen Heng in the refugee camp on the Thai-Cambodian border that he was Sokha's son, and Nigel had done everything in his power to help him. He had brought him to Bangkok. He had paid for Heng's education and seen that he'd had a good start in his chosen field when he grew older. He had remained friends with Heng and tried to be a parental figure, helping Heng navigate tough times. As Heng had grown and matured into a stellar student and scholar of Khmer art, his knowledge of the field and the sites, even the smallest ones in the countryside, had become encyclopedic. Over the years, Nigel had thought about asking Heng to help him out with some of his work. But he never had. And through all this, Nigel had never told Heng that he had known his father in the 1970s.

Last week, Heng had told Nigel about an old diary he had found at the national museum. Nigel had asked him some questions about it and had assumed that Heng would bring it to Bangkok with him when he came, but he had not, which had ended the conversation. Still, Nigel remained concerned about Heng's description of it, as well as his suddenly quiet and removed demeanor. Heng's comment, that he thought they might be able to use some of the contents in one of the galleries of the exhibition, also unsettled Nigel. Still later, Heng had spent some time alone in Nigel's office—something he'd never done before—and there were certain things there that Nigel wanted to keep private. Now he wasn't sure what Heng may or may not have seen. As much as he tried to put all this out of his mind, he found it impossible to do.

CHAPTER 5

Phnom Penh
Tuesday morning

James Carlyle thoughtfully replaced the landline phone's receiver into its cradle. He drummed his fingers on the desk as he looked out the window of his office in the US embassy in Phnom Penh. The conversation he had just finished had gone better than he could have imagined, and it seemed that his new informant, an integral member of the last remaining major antiquities trafficking gang in the region, would deliver on his promise. This might just be the light at the end of a very long and dark tunnel.

He picked up the phone to call the public affairs office at the embassy. He had an idea about how he might leverage an upcoming meeting he had seen on the calendar and hoped they would agree to it.

James had arrived in Phnom Penh three years ago after requesting the posting here with his agency, Homeland Security Investigations. The capital city of Cambodia wasn't a posting that many investigators wanted, and the agency had readily agreed to bring him in to investigate and disrupt the illicit trafficking of antiquities out of Cambodia and into the US. He was passionate about fighting against this criminal activity in Southeast Asia—James did his job well. But the Department of Homeland Security wasn't aware of an equally important motive for his request for a post in Phnom Penh. Over the years, he had become fixated on finding out what had happened to his father many years ago in Vietnam. He had read every report and pursued every channel available to him in DC. But he never found the information he craved about his father's fate. He had hoped this posting would give him the opportunity to meet with the one person who knew exactly what had happened that night outside Tay Ninh.

Finally, his efforts within the department were falling into place. His relationships with authorities in both Thailand and Cambodia were excellent, and now an American curator of Asian art had arrived to talk to embassy staff about the exhibition she was organizing.

His personal quest and his professional work were headed for a major collision.

CHAPTER 6

Bangkok
Tuesday morning

Half an hour after leaving the hotel, Sarah negotiated Soi Kasem San 3, the narrow street that led to Nigel's apartment. She was glad she had worn sandals and a loose-fitting dress. At this instant, her phone registered 92 degrees and 98 percent humidity, and it wasn't even 10:00 a.m. Sweat poured down her back as she rang the bell at Nigel's door.

"Yes?" came the disembodied voice of Nigel's housekeeper from the intercom box.

"Ahmi, help! It's Sarah. I'm early but I'm melting out here. Can you let me in?"

The door buzzed, and she pushed it open into the blessed coolness of the building's lobby. Nigel's apartment was on the fifth and sixth floors, at the top, and he had his own roof deck that had a panoramic view of the city. It overlooked the nearby Jim Thompson House, famous for its art collection and beautiful gardens—and doubly famous for the mystery surrounding what had happened to its owner. She turned to look at herself in the elevator mirror. It was a good thing she and Nigel had known each other for so many years. Her hair was flat and her makeup melting, and sweat stains were beginning to creep across part of her linen dress. She laughed out loud.

On the fifth floor, Ahmi opened the apartment door and looked her up and down, politely saying nothing, and beckoning her onto the polished floor of the foyer. Sarah couldn't remember when Ahmi had come to work for Nigel. It had been a long time ago. She was a tiny ethnically Akha woman with long black hair that she wore pinned up. Sometimes, if no guests were expected, she dressed in the bright traditional textiles of the Akha. Today, though, she had on a plain black dress. Sarah felt like a giant standing next to her.

"Sarah, my dear!" Nigel came bursting through his office door, situated directly across the entrance foyer from the front door. His assistant, Bona, followed several steps behind him. Nigel stopped abruptly before hugging her. "Oh, my dear Sarah . . . hmm, hot enough for you here in our city of the angels? Have you been swimming in Khlong Saen Saep? But of course, you were a champion swimmer in college! Me, I never learned to swim. I was never able to figure out the coordination required."

Nigel glanced at his assistant, who seemed to Sarah to be as wide as he was tall. "Bona, I think we were finished?" Bona pivoted and headed for the kitchen without responding. Returning his attention to Sarah, Nigel's tone was as crisp as always. "Sarah, you're early. But let's get started." He then shook his head and practically barked at his housekeeper. "How about some iced tea, Ahmi, please?"

As Ahmi headed toward the kitchen, Sarah called after her. "Ahmi, Western iced tea? No sweetened condensed milk, please."

Ahmi nodded.

Attired in his Southeast Asian uniform, Nigel wore a white polo shirt and khakis with Birkenstock sandals. Aside from the times they had been in formal meetings, Sarah had never seen him dressed in anything else. He looked older and more fragile than the last time she had seen him, but he was still quite remarkable, lively and quick in both his movements and his thought process. He enveloped her in a massive hug.

He pointed to his right. "And Sarah, you know where you can freshen up in the guest bathroom, just over there." He had already turned away from her before she could reply and was striding quickly toward his office. In the bathroom, she combed her hair and pulled it up into a ponytail, polished her smudged glasses, and then managed to dry off her skin. The air-conditioning would soon take care of drying her clothes.

A few minutes later, Sarah met up with Nigel in his office. She relaxed now that she was back in the familiar welcoming, cluttered, and cheerful environment, though at the same time she felt a familiar envy of Nigel's magazine-worthy apartment, with its teak furnishings and ancient works of art. It was a far cry from her small, cramped condo, with its furniture only a slight upgrade from IKEA, back in San Diego. She thought wryly, not for the first time, that though she loved her job and had a classy title and great job benefits, her income only allowed her to live like a graduate student, albeit a rich one.

As she walked into Nigel's office, Sarah felt a flood of affection and respect. She truly loved this man for all he had done for her and for the field. She had been lucky to have him as a friend and mentor, and she didn't know where she would be today if he had not helped her.

The iced tea was already waiting for her on a small table next to one of the chairs. After picking up the glass and drinking most of the tea in one long gulp, she felt better. "I hope I didn't look this bedraggled the first time we met at Ban Chiang, when you visited the excavation site to see Heng and Anada and me."

Sarah remembered vividly that summer at Ban Chiang, her first prolonged experience in Southeast Asia. She had sent a blind letter to the excavation director asking whether she might join the work site to gain experience. He had agreed and referred her to Nigel, who was funding some of the work. Nigel had also agreed that the excavation would take her on, sight unseen, and he could provide a small stipend, simply on the basis of a short phone call. The project had been an extraordinary learning experience for her, and in addition to the team's remarkable finds, she would never forget the intense heat of the day followed by the relative cooling of the afternoon monsoon rains.

The Ban Chiang excavation had been her introduction to the early civilizations of Southeast Asia, and she had been hooked from the minute she stepped off the plane at the Udon Thani airport, where Heng had picked her up. She had also met Anada then, a graduate student at the National University of Singapore and a lifelong friend of Heng's. The three of them had spent an intensely close summer together. It was a glorious and special time in her life.

As she looked around Nigel's office, two pots on an upper shelf caught her eye. "I see that you still have those two pots that the Ban Chiang excavation director gave you. I thought you were going to return them to the ministry of culture."

"Yes, they are still among my favorite pieces—so many memories!—and yes, as I've told you, after this exhibition is put to bed, I intend to start the paperwork process of sending them and everything else back once I am no longer around."

He paused and looked at her again before continuing, "I am thrilled to see you, my dear Sarah. Though you *are* wet! Come, we have much to talk about. Will Heng be joining us? He was supposed to call on Zoom earlier so that he and I could catch up on more personal news, but he didn't show up."

"That's odd and also annoying. I tried calling him multiple times this morning and there was no answer. Crap," she said, shaking her head. "I can't believe he would blow off this meeting and discussion. I'll try again."

She once again rang Heng's mobile phone, which once again went to voicemail after four rings. "Heng, where are you? I'm at Nigel's apartment and we're waiting for you. Sending you another Zoom invitation in case you've lost it." Sarah hung up and cut and pasted the Zoom link into an email before hitting the send arrow.

Nigel seemed fidgety, which she knew meant he was impatient to begin. Everything always had to be on Nigel's timetable. As if to reinforce her thoughts, he said, "In the meantime, dear Sarah, we need to begin. Heng can catch up when he calls, and I certainly hope that will be soon. The three of us are like Dumas's musketeers—one for all and all for one. And seriously, we do need Heng's brain to get through this."

The next several hours were filled with serious discussions of exhibition planning, budgets, catalog entries, and technology, broken only by Nigel leaving the room to take a short call. Neither of them was an expert on some of these topics, but they had good colleagues in the US who were going to handle the technical and financial aspects of the exhibition. Still, deep down, Sarah was not completely convinced that this installation was possible, and Nigel was so old that he really had no understanding of how it was going to be done. They were relying heavily on Heng and their technical colleagues, whom Nigel had christened "the wizards," to figure it out and ensure the event would be both a rigorous scholarly exhibition and an appealing experience for the general public.

By the time they had reviewed almost their entire agenda, Sarah had become increasingly concerned about Heng and his lack of communication. Heng did his own thing at times, but this meeting was important, and he should have been here.

Lunch included Ahmi's panang curry, which was famously craved by all in the ex-pat community in Bangkok, and som tam, a lovely spicy papaya salad. When they finished eating, Sarah called Heng's phone yet again. And again, no answer. Nigel started back to his office to take up working again.

"Nigel, stop a minute, please," Sarah said as she stood up from the table. "I don't know what to do, and I'm beginning to worry. Heng can be fanatical and obsessive about whatever he is working on at the moment. We both know that. We also know that he misses calls and deadlines when it suits him. But he would never miss today's work session. He knows how critical he is to all of this. Where is he?"

Nigel paused in the foyer. "You know, Sarah, I am glad you feel that way, because I know I have a tendency to worry more than I should. And I, too, am worried and not sure what to do. If he were in Bangkok, I would call my contacts in the police department and ask them for advice. But since he is in Phnom Penh, I just don't know. Maybe the best we can do is get back to work and hope for the best? What do you think? Honestly, it's not as if we could report him missing at this point. And who would we report him to?"

Reluctantly, Sarah agreed. While it would not be the first time Heng had temporarily disappeared, this time definitely did not seem in character. There was too much at stake, and their time was short. It was not the air-conditioning that sent the shiver up her spine. She strongly felt that something was wrong and that Heng might not be voluntarily incommunicado. Staying behind as Nigel walked into his office, Sarah pulled out her phone again and punched in the mobile number for Heng's wife, Som Jorani, who also did not answer. Sarah left a message for Jorani to call her back.

CHAPTER 7

Phnom Penh
Tuesday afternoon

Heng slowly opened his eyes and rapidly closed them again as the room spun around him. He was lying on a concrete floor in the midst of an expansive, mostly empty space. The surrounding air was surprisingly cool considering the heat and humidity of the city, and he could smell the funk of one of Phnom Penh's three rivers. He also heard the sounds of boat traffic.

His brain was fuzzy as he tried to figure out what was happening. He grunted reflexively as he tried to move his body, and he looked around, wondering if anyone had heard him. From the size and condition of the room, he surmised that he might be in one of the old warehouses along the Bassac River, south of the city center. While the city's riverfronts had been gentrified in the past few years, there were still some warehouses on the outskirts of Phnom Penh. Some were still used. Some, like this one appeared to be, were deserted.

"He's coming to." Heng shifted his gaze and spotted two men in the room. The smaller of the two seemed to be missing quite a few of his teeth. He was poorly dressed and spoke roughly.

"OK, let's get him off the floor and into the cell," said the other, much larger man, who was better dressed and clearly in charge. "Now that we know he's OK, we need to call to find out what we're supposed to do next."

Four strong hands under his armpits and at his feet lifted Heng off the floor and carried him across the concrete to a small caged area in the corner of the space. The men gently placed him down on the floor. Before the lock snapped shut, one of the men tied Heng's wrists and ankles together with duct tape, stuffed a rancid cloth in his mouth, and wrapped more tape around his head to hold the rag in place. While he wondered why they hadn't blindfolded him, Heng was grateful that he could at least see and breathe through his nose.

He tried to make out a conversation he was overhearing. He couldn't make much sense of the words, although he could discern that he was only hearing one side of a telephone discussion. Who were these guys, and why were they doing this to him? It didn't seem they knew much more about the situation than he did. They needed to talk to someone else on the phone to get instructions.

"What do we do with him now?" The big one muttered into his phone. Heng couldn't hear the response, and although he did hear the next sentence, it was incomprehensible to him. "No, nothing. Just some loose papers, and his phone, which we have turned off, and his wallet." There was a pause before he added, "OK. OK. Got it."

He abruptly hung up. "We're supposed to feed him and give him some water and let him take a leak," he told his fellow abductor. "Also, toss his phone and wallet into the river. You go take care of that."

Heng thought fleetingly about how worried Jorani and Nigel and Sarah would be before the smaller of the two once again jabbed him in the arm with a needle. This time, before he lost consciousness, he heard one of them say to the other that it was the easiest US $1,000 in cash they had ever earned.

CHAPTER 8

Bangkok
Tuesday afternoon

Sarah stood at the window of Nigel's office and surveyed Bangkok. There wasn't a lot of open space, but it calmed her to contemplate the immaculate green patch of the Jim Thompson House's garden. Bangkok had changed a lot during the time she had been visiting the region. Some of it was definitely for the better—the BTS and metro systems in the city had made getting around much less of a challenge, and even a pleasure in some cases. But she viewed some changes as more problematic. There was a lot that she preferred about the Southeast Asia of a few decades ago, when people seemed less hurried and stressed. Maybe she was showing her age.

Now that she was approaching that mid-century milestone, Sarah felt seriously middle-aged and accepted the likelihood she would probably be alone and working for the rest of her life. Given some of the alternatives, she didn't think this was necessarily a bad outcome. She sometimes thought Nigel was an excellent example of how to age well and alone. She often watched him when she thought he wasn't paying attention, and right now, she peered over at him as he sat at his desk intently studying documentation of his collection.

As a young man in the 1960s and 1970s, Nigel had been in Vietnam and Cambodia as a junior officer with some governmental agency or other. He had decided to stay in the region after he was discharged from his post. After they had met at the Ban Chiang excavation site in 1995, Sarah had eagerly kept in touch with him, and when he was later invited to teach a course and seminar on Khmer art in the department of art history and archaeology at Columbia while she was earning her doctorate, she was thrilled. At the time, there was little, though definitely expanding, expertise on Cambodian art in the US, and to have someone like Nigel, highly knowledgeable and straddling the worlds of the US and Southeast Asia, had seemed miraculous. Nigel had enthusiastically worked with Sarah at Columbia when the other professors, who had been immersed in art from Italy and France, had written her off as a not-very-smart fringe player unworthy of their attention. But not Nigel. He had taken her, and her passion for Khmer art, seriously. She had been about to drop out, and he had believed in her when others hadn't. And that was enough.

Of course, unfounded rumors and gossip swirled about the two of them. There *had* been that one weekend, which they both decided was better forgotten and never spoken about again, though Sarah did think about it from time to time. She sometimes wondered if Nigel did as well. But for the most part, their relationship was professional, even if it wasn't always entirely on the up-and-up, like when the employment market was poor and he offered her a job working with his collection. In retrospect, she realized that she had been used as cheap labor, quite possibly in the service of legitimizing his illegitimate collection.

That was a period in her life about which she had mixed feelings. She had learned a tremendous amount, but at what price? She still wondered how much longer she would feel she owed him something, and she knew he would always believe that she did. Even so, despite any disagreements she might have with him, she rarely questioned or crossed him, and she had deep respect for him and the disappearing world that he represented, one in which a long life of practical, on-the-ground experience counted for as much, or more, than diplomas on the wall, and in which art was highly valued for its beauty and what it could tell us about humanity and its achievements.

She realized he had been staring at the same piece of paper for the past few minutes while she had been daydreaming. Now his eyes were closed. She assumed he was thinking about Heng.

"Nigel, Heng marches to the beat of his own drum at times, but he would never blow off today's meeting." She paused before repeating, "There's something wrong." She stepped closer to his desk. "I am now officially worried."

Nigel opened his eyes and shook his head as if shaking off thoughts, the way a dog shakes water from its body. "I am worried too. But I'm still not sure what to do." He repeated what he had said earlier about Heng being an adult and how they couldn't just call in the cavalry. "We also certainly can't jump on a flight to Cambodia and start calling his name in the streets of Phnom Penh." Sometimes Nigel could be a harsh businessman or dealmaker. But other times he seemed more like a kind grandfather. "Maybe the internet is down. Maybe he got held up in horrific traffic. Maybe he just forgot and took a detour into the storerooms of the museum. None of these would be unusual for Heng. There are multiple explanations for why he isn't answering his phone or connecting on Zoom." He offered a warm smile. "Have you come up with any ideas about what we should be doing?"

Sarah remained at a loss. This was Nigel's territory, and she had always leaned on him to have the answers, though she realized increasingly that he may be unable to provide them. She knew the region, and a little bit about its politics and dangers and issues, but she had to admit to herself that she knew little about how to solve problems here beyond those related to art and cultural history without asking Nigel what to do. "No, Nigel, I don't know what to do."

With a little effort, Nigel pushed himself out of his chair, faced her, and placed his hands on her shoulders. "I know you're unconvinced that everything is OK, and I must admit I'm not completely convinced either. If he doesn't turn up by tomorrow morning, we'll call my contacts at the US embassy and alert the Cambodian authorities. Remember, Heng is like a son to me. I understand his ups and downs better than almost anyone. I must believe that he will turn up."

Then he switched gears abruptly and said, "I need to go upstairs to my file cabinets to collect some older documentation that's up there. I'll be back in a few minutes."

While he was gone, she surveyed the barely controlled chaos of books, papers, and objects. Nigel was the consummate old-school, paper-based scholar-adventurer. The field and the world had moved on, but he had not.

She reminded herself to focus on what she was here to do. Her intention had been to look for a specific article in an early issue of the *Bulletin de l'École française d'Extrême-Orient*, which she already knew was housed on the second-to-top shelf of Nigel's idiosyncratically organized library. She surveyed the volumes on one of the upper shelves of an overstuffed bookcase, well above eye level. On the shelf above the *Bulletin* volumes, a group of small stone Khmer heads had been placed. They appeared dusty, and as they were shoved back from the edge of the shelf, they were difficult to see, but she didn't think she had ever noticed them before. Certainly, they had never been prominently displayed in his home for others to observe. For a moment, she wondered if they were modern copies, though she knew they were most probably the real thing. This was in fact the part of dealing with Nigel that caused her the most distress—the fact that he continued to keep authentic works of art that had clearly been taken, possibly illegally, from their original context. These sculptures certainly seemed genuine. And if they were, they should not be here. She did not remember researching and cataloging them for Nigel years ago. Maybe she wasn't remembering everything that she should.

There were several heads, and she peered more closely up at them. One of them felt very familiar, but in her worried and still-jet-lagged state, she couldn't place it. She thought that she might've seen all of them as illustrations in a book somewhere, but she couldn't remember where or when. Maybe Nigel had sent a photo to her at some point? She just didn't know. She looked around for the rolling library ladder and was positioning it in front of the shelf when Nigel returned with a sheaf of yellowed file folders in his arms.

"What are you doing, Sarah?"

Later, as she thought back, she wasn't sure why she had not been completely honest with him about wanting to examine the row of stone heads in more detail. But she didn't tell him that. "I wanted to grab the volume of the *EFEO Bulletin* with the long article about the sculpture of Indravarman II to look for a reference." She pointed to the top shelf. "It's up there and I couldn't reach it without the ladder."

Nigel waved his hand and said, "Leave it. Our time is limited. I'll give you the book to take back to your hotel to read tonight. Let's finish going through the World Monuments Fund documentation about the Preah Khan architecture, and then we will call it a day. In fact, why don't we just stop working in about half an hour? We can continue when you are back from Phnom Penh. I'm sure you'll be happy to get back to the hotel and take a rest. Your jet lag must be fierce." He rolled the ladder and climbed up slowly and stiffly to grab the dusty volume, which he handed down to her.

Sarah nodded. He was right; she was more tired than she had admitted to herself, and returning to the hotel seemed like a great idea. It would also give her time to think through some of the remaining issues they had and how she was going to present them to the museum when she got home. This whole thing might end up costing more money, and the exhibition was already over budget. That could be a big problem.

But she remained resolute that they had to accomplish their goals because they were aiming for something that had never been done. While there had been major exhibitions of Khmer art since Cambodia had reemerged from the dark days that Cambodians still sometimes referenced as "Pol Pot Time" and the Vietnamese occupation that followed, there had never been an exhibition that did what the three of them were attempting. They had all believed—and now they knew—that there was enough material scattered in museums and private collections around the world to create solid reconstructions of parts of three of the major temples of Angkor from three distinct historical and stylistic periods.

They had chosen Prasat Krachap at Koh Ker, an early Khmer capital that had been the target of looters over the past decades; Banteay Srei, a tenth-century temple northeast of the main Angkor site; and Preah Khan, the temple that the god-king Jayavarman VII had built in honor of his father.

Nigel had directed some of their activity from his home office, while Sarah and Heng had spent the last three years scouring museums and private collections to ask, and at times beg, for loans, based on Nigel's scrupulous reading and researching of catalogs and auction records. They had found sufficient sculptures to reconstruct enough of the temples to bring them alive for the visitors. The virtual reconstructions, of course, would not be on the scale of the originals, but with well-done labels and technology, they hoped that each visitor would feel present at the site.

The politics of the exhibition had proved difficult but not insurmountable. Sarah knew that some of the objects they planned to include were of sketchy provenance, and both museums and private collectors had expressed their concerns about potential seizure of their objects during the run of the exhibition in San Diego. But the government of Cambodia had agreed not to press for the return of any of these objects at this time, though they did not rule out future action. Some collectors had asked to loan their objects anonymously, but after discussions with the museum's administration and legal advisers, the curators had decided against this. Every object would be connected with a collector or museum.

In addition, the logistics of an exhibition like this were stunningly complex. Not only did the San Diego Museum of Asian Art building need to be checked for structural integrity to ensure the floors could handle tens of thousands of pounds of stone, but there were limits on the size and weight of objects that could be shipped by air. One object they had found, after an intensive search, had actually been structurally embedded in the wall of the house of a senior Cambodian official in Phnom Penh. It was exhausting just to think about it, but Sarah and her colleagues all hoped that, in the end, it would be worth it. They were also tackling the thorny issues related to illicit trafficking of objects. For a country like Cambodia, which was culturally rich and economically poor, this was huge.

Why would Heng blow off *this* meeting, which surely he'd known was critical to finalizing details?

Sarah and Nigel worked for a few more minutes in silence, and then Sarah took a short break to leave the room and call Jorani again. When there was still no answer, Sarah felt a slow panic rising and began to wonder if something had happened to both of them. She was going to Phnom Penh the next morning, but as Nigel had intimated, she wasn't sure what more she would be able to do once she was there.

When she returned to the office, Nigel was sitting in his customary space behind his desk with a businesslike look on his face. "Sarah, I have other business to attend to now." But his face then softened, and with one of his characteristic displays of humor, he added, "That means I need to take a nap."

She laughed, but she knew this idea of a nap wasn't something the Nigel of yesterday would have done. His age was becoming clearer every day.

"Feel free to stay here and finish up any loose ends and prepare for your meetings tomorrow, and good luck on your trip to Phnom Penh. I'll look forward to hearing about progress with the ministry, which seems to be dragging its heels. Call me when you can. I don't know what to tell you about Heng. The boy is more impetuous than is good for him. If we don't hear anything by tomorrow, I'll begin to make phone calls." He hugged her tightly and left.

Sarah worked for a few more minutes and then sat for a moment, thoughts of Heng and the exhibition and Nigel and Khmer art swirling around her fatigued brain. As she stood and gathered her papers and the book to leave, she glanced up again at the shelf with all the heads. She realized, as she looked at them, that most of them were not of the highest quality, possibly from the late Khmer period or from an outlying provincial temple, though there was one that was intricately and beautifully carved, and she was annoyed with herself that she couldn't seem to place it. Perhaps there would be time to look at these later in the week.

Wordlessly, Ahmi led Sarah out of the apartment, and the elevator delivered Sarah to the ground floor. As she stepped into the steamy Bangkok afternoon, she glanced up at the towering clouds, full of water about to be dumped on the city, and hurried toward the National Stadium BTS station, hoping to beat the unseasonable incoming rain.

CHAPTER 9

Bangkok
Tuesday evening

Sarah awoke to the chirping of her mobile phone. She stared at the ceiling of her hotel room, not understanding for a moment where she was. She must have dozed off. What time was it, and more importantly, where was she? The memory of the afternoon came flooding back to her as she remembered Heng's absence, being at Nigel's apartment, and their mutual confusion and concern about what might have happened to him.

She sat up and looked at the phone on the bedside table. It was 7:23 p.m., and she had just missed a call from Jorani, Heng's wife. She grabbed her phone and tapped Jorani's number. It rang once before Jorani picked up.

"Hi, Sarah, I see that you called several times earlier today. My apologies. I was in the studio with my phone off working on my new piece—did I tell you about it? It's a commission for the new office of the UN Refugee Agency in Geneva. I'm very excited about it—thrilled!

I still can't believe they chose me! So important for conveying the plight of refugees worldwide."

Sarah wanted to interrupt Jorani and ask about Heng but didn't want to alarm her. She let her go on for another minute or two.

"I'll get to go to Switzerland. I can't imagine a country with that much snow and that many mountains, and it just all looks so insanely adorable. Anyway, I'll send you some photos, though it's very much a work in progress at this point. How are you? How was your trip from California? I can't believe sometimes that people actually encase themselves in a metal tube and fling themselves halfway around the world at a moment's notice. I never thought I could ever do it—though I guess I will when I go to Switzerland!"

Jorani paused to catch her breath. Sarah was about to try to break into the monologue to ask about Heng, when Jorani continued.

"By the way, did Heng say anything today about changing his plans? He left the house early this morning to go to the museum. He hasn't returned or called and isn't answering his mobile."

Sarah's heart sank. She tried to unravel her thoughts and feelings and arrange them into some kind of order without causing undue worry for Jorani.

"Also, the museum says he never came into the office," Jorani said. "I'm guessing he must have decided to go to an internet café or one of the local hotel lobbies with a good Wi-Fi connection for his Zoom with you and Nigel. There have been Wi-Fi issues throughout the city over the past couple of days, and I know the museum was affected by them. Anyway, I'm hoping you can solve the mystery of where he has been all day. It's puzzling because we had a plan to meet up with friends tonight."

Sarah took a deep breath. "Jorani, Heng never got in touch with either Nigel or me today. He did not call in for the Zoom. We assumed that something had happened in Phnom Penh to prevent him from joining us. I haven't talked to him since I arrived in Bangkok last night, and I frankly don't know where he is. I was a little worried this morning when he didn't show. But now that I've heard from you, I am very concerned." She clambered off the bed, knowing she had to do something, although she still had no idea what that might be. "And I know Nigel is too."

She didn't know what to make of Jorani's silence. Was she worried? Confused? Angry at Heng for being so inconsiderate?

"Well. Heng can be a little obsessed with his work," Jorani said. "But this? No, not like him. I will call the museum director back and send out a WhatsApp to his friends to find out if any of them has any further information. If you hear anything from him, let me know. Maybe he got buried in a museum storeroom, though that's doubtful. Maybe he had a brainstorm and went up to Siem Reap to look at the temples or talk to the staff at Conservation d'Angkor. It wouldn't be the first time he's gone AWOL. But he knows it makes me crazy when he does. And also this exhibition means everything to him right now, and I can't see him just blowing off a meeting about it. I don't know . . ." Her voice trailed off.

"Jorani, I'm coming to Phnom Penh for meetings tomorrow. I have an appointment at the US embassy, and then at the national museum. I'm sure Heng is fine, but is there anything I can do to help you once I'm there?"

"I can't think of anything for now. Call me when you get to Phnom Penh and also if Heng gets in touch with you. At the very least we can keep in touch with each other. At best, we can beat up on him together for scaring all of us."

At least Jorani could bring some levity into the situation. After she hung up, Sarah realized just how exhausted she was—despite squeezing in a nap—not to mention disquieted and unable to focus on anything but Heng. If she, Jorani, and Nigel were all worried, there *was* something to worry about. She sat for a moment to muster enough energy for a short walk through the streets around the hotel. Maybe a meal would help. But after a quick and delicious dinner of pad thai with shrimp at one of the local restaurants and a Singha to quench her thirst, her feelings of unease and worry grew.

She was glad she would be going to Phnom Penh tomorrow.

CHAPTER 10

Phnom Penh
Wednesday afternoon

Why were these chairs so uncomfortable? Sarah sat in the waiting room of the consular section of the US embassy. The cynic in her thought it was probably to discourage people from coming in to ask for assistance. She observed, too, that the wall decor could have used some updating; the posters of Yellowstone National Park, New York City, and New Orleans, on two of the four walls, were terribly faded. *My tax dollars at work,* she thought. She did give this embassy points for being more open than most, however. She had always felt uncomfortable in other US embassies around the world that looked more like federal prisons than beacons of freedom and democracy.

Her flight from Bangkok to Phnom Penh had been short, and immigration had been efficient, and her hotel had sent a driver to meet her at the airport. The drive into the city had also been uneventful, unlike the time years ago when one of her colleagues had been robbed en route from the airport to meetings at the national museum. Those days were gone now—or at least she hoped they were.

She had checked into Raffles Hotel Le Royal, an old French colonial hotel that had been beautifully restored and updated. One of the major perks of her job was the ability to stay in nice hotels in the center of cities. The higher-ups at her museum back home were concerned about staff safety when traveling, and she took full advantage of this. And she felt this was one of the most beautiful hotels to which she'd been given access. It was also one of the sponsors of the exhibition and would be providing funding for the opening night when the exhibition moved from San Diego to Phnom Penh. The management at Le Royal knew her well at this point, and they were always very gracious and excited about accommodating her whenever she was in the city. In turn, Sarah loved seeing people she recognized from previous stays, and she had already dropped in to see the general manager, confirming they would meet the next morning to review the details surrounding the hotel's participation in the exhibition's opening event.

In the late morning, after checking in with Jorani and learning that no news about Heng had surfaced, she had taken a walk around the heart of Phnom Penh. The city was certainly no longer the gem it once was, but Sarah recognized that a core of its elegance remained despite the horrors of the 1970s. Civil war, during the rise of the Khmer Rouge, had forced multitudes to flee the countryside and head for Phnom Penh for safety. Less than two years later, Khmer Rouge soldiers entered the city and forced most of the population back out into the countryside. Many died of overwork, disease, and starvation; others were executed by the Khmer Rouge.

But ironically, many—though certainly not all—of the city's buildings had been left as they were. Most important for her and her work, the collection in the national museum, which was the greatest collection of Khmer antiquities in the world, had remained virtually untouched, though the museum was in ruinous condition by the end of the 1970s. She had only recently learned that while many of the museum workers, especially those who had been educated in France, had been killed, a few had been spared as essential to the care of the collections, at least for a short time after the Khmer Rouge occupation.

Her route had taken her past the museum, which was a wonder and a story unto itself. Opened in 1920 as the Musée Albert Sarraut, it was a faux Khmer palace with a beautiful central courtyard surrounded by galleries exhibiting treasures from the Khmer Empire, mostly from Angkor and its adjacent sites. She'd never tired of walking through these galleries, marveling at the abilities of the ancient sculptors and the overall history of that time and the people. The astonishing empire, ruled by god-kings, had lasted from the ninth to the fifteenth centuries and was most powerful in the eleventh and twelfth centuries. It encompassed a vast geographic region, including much of what is now mainland Southeast Asia—all of Cambodia, northeast Thailand, southern Laos, and parts of Vietnam and Malaysia. Scholars have estimated that at the height of the empire, the capital at Angkor had a population of close to a million people, roughly comparable to the population of ancient Rome in its heyday. And the enormous sculptures created by this civilization, some of which were now in the national museum, projected power and assurance, the product of a confident and stable empire, before its ultimate demise. The reasons why the Khmer Empire fell were still debated, though Sarah subscribed to the theory that the weakened empire had lost control of the water it had managed so brilliantly for centuries.

She had always considered all this to be just short of mind-blowing in its scale and complexity. What had these people, and particularly the god-kings, thought about themselves? Who created buildings and sculptures on this scale? What could their history teach our modern society?

After weaving her way through the lively streets south of Wat Phnom, she'd returned to her hotel to get ready for her meeting. From there, it had been just a short walk through the old colonial quarter of the city, past the national library. She had learned early from the travel required for her career, and visits to numerous national museums in other countries, that US embassies were frequently located in the most expensive sections of cities and surrounded by tall, forbidding walls. But the embassy in Phnom Penh was different, more welcoming, though still enclosed by substantial walls. The receptionist had received her politely and directed her to the waiting room after she surrendered her phone and the flash drives in her handbag.

She now riffled through her bag, which contained only her papers and a small notebook, until a voice startled her.

"Dr. Burroughs? I'm pleased to meet you. I'm James Carlyle."

Sarah had asked to meet with a consular public affairs official, but this guy standing in front of her, extending his hand to shake hers, did not fit her vision of someone in that position. These types of officials were liaisons for communications, diplomacy, and cultural activities throughout the country, and she frequently envisioned them as earnest do-gooders, eager to spread the gospel of American democracy. He seemed different. She shook his hand.

James Carlyle was tall, and it was obvious that, under his suit—which she suspected had been custom tailored in Bangkok—he was both muscular and graceful. He looked more like a military attaché in civilian clothing than a US consular official. And she couldn't help but notice that he was nice looking in an unprepossessing way, with even features and large brown eyes. Lightly tanned, with moderately graying hair cut short, he looked to be in his late forties or early fifties. He obviously took care of himself, and for some inexplicable reason she found herself speechless.

"Please, Dr. Burroughs, my office is down the hall." He extended his arm to show her the way.

Sarah hooked her bag over her shoulder and followed him down a drab institutional corridor, which was in dire need of a coat of paint or two, and into an office that was too tidy for someone involved in bureaucratic, paper-intensive work.

"Thanks for taking the time to see me, Mr. Carlyle," she said, unsure whether, or where, to sit.

"Please call me James," he said as he circled to the back side of a large desk.

"Thank you, and please call me Sarah." At his invitation, she sat in the chair opposite his desk, then glanced around the office. Her first thought had been that it was tidy, but now it almost seemed as if no one worked there. The books on the shelves, the paintings on the walls—everything looked generic and standard issue.

He interrupted her survey by asking where she was from back home.

"California native, Bay Area born and raised. After a stint in New York at grad school, at Columbia University, I came back and now live in San Diego. I think I told the consulate in my email requesting a meeting that I'm a curator at the San Diego Museum of Asian Art."

He nodded and said he'd seen the email.

"What about you?" she asked.

"I'm from the Golden State too. Small world! Though my roots are in Southern California. Do you like living in the Southland?"

She laughed. "Despite my roots and family in the Bay Area, I've become enamored of the energy and openness of Southern California and can't really see myself up north anymore. Not that I could afford it if I had the opportunity!"

James nodded. "So true, so true." He leaned back in his chair and crossed one leg over the other. "I'm sure your time today is valuable, so what can I do for you? Your email indicated that you wanted to talk to us about an upcoming exhibition, which I will say is much more interesting than most of the topics I get to deal with."

She wondered what some of these other topics might be but knew now wasn't the time to change the subject.

"So I'm all ears," he added.

"That's right," she said, suddenly embarrassed when she realized her comment could be interpreted as a referral to his ears. "About the exhibition, I mean. I've been working with an American ex-pat expert on Southeast Asian art—Nigel Sanderson, who lives in Bangkok—along with Sam Heng, a curator at the national museum here in Phnom Penh. We're organizing a massive world-class exhibition with the assistance of outside experts, including collaborating curators at most of the national museums around the region. We open in five months in San Diego, after which the show will come to the national museum here in Phnom Penh. When the show arrives here, it will be partially sponsored by Le Royal. We kind of need help with some of the outreach and governmental interactions that we have found challenging—to say the least—thus far. Everyone on the front lines is anxious to move forward with the exhibition, but the ministry of culture in particular is dragging its feet. We don't know why."

James uncrossed his legs and pulled his chair forward as he made a note on the pad in front of him. She hoped it didn't have anything to do with the ear faux pas.

"You wouldn't be the first to have that challenge with government agencies." He lifted his hand to indicate she should go on.

"At this point, we're down to the wire with needing signed

documents. They keep assuring us they will sign, but they haven't. And we need them now. The delay may be due to a change in leadership at the ministry, but I don't know. The thing is, this is mission critical because it takes a lot of time to make the logistic arrangements—deinstalling, packing, shipping, unpacking, you get the picture—to transport these kinds of massive objects around the world. We think—we hope—that the intervention of the embassy might help us move forward."

He seemed interested, now leaning forward at his desk. "I am at your service, so shoot."

She pulled out a notebook she'd been carrying everywhere she went, ever since starting this project, and flipped to a dog-eared page. "First, could you get in touch with any contacts you may have at the ministry of culture and ask what the holdup is? We have been told through informal conversations that the loans of artwork have been approved, but as I said, we haven't seen anything in writing. What more information do they need? Then, if you could ask about my request to actually see some of the works, which are in storage at Conservation d'Angkor in Siem Reap? I need to get in there later this week." Sarah finished going through the rest of the items on her list, enumerating her concerns and thoughts about each one. After finally addressing the last item on the page, she looked up and saw that he'd been making his own list of notes on a memo pad on his desk. "In case I wasn't clear, this exhibition is a very big deal in the museum world, and it's a huge step for me professionally. I want everything to go well."

James nodded, although she admitted to herself that it was unlikely any embassy personnel would care much about her own career. But he promised to contact the various ministries, and especially the ministry of culture, to move her requests through in as timely a manner as he could. He also seemed to be familiar with Heng's reputation and work and had nodded at the mention of Nigel, both of which surprised her. He hadn't bombarded her with any pressing questions, and his face had actually seemed to light up when she described the exhibition's scope and approach. So maybe he was at least a little impressed. And anyway, it was always good to have Uncle Sam on your side. She made a few notes in her notebook and slipped it back into her bag.

"Anything else I can do for you, Sarah?"

She hesitated. Should she tell him about Heng's seeming disappearance, or was that something that Jorani was better equipped to handle without intervention from a foreign diplomatic officer? What could *he* do? And, honestly, what would she say? That a grown man who was a Cambodian national, not a US citizen—and capable of taking care of himself—had been incommunicado for thirty-six hours? She decided to say nothing and shook her head. "No, thanks. I won't take any more of your time, James." She stood up to leave.

"If you have a few minutes, there is another topic that I want to talk to you about."

This was a surprise. She hadn't expected the embassy would ask anything of her.

"Nigel Sanderson, your collaborator on this exhibition."

Sarah looked up from her bag and slowly sat down again. This certainly had come out of left field. "OK, what do you want to know?"

"His name comes up in conversation from time to time as someone who has been around Southeast Asia for many decades and who seems to know everyone and everything. I'm always interested in knowing these ex-pats—how they are viewed, what their local friends think and are talking about."

It was true Nigel was quite a character and certainly well known in the art world. But this was curious, and there was something about his expression that unsettled her.

"This isn't meant to be an interrogation, Sarah, and I'm sorry if I'm out of bounds. Just interested in knowing more about prominent Americans in the region."

Sarah thought for a minute. "Nigel is a long-standing colleague. He's an expert in the art of Southeast Asia, with an emphasis on the art of Angkor and the Khmer Empire. I have known him for decades. He was probably the first Westerner to return to Cambodia after the Vietnamese withdrawal in 1989 to assess the situation on the ground. No information had come out of the country in almost fifteen years, and no one knew what was going on, and there had been rumors of sculptures being carted off by the truckload, but there was no proof. He had no official standing then. Really, he has none now. But his work constituted a very early, rough inventory that helped organizations like UNESCO and the APSARA National Authority to understand the magnitude of the problems they were facing with the cultural patrimony of the country. Are you familiar with these groups?"

James laughed. "Yes, of course. And I wholeheartedly endorse their work in preserving sites and regions that are culturally and historically significant. Go on, please."

She worried she may have insulted him but for now set that concern aside. "These organizations built on what Nigel had done; they could not have accomplished what they did without him. It's doubtful that the Angkor Archaeological Park would have achieved World Heritage status as quickly as it did without his assistance and help, which in some cases predated the arrival of the French and Japanese teams that worked here. His work was invaluable—and at times conducted at great risk to himself."

She was able to spew out his bio without missing a beat, but all the while was genuinely curious about why Nigel had become a topic of conversation in this US consular official's office. "Why, exactly, the interest?"

James held up his hands as if trying to settle her down, even though she didn't think she'd necessarily acted defensively. "I'm just trying to keep up with prominent Americans in the region, particularly those who have been here a long time and who have influence. Nigel falls into both of those categories."

Although James was correct about Nigel having been here a long time and having influence, Sarah realized uncomfortably that his words did not ring entirely true to her. It was time to leave. "Nigel is definitely one of a kind," she said as she stood up again. "The world won't ever see another like him. Now I have definitely taken enough of your time today. If you can keep me updated about any conversations that you have with any of the ministries involved with this exhibition, I would appreciate it a great deal. I'll be staying at Le Royal for a few more days, though I will be back and forth to Siem Reap. The consulate has my mobile number—but you already know that if you read my email. Texting or WhatsApp is usually the easiest way to get hold of me, though please identify yourself the first time you text so I know who is contacting me." He started to stand. "No need to get up. I know you're busy, and I think I can see myself out. I am due at the national museum in half an hour."

"The consulate is not generally enthusiastic about unescorted visitors in the corridors," James said, pressing the wrinkles out from his slacks when he straightened. "I'll see you out." When they reached the security station near the embassy's entry, he extended his hand. "Always great to meet a fellow Californian, Sarah. Look forward to following the progress of your fascinating exhibition."

"Thank you, James, and I look forward to your being in touch." As she walked out, she realized how this could be misinterpreted as a double entendre. *Oh well.* She grinned. He probably had a wife and five children, though deep down she sensed that was not true. *Didn't seem like the type.* When she retrieved her phone at the embassy security desk and booted it up, she found three text messages and a call, all from Jorani. She tapped the call-back button. Jorani picked up after two rings. They spoke briefly and agreed they would meet in the lobby of Le Royal at 7:00 p.m.

Late that afternoon, after a meeting at the national museum, Sarah's phone exploded with messages and calls from Cambodian officials from the ministry, Conservation d'Angkor, and the Angkor National Museum in Siem Reap. All were apologetic about not responding earlier to her queries. Virtually everything that she, Heng, and Nigel were asking for was granted, though they did ask that she come to Siem Reap the next day to review some of the requests. These calls were followed by texts from her colleagues at the national museum, wanting to know what she had done to get such a move on after they had waited for so long.

She shook her head. James Carlyle certainly knew how to put pressure on all the right people.

CHAPTER 11

Phnom Penh
Wednesday afternoon

Heng again swam back into consciousness, spurred by rough voices speaking at the edge of his range of hearing. He could still smell the river and hear the sounds of boat traffic passing but had no further idea about where he was. He also had no notion of how long he had been there or, more importantly, why he had been abducted on his way to work.

He no longer just wondered what was going on. Now he was terrified. His heart was beating fast, his breathing was shallow, and his arms and legs were stiff and cold, or asleep—he couldn't tell which. He was also angry. *Why am I here? Who are these people?* It must all be a mistake. And they were making no attempt to hide who they were. He knew from watching too many American movies that when people were kidnapped but not blindfolded, it generally meant it wouldn't end well for them.

But for the moment he needed to put these thoughts out of his mind and concentrate on his bladder, which was about to burst.

As he lay there, eyes closed, the voices moved closer to him. The deeper one, the one he had determined belonged to the man in charge, said they would be moving out at nightfall. "The order is to take him to the local safe house and keep him tied up there and await further instructions. I guess the plan then will be to move him to Siem Reap. The operation is scheduled for Sunday, and the boss wants him in good shape then to ensure that—" Heng lost the rest as the voices passed out of hearing range.

As he realized this was not some random kidnapping, his panic began to escalate. It was definitely *him* they wanted. But why? And the word *operation* sent a shiver up his spine. What on earth did that mean, and why did they need him for whatever was happening in Siem Reap, the town nearest the Angkor Archaeological Park? He thought back to the past few weeks. The only thing out of the ordinary that had happened recently was that he had found that diary in the storage area of the museum. Maybe someone knew about it. Maybe *that* was what they wanted. He had made it through several pages of the diary, including the shocking discovery on the first page about the events of 1975, before he couldn't read any more. He had digested enough, though, to recognize that the content was important for him personally and to many more people beyond that. It might even be important for history. But he didn't have it with him. If this was what they wanted, there was no point to his kidnapping unless they wanted to hold him hostage until they could force Jorani to turn it over. And that was the problem. While Jorani was one of the most resourceful and capable people he knew, she would likely not be sitting around wondering what had happened to him. Instead, she was probably already out looking for him, trying to find him, and that could spell disaster for both of them. That was what worried him the most.

Jorani was certainly his soulmate, but it had definitely not been love at first sight. They had been introduced to one another, and they had seen each other at lectures, and at restaurants and coffee shops around the university and the museum. But neither had been interested in anything further. No commonalities. Nothing on which to hang even a friendship, and certainly nothing more.

She had later told him that though she had found him attractive, she had also thought he was a cocky, foreign-educated snob, someone who thought he was better than all the Cambodians around him who had grown up in the gritty post–Khmer Rouge period in Phnom Penh. Jorani had said everyone seemed to think he wondered how *they*, Cambodia's present and up-and-coming artists, could possibly work in the shadow of the great artists of the Khmer Empire. How could *they* possibly believe they would be able to create anything that even began to approach the brilliance of their forebearers? What did *they* even think they were doing? Jorani had told him she'd found him irritating in the extreme.

He hadn't been much taken with her either. He'd thought she was a dilettante and a mediocre artist just passing the time until something, or someone, more interesting came along.

All of that had changed, however, at the exhibition of graduate student work at the Royal University of Fine Arts, not too long after he'd begun working at the national museum next door. He had gone to the art show thinking there might be beer and some food available at the reception without a thought as to whether the art might be of interest.

While much of it had not been to his taste or terribly fascinating, he'd had to admit that he had underestimated the abilities of the art students. There had been a lot of talent on display, and as he had been drawn into the exhibition and looked more closely at the art, he had also engaged in conversations with the artists, most of whom were in attendance. As he'd progressed through the gallery, he'd begun thinking about proposing a small installation in one of the galleries of the national museum that might pair ancient sculptures with modern art. It could be an interesting and thought-provoking little exhibit that might even help cement relations between the two institutions and give exposure to a group of young artists. He'd been surprised by how excited he was at the possibility.

And then he'd come to the last gallery and seen Jorani and her work. She had just finished speaking to a wealthy Cambodian couple, whom he'd recognized from the pages of *The Phnom Penh Post*, the English-language newspaper in the city. They were prominent businesspeople in the city, one of the few couples who seemed to have made a fortune without graft and corruption. She'd clearly known them well and hugged both before they left.

She must have sensed the presence of someone else in the gallery because she'd turned around with a big smile on her face. But when she'd seen who it was, the smile had disappeared, to be replaced by a quizzical look, as if to ask what exactly Heng was doing at an exhibition of student work. He could no longer remember if she'd actually said anything, but her face had said it all: *Why on earth are you here?* And throughout all the years since then, he had never told her that he had just been in search of dinner and a beer.

At the gallery that night, Jorani had been livelier, and definitely more attractive, than he remembered from their past encounters, but it had been her art that had first drawn him deeper into the space. He'd immediately understood why her work occupied the final room of the exhibition on its own. The scale of her stone-carved sculpture was enormous. There were clear influences from the sculptures of the ancient Khmer Empire, but she had made something completely new. Somewhere along the way, he had heard that she was a practicing Buddhist—which he no longer was—and he'd seen then how she had skillfully taken the motifs from both the Hindu and Buddhist temples of Angkor and incorporated them into her work in a meaningful way. He had never seen anything like it. And he'd told her so.

And at that moment, they'd clicked. He'd stayed until the exhibition closed. They had talked most of the rest of the night and had been inseparable ever since. More than twenty years later, they still rarely spent time apart. It would not be an exaggeration to say she had profoundly changed his life.

And during these last few hours in captivity, he wondered if somehow his discovery of that diary might also be life-changing. The contents in just those few opening pages seemed to carry immense importance for him. But why would someone else care so much about what was on the pages that it would be worth kidnapping him? There had to be another reason he was lying there with his mouth taped up.

The voices came back into his hearing range, along with the sounds of footsteps. Two sets of arms peeled him off the floor, carried him outside, and untied his hands before letting him pee against the side of the building. They placed him into the back of a car again. As the driver started the ignition and backed out onto the bumpy road, the other man looked back at Heng in the back seat, as if he was going to try some herculean effort to escape from his restraints. But that would be impossible, so Heng turned away from the man's glare and leaned his head against the window once the car veered onto a better-paved road, and watched the river drift past.

CHAPTER 12

Phnom Penh
Wednesday evening

Som Jorani walked into the lobby of Le Royal, dressed in clean jeans, a T-shirt, and a pair of flat sandals, with a stylish cotton scarf around her neck and a cotton bag slung over her right shoulder. Sarah was seated there, waiting for her. Every time Sarah had seen Jorani, she was filled with awe at her bearing and grace, and the same was true now. A small woman at just over five feet tall, Jorani was one of the most beautiful Cambodian women that Sarah had ever met.

And her story, like many stories in Cambodia, was very moving. Unlike Heng's parents, who had disappeared during the Khmer Rouge reign of terror, Jorani's family had been classified as peasants and had managed to stay alive. But her father had died eventually from the effects of overwork and malnutrition in the early 1980s, and her mother had died from lack of medical care a few years later. Jorani had previously shared a few vague memories of her mother with Sarah, though nothing too specific, and she had no memory of her father. Like many Cambodians of her generation, she had never really been clear on the details of the deaths of her parents, nor would she ever be. Unlike Heng, Jorani had not ended up in a refugee camp but instead had gone to live with an aunt in Phnom Penh once both parents were gone. Fortunately, her aunt had been committed to helping Jorani overcome her tragic losses, and she'd lived long enough to ensure this happened and to see the beginning of Jorani's success as a sculptor.

Through determination and grit, along with some help from UN officials in the 1990s, Jorani had worked her way into the Royal University and had ultimately become one of the country's important young sculptors. She and her generation had learned quickly that they were tasked with the reconstruction of the cultural life of the country, so her work was founded in a traditional Khmer style. But she imbued it with an edge and contemporary sensibility that appealed to a wide audience.

Although she and Heng had been together for many years since their first meeting at the gallery exhibition, they had been married only recently. During the intervening years, they had both been tre-mendously dedicated to their careers, rebuilding the traditions of arts and scholarship in Cambodia. Heng was now forty-seven, and Jorani was forty-two. Heng had once told Sarah that because of the trauma of their childhoods, the couple did not plan to have children.

Sarah waved to Jorani as she stood up to greet her. At five feet, ten inches, Sarah towered over, and often felt clumsy around, Jorani, whose graceful, gliding walk was nearly mesmerizing. But despite their differences in stature and background, their friendship, based originally on their mutual admiration and love for Heng, was strong. In some ways, Sarah considered Jorani as much a sister as the wife of one of her best friends. More than occasionally, Sarah found Jorani to be unreasonably stubborn, and she was sure that Jorani felt the same about her. But there was nothing that Sarah wouldn't do for Jorani, and she suspected that the opposite was true as well. They'd had some exhilarating times over the years, climbing temples at Angkor and ex-ploring the outlying archaeological sites that had been the outposts of the Khmer Empire. Those had been the best of times.

These were not the best of times.

The women embraced in a tight hug. "Jorani, I have missed you so much. Let's go to my room, where we can talk," Sarah said. Jorani nodded, and they rode up the elevator in silence. After opening the door with the metal key, another element of Le Royal that she loved, Sarah tossed the key and her bag on top of the TV cabinet. Jorani hesitated, hanging on to her cotton bag. Her discomfort was unmistakable.

Sarah sat on the bed and patted the duvet, inviting Jorani to join her. She had never seen Jorani look so lost and frightened. "Talk to me."

"I'm scared."

Sarah put her arm around her friend's shoulders. "I can see that. Tell me everything."

Still hugging her bag to her chest like a little girl with a teddy bear, Jorani gazed out the window for a moment before turning her attention to Sarah. "I'm not sure where to start or what to say other than that Heng has not been himself for the past couple of weeks. He's been moody and distant and hasn't paid a lot of attention to me, or to anything or anyone else, really. He hasn't been eating, either, even when I prepare his favorite meals. I've caught him staring off into space more times than I can count. I can't pinpoint a start date, but it was before he went to Bangkok that this all started, and I can tell you that the situation was exacerbated by his trip there last week, when he stayed with Nigel. He came back even more distracted. I finally told him that until and unless he told me what was going on, or until he resolved whatever was bothering him, I was just going to work, and although I would come home to sleep and eat, I'd otherwise just ignore him. I expected some kind of reaction from him. But it was as if he hardly knew me. He nodded distractedly and looked off into the distance, almost as if he hadn't heard me. He barely responded, and he certainly never told me anything about what was troubling him."

"Nothing at all?" Sarah asked.

"No, and that wasn't like him. I told him that I was confused and hurt and that he needed to talk to me about what was wrong. He said he couldn't tell me what was on his mind at that moment but that in good time, he would explain everything." She groaned and shook her head.

"I guess that 'good time' never came, because he never did tell me anything. So I still have no idea what was wrong or why he was acting so peculiarly. I finally notified the police—just a few hours ago. I came straight here from the station."

Sarah asked how the police had responded and if they'd been helpful.

"I'm not sure. They took down my information and were, surprisingly, more sympathetic than I thought they would be. But they said there's not much they can do when an adult disappears like this and they would be in contact if they learned anything. Frankly, it seemed to me they thought Heng had probably left with another woman or gone drinking with his friends. But you know Heng. He's not like that, and I told the police that I was positive that is *not* what's happening here. I even called Anada several times to find out if Heng had talked to him recently, but he hasn't called me back, which is unusual for him."

Sarah twisted the caps off two bottles of water and handed one to Jorani, who gulped half the bottle down quickly.

"But there is something I discovered, and I'm not sure what to do about it. I didn't mention it to the police. I looked through the papers on Heng's desk and in the cabinet at home, after your call yesterday. I was looking for something, anything, that might indicate what might have happened. I found this. I think it may be important."

She reached into her bag and pulled out a small battered notebook, which looked as if it had been untouched for many years.

"This was in a drawer in the cabinet where he keeps a lot of his files. I certainly don't know everything that Heng works on and studies. But I know I've never seen any notebook like this in our house before. You can tell it's quite old and that it has been through a lot." She gently ran the palm of her hand over the surface. "But it's the inscription that made me gasp when I first saw it."

As someone who had studied ancient artifacts for most of her adult life, Sarah recognized when objects needed to be handled with great care. And this was one such item. She wished she had a pair of cotton gloves as she carefully flipped the cover open to reveal the handwritten inscription on the inside cover. It was in Khmer, and Sarah handed it back to Jorani, asking her to translate.

"This is the diary of Sam Sokha of Phnom Penh and the National Museum of Cambodia, April 1975." She looked up at Sarah, her voice barely a whisper. "Sokha was Heng's father. Heng knows his name but almost nothing else about him."

Sarah gasped and put her hand over her mouth. "Oh my God."

"I don't know where this diary came from or when Heng got it," Jorani said, "but I know he hasn't had it for long. I suspect that it was the reason for his odd behavior over the past weeks, though I suppose I shouldn't be surprised that Heng's father was also a staff member at the national museum. I can only imagine what might have happened to Sokha after the Khmer Rouge takeover in 1975. I do know that while the Khmer Rouge did leave thousands of landmines around the site at Angkor, they also left the temples more or less intact as a testament to the glories of the past and an inspiration to the future Khmer civilization. The national museum was also allowed to remain untouched for at least part of their time in power."

Sarah leaned over to look at the book and let her hand hover above it, almost as if she was afraid to touch it again. She started to say something but instead shook her head and waved at Jorani to continue.

"I've heard that some of the regime leaders lived at the museum and used the building as offices. But even though they allegedly respected the cultural works of art, they were brutal toward the museum staff and other scholars in the field. Most of those people didn't last much beyond the first few months after the Khmer Rouge arrived. My assumption is that his father was one of those who were terrorized, and I can't imagine what Heng must have been going through after finding this diary."

Sarah asked if Jorani had read any of its contents.

"I began to read it. It seems to be the account of what happened at the museum between April and June of 1975, beginning with the day the Americans left, which was April 12. Sokha then describes the downward spiral of life at the museum and what happened to its staff." Her tears seemed to interrupt her thoughts, but she gathered herself together. "Heng must have found it somewhere in the museum, probably dumped at some point into a box in the archives or even into a cabinet in an unused room somewhere. Once he read the inscription, he would have known that it had belonged to his father. He probably brought it home to study further."

Now Jorani's tears devolved into a near torrent, and Sarah once again put an arm around her and pulled her close. But it didn't surprise Sarah that Jorani was able to settle her emotions quickly, given how strong she had always seemed.

"Sarah, the fact that this diary exists brings back so much horror and pain. I can't imagine what Heng went through looking at this. I just *know* this has something to do with his disappearance, but I can't tell you why I believe that. Could there be something in this diary that someone or some institution doesn't want to be made public knowledge?" She paused. "But why would anyone kidnap him if he doesn't have the diary with him?"

"Whoa, Jorani, who said anything about kidnapping?" Sarah knew her voice sounded more confident than she actually felt. "We don't know yet if he was kidnapped or what has happened to him. We need to stay calm and try to think through all this. He may just have needed time and space to think about this diary and what it means. You've already contacted the police. Have you done anything else?"

"Yes, I did leave messages for the director of the museum, and with some of his curatorial colleagues, to let them know I'm worried about what has happened, but I'm not sure they will have any ideas beyond contacting the police. I did not tell them about the diary. I don't know why I didn't tell them, but I didn't."

"Can I see the diary again?" Sarah extended her hand and gestured at the book in Jorani's lap. "I'm surprised you've only read a few pages. If you're so convinced the diary has something to do with all this, why didn't you read more? I think, if it were me, I'd devour it."

Jorani continued to clutch the diary in her lap. "I guess it just seemed invasive for me to dig into it too deeply without talking to Heng about it. Also, in this humid climate, the pages have really suffered. Some of the pages are stuck together, and they need to be separated by someone who knows what they're doing. I'm afraid I may rip them if I try. I did read the first entry in the diary, which is so tragic and personal, and I was so moved that I couldn't really read much more of it without Heng. I could translate it for you if you think it will help."

After Jorani read the passage dated April 12, 1975, about the Americans leaving Phnom Penh and the last visit from an American who had worked with museum staff for several years, they both sat speechless.

"Crap," Sarah said, taking Jorani's hands in hers. "I can't even imagine what Heng was going through after he read this. This must have hit him like a hammer. He must have been in terrible pain."

Jorani reminded Sarah how Heng had never known his father and had only vague memories of his mother at the camp on the Thai-Cambodian border. "I don't know how much Heng has told you about his life, and I'm so sorry if this is old news to you. He doesn't like to talk about it and sometimes pretends that his background and lack of family have not been that big a deal. But I know him better than that, and I know that all of this hurts him a lot." She paused. "*A lot.* We all suffered, but some of us suffered more than others."

Jorani tried to offer Sarah a quick smile, but it faded rapidly. Meanwhile, Sarah's mind and heart were racing. She had left San Diego four days ago, embarking on this trip thinking that her greatest challenges were going to be convincing officials in Phnom Penh to sign the paperwork regarding loans of objects from the national museum and worrying about how many cargo flights it would take to get the sculptures to the US. Instead, she had one missing colleague in Heng and one distraught friend in Jorani, and one friend whose reaction, she began to realize, she didn't really understand. Nigel could have taken more action yesterday when Heng didn't show up. Although, she admitted to herself, while she didn't know what that would have been, she believed he probably had some powerful allies to help figure out what was happening. All this added up to the fact that she herself was now feeling frightened and trying to navigate scary territory—not to mention feeling taken aback by what Jorani had translated for her.

In particular, there was something in the passage about that day at the national museum, in April of 1975, that jarred something in her brain. But as tired and rattled as she was, she couldn't make any specific connection. So, she did what she normally did in times of great stress.

"OK, Jorani. I don't know about you, but I haven't really eaten since the plastic-wrapped food on the plane, and I am starving. Want to head out for a little dinner with me right now? It might give us a chance to look more closely at this diary. We can think a little more about it beyond that one entry."

Jorani hesitated for a moment but then nodded. "Yes, let's go and get something to eat, but I think, if it's OK, I'd like to leave the diary here in your hotel-room safe rather than taking it out. OK with you?"

Sarah agreed and placed the diary inside the safe, which was tucked into the cabinet under the TV. After entering the same code she had used for as long as she could remember, she spun the dial.

CHAPTER 13

Phnom Penh
Wednesday night

As they walked through the hotel lobby, Sarah waved at the general manager, who was coming out of his office. "See you tomorrow!" He waved back.

She and Jorani walked over to a local Chinese restaurant on Street 61 in silence. Sarah couldn't figure out what to say to Jorani, and Jorani seemed lost in her thoughts. Though it was clear why Jorani was distracted, given all the recent events, she remained uncharacteristically quiet throughout the meal, which was excellent. It never ceased to amaze Sarah how the Chinese diaspora was able to size up local tastes, incorporate spices and food preferences of the target audience, and come up with solid, reasonably priced food all over the world. Their culinary skills were validated by Jorani's appetite—she ate as much as Sarah did despite her reserved demeanor. They were both surprised that their serving plates were empty by the time they were done. After Sarah paid the bill and saved the receipt for her expense report, they walked out of the restaurant onto the street.

Traffic had quieted down for the evening as merchants were closing up their shops, and it seemed safe to cross the street in the center
of the block. The sound of a motorbike starting up in the distance was
the only vehicle Sarah specifically heard, and as they crossed toward
the hotel, the bike got closer and louder. As Sarah watched Jorani turn
around to look back, she came to the dawning realization that the motorbike was heading straight for them.

"Sarah, run!" Jorani screamed as the motorbike rammed between
them and the rider grabbed Jorani's shoulder tote bag. Jorani initially
refused to let it go, hanging on to it while being dragged down the
street.

Sarah, who had been knocked down by the force of the motorbike
and had hit her head on the pavement, momentarily saw stars. Her
glasses had flown off, and she squinted as she searched around for
them. They were on the sidewalk just a few feet away, miraculously still
in one piece. She grabbed them and stood up quickly, but the wind had
been knocked out of her as well, and feeling unsteady, she immediately
sat down hard on the curb before making a superhuman effort to pull
herself up again and run after the motorbike and Jorani. "Jorani, let go
of the bag!" she hollered before the world began to spin and she fell to
the sidewalk pavement. It sounded as if the motorbike was approaching full speed, and in her fog, she knew Jorani would no longer be able
to hang on. The next thing she knew, Jorani was moaning in pain a
short distance away.

What had been a semideserted street became instantly full as people came out of nowhere to assist the two women. Men took off their
jackets and shirts to put under their heads, and a woman who Sarah
had seen closing up a T-shirt shop took charge of the scene, insist-
ing that Sarah and Jorani go to the hospital. Someone whistled for a
tuk-tuk driver, and the local crowd carefully lifted both of them into
the little three-wheeled carriage, which then whisked them off in the
direction of the Royal Phnom Penh Hospital on Monivong Boulevard
near the airport.

Although Sarah and Jorani were conscious, they were both hurting.
Sarah had a throbbing headache and couldn't move her neck without
stabbing pain. But she somehow managed to glance in Jorani's direction. Her friend was bleeding from a number of deep cuts and scrapes,

which Sarah assumed had been sustained when the bike dragged her down the street. Jorani, who was holding her arm gingerly as if it had been broken or dislocated, was muttering incoherently. "The diary, the diary. He was after the diary. Sarah will keep it safe, Heng. Sarah will keep it in the safe."

Sarah was barely conscious, but she did manage to reply. "We need help. What should I do? Call the police?" There was no response from Jorani. Sarah carefully turned her head once more. Jorani had passed out.

CHAPTER 14

Phnom Penh
Early Thursday morning

Heng awakened to discover he was no longer moving in a vehicle. He was now lying on what seemed to be a clean bed, and one of his hands was bound and handcuffed to the bedframe. His mouth was taped shut, but he wasn't blindfolded. Light streamed in through a window high on the wall. It must be morning, he figured, and they had arrived at the safe house, wherever that was, but he still had no idea why he was there.

The good news was that his head felt clearer now, and he forced himself to assess and compartmentalize his current situation and why this was happening. The more he thought about it, the more he became convinced of the source of all this chaos. The diary.

Even forty years after the overthrow of the Khmer Rouge by the Vietnamese, the national museum had still not completely recovered from the decades of neglect. Information was still stuffed and scattered in various places around the building. With so much history lost, most evidence for the recent past came from the sketchy documentation that the staff kept unearthing in the museum building and from the sometimes-vague memories of those few who had survived and were still alive. Heng had recently been searching for old files that might shed more background light on some of the exhibition's installations, and he'd been told he might find something useful in one of the museum's storerooms. And, quite unexpectedly, he did. But what he'd found was a treasure far more valuable—to him, anyway—than the initial target of his search. The diary had been buried in the bottom of a box, stuffed with other papers, which had been crammed into a metal cabinet drawer in a little-used back room. It had clearly been sitting there for decades.

But it wasn't until after he had been through all the paper files, and completed a rough organization of them, that he'd turned his attention to the small notebook. He hadn't even known, initially, that it was a diary. But he had known it was old, so he had been careful when opening it up, to avoid damaging the pages.

The mere presence of handwritten Khmer script on the inside cover had sent a bolt of lightning throughout his body. And then he'd seen his father's name.

"This is the diary of Sam Sokha of Phnom Penh and the National Museum of Cambodia, April 1975."

Heng's heart had begun to race. He had felt so dizzy and disoriented that he had to sit down in that dingy, messy storeroom. Could it be true that his father had also worked at the national museum? Had he been there at the time of the Khmer Rouge takeover of the country and its institutions?

A short sentence beneath his father's inscription had confirmed his suspicion. Sokha had been a conservator and restorer of sculpture at the national museum in Phnom Penh and had been present for the fall of Phnom Penh and the departure of the Americans. Heng had then gone on to read an entry on one of the first pages. It was dated April 12, 1975.

> Today was a sad day and one I will remember for as long as I live, though at this point I do not know how long that will be. The staff of the museum is anxious about the future. I am as well, and it seems to be a

bad omen that the foreigners, and in particular the Americans, are leaving the country after helping us for so many years. I will miss them and their optimism and passion and their belief in a better Cambodia and Southeast Asia.

Early this morning, our American colleague, whom I am not going to name because the future seems so uncertain, came to visit us for the last time, telling us that he, along with the rest of the Americans, would be evacuated this afternoon from a landing zone near the US embassy. It was awkward. We all didn't have much to say to him, but we shook hands and embraced, and then the little group broke up, seemingly knowing that we would never see one another again but hoping irrationally that we might. I have always respected and loved the confidence that this American had in us and our ability to preserve our own cultural heritage. He seemed truly to believe in Cambodia and its future, and his departure was very, very sad. He took me aside before he left and suggested to me that my family and I should leave the city. But I told him we had decided to stay.

Perhaps to cling to one of our last connections with the outside world for as long as I could, I followed him at a little distance as he left the building. He seemed distracted and sad, probably lost in thought as he often had been during the time we had known him. I had always thought there was something resigned and defeated about him, as if something terrible had happened to him from which he might never recover. After the departure of the French, I never thought there could be a Westerner who would be as devoted to the art of the Khmer Empire as he has proven to be. I will never forget him.

As he passed the tenth-century sculpture of Uma and Shiva from Banteay Srei, the one for which he had helped me when I had worked to rejoin the head of Uma to her body, he stopped. I stopped walking as well, embarrassed that someone who had been such a friend to me and to the museum might see me following him through the galleries. As I watched from the shadows, to my astonishment and dismay, he pulled the head of the goddess Uma from the sculpture and put it into his bag. I was paralyzed. I let a piece of one of the great treasures of the collection walk out of the museum with him as he headed back into his comfortable and safe Western life. I stood there almost in tears and thought, sadly, that it might well be that all of us, and all of the collection, would be better off out of the country for the next few years. But we have taken our stand. We await the arrival of the Khmer Rouge, who cannot be far off as we hear gunfire and explosions that now seem very close.

What will become of this museum, to which I have devoted and dedicated my life? I alternate between fear and deep depression. What will become of my wife and our unborn child? I feel so helpless, but I am determined to survive to bear witness to whatever happens.

The entry had hit Heng hard, but the next one had been even worse.

Nothing good can come from what I have seen today in the city. Just after the midday meal, Khmer Rouge operatives began to order people to leave the city, and as I write this, late at night on 17 April 1975, I have watched columns of uncomprehending and terrified people begin to evacuate the city. Everyone is bewildered and confused. I have heard much talk of the Year Zero, the point in time to which the Khmer Rouge wishes to bring us back. These people, these Khmer Rouge, are not used to cities and city people. They do not know how to behave. Yet they have become our masters.

Apparently, all those being evacuated are being asked to return to their ancestral towns, where they will be processed. There seems to be no explanation for what the future will hold or how this new regime plans to govern the country. But it is clear that there is no place for compromise or half measures. Everyone who is told to leave must leave. Some of us in the museum have been exempted so far, but we are confined to the building. I have not been able to get home to check on Bopha.

We have been told that those foreigners who have stayed are all in the French embassy building north of us and that the Cambodians who entered the embassy with them are being asked to leave. I suspect the foreigners will all be allowed to leave the country, but when? I have tried to get word to Bopha to come to the museum but have been unable to do so. I am terrified that, in her pregnant state, she will not be able to make a long journey. I am torn between staying here and continuing to wonder about her and going home and risk being beaten to death as the rumors and our young minders, who can't be more than fifteen or sixteen years old, have suggested will happen.

I don't know what to do.

The next short entry, dated April 20, 1975, read:

I have worked myself into a state of exhaustion. I had finally made the decision to go home and find Bopha. I went under cover of dark and made it only to find a note from her that she has been forced to begin walking to her ancestral home of Siem Reap. I returned to the museum, and I do not know if she, and the baby who was planning to come into our world any day now, will make it. I have also learned that many of us are going to be taken from the museum in the next day or two.

I have failed on both fronts of my responsibilities—to my family and to the national collections of Cambodia. I have fallen into despair. Now I wait for whatever may come next and pray several times a day in front of the head of Jayavarman VII in the gallery. For many, his head has become a stand-in for the Buddha himself, and in my hopelessness, I find myself falling into this trap as well.

The final entry that Heng had read before he'd been unable to go on was from later in 1975. The exact date was smeared and illegible.

I have heard rumors that the offices of the Ecole française have been raided and that all the papers documenting the temples at Angkor have been destroyed. I weep for my country. The new regime is now calling our homeland "Democratic Kampuchea" and the new leaders claim they want to recapture the greatness of Angkor.

Sadly, we have been told that another group of us needs to be ready to leave the museum in the next day or so. Apparently, I have been spared departure so far because of my work. The leaders of our new world, who hailed from the nameless, faceless "Organization" known as Angkar, and who rule our lives, seem to believe I am important for maintaining the collection which will, presumably, inspire us to achieve the heights that our people reached nine hundred years ago. I do not know if I will be spared my life. Or if I am one of those who will be forced out into the countryside. Or if I will be taken to the Cercle Sportif, or S-21, the old high school that has recently been repurposed as an extermination center for enemies of the state.

I try to remain calm about my fate and pray and light incense and leave offerings to the Buddha every day asking that my wife make it to Siem Reap and that she, and our child, are alive.

Devastated, Heng hadn't been able to read any more. How could he not have known that his father had worked at the museum and that he was following in his footsteps? How could he not have known? After a few minutes, he had made the decision to break museum policy and bring the diary home to read and examine further, justifying his action by thinking that the diary was really more his father's personal thoughts than about the museum's work.

But he had needed time before reading any more, so he had not taken the diary with him to Bangkok. He had not mentioned it to Jorani, though when he was in Bangkok, he had mentioned it to Anada, who'd perked up but only briefly, as Heng hadn't shared any details. And he'd told Nigel about it. Though he'd made it clear he had not yet been through the entire document, he'd thought Nigel might find the first section about the American interesting. Heng had also suggested that an excerpt from the diary's narrative might make an excellent label in the exhibition, or even provide narrative content for the video about Shiva and Uma they were producing for the show.

Nigel had initially been very intrigued, explaining that he knew some of the Americans who had been in Phnom Penh until the 1975 evacuation. He had even asked Heng about any specific names and to bring the diary to Bangkok so he could inspect it directly. Of course, Heng hadn't brought it with him, which meant Nigel never had a chance to look at it. He had told Nigel, though, that the diary's author had not specifically named any of the people about whom he had written, except his wife.

Now, as Heng lay here imprisoned in a room somewhere, presumably in Phnom Penh, he just couldn't shake the suspicion that his father's diary had something to do with his situation. He thought again of Jorani, and of Nigel and Sarah and Anada, all of whom must be worried about him by now. They would know even less about his predicament than he did, which wasn't much except that he believed he was next going to be taken to Siem Reap, a town he knew well. If he did end up there, he hoped that someone would be able to help him. But for now, his priority was to get out of this room.

CHAPTER 15

Phnom Penh
Early Thursday morning

Sarah had a splitting headache. She carefully opened one eye. The room where she lay appeared sterile, and a window to her right revealed Phnom Penh's predawn darkness. Glancing down at her arm, she found a tube connecting her to an IV bag hanging from a pole. Every muscle and nerve of her body then seemed to awaken at once, on fire. *What happened?* She and Jorani had been eating dinner . . . and then what? Why did she feel so awful? And where was she?

Suddenly, her memory kicked in, and she sat bolt upright in the hospital bed before promptly collapsing back down. Where was Jorani? She looked to her left and saw someone lying on the other bed in the room. The face of the figure was covered in bandages, but she recognized Jorani's hair and her arms, which were folded across her chest on top of the blanket, one with an IV tube attached to a bag, the other in a soft cast.

"Jorani?" she croaked in a voice she didn't recognize.

No response. Sarah was just attempting to get out of her bed, when a crisply efficient Cambodian nurse opened the door and entered the room.

"Not so fast, please," the nurse said in excellent English. "You are badly bruised, and you hit your head. It is better if you just lie there and let the medicine and rest do their work. You are both very lucky there were people on the street who took action and that the tuk-tuk driver brought you here to our hospital. We are one of the best equipped trauma and emergency hospitals in the city."

"Is my friend OK?"

The nurse hesitated. "I'm not really supposed to talk to patients about other patients. Your friend is quite injured, and we have her lightly sedated right now. She has a couple of cracked ribs, a broken arm, and some significant bruising and scratches, but the scan of her head seems to be normal, though she also seems to have hit her head. The doctors don't think she has a concussion, however. They think she is going to be OK. You also have some significant external bruising and need to rest. Would you like some water or juice?"

Sarah realized her mouth was very dry. "Yes," she said. "Some water, thank you."

After taking a sip through a straw, she asked the nurse if she had any further details about what had happened.

The nurse hesitated again before answering. "The tuk-tuk driver who dropped you off said two people on the street had told him that you both had been the victims of a grab-and-go theft. Apparently a motorbike driver came after you as you began to cross the street and made off with your friend's tote bag. I've heard that the police took some basic information from the witnesses, but I'm sure they are going to want to talk to you both at some point soon. You're lucky there were several local merchants and other people who were there to help the two of you."

Sarah nodded, grateful for the water and the information. She lay back down on the bed. She was quite sure Jorani didn't carry large quantities of money or valuables in her bag. And she always kept her phone in her pocket. Why would a motorbike thief target Jorani instead of Sarah, especially given that she looked as if she belonged in Phnom Penh more than Sarah did? Her brain was still too muddled and she was in too much pain to think this through right now. She decided to take the nurse's advice and rest, though as she drifted off, she had the feeling there was much more going on with all of this than she understood.

CHAPTER 16

Phnom Penh
Thursday afternoon

Both Jorani and Sarah had only picked at their hospital lunches. It was now late afternoon, and they were awake, though quiet in their beds. Jorani seemed to have lost her voice and could only whisper. "It hurts to talk, but there is so much that we need to talk about."

Sarah said, "Shh, Jorani, we should rest." Ignoring her own advice, she went on. "But I understand. Do you remember what happened at any point before we woke up in this hospital room?"

Jorani thought for a minute. "I remember having dinner. Crossing Street 61. Hearing a motorbike. The driver yanked at my bag. He must have gotten it. We were in a tuk-tuk, and then we were here and I was going in and out of rooms. Then I woke up, and I think I knew you were here. Then I must've gone back to sleep."

"Yeah, that's what I remember too. Did you get a look at the motorbike rider?"

"No, he was wearing a helmet and sunglasses, at night. Impossible to see anything."

"Jorani, you said something in the tuk-tuk about the thief wanting the diary. Do you think the motorbike rider was after that diary Heng found? Did you tell anyone else about it? Or did you have anything of value in your bag?"

There was no answer from the other bed.

"Jorani? Are you awake?"

Jorani had drifted off, and Sarah lay in the bed looking at the ceiling and wondering what, exactly, she was doing there in a hospital in Phnom Penh when she was supposed to be in Siem Reap meeting with the directors of Conservation d'Angkor and the Angkor National Museum. They must be wondering why she hadn't shown up for their conversations. She didn't have their numbers in her phone and couldn't call but wished she could somehow reach them. Her head still hurt, but she definitely didn't feel as if she needed to sleep again.

"Sarah! How are you feeling?" Sarah snapped her head toward a voice at her open door. James Carlyle stood there, knocking on the doorframe. "May I come in?"

Sarah's head cautioned her not to move so quickly anytime soon. Maybe she was worse off than she'd thought. She nodded just slightly at her unexpected visitor.

James walked in and asked if he could sit down. She nodded again, and he pulled up a chair next to her bed. Self-consciously, and she realized somewhat absurdly, she wondered how bad she looked. She wished she had been able to comb her hair and wash her face before seeing him, or anyone, and hoped she didn't look too much of a hot mess. Then she made an invisible eye roll to herself given the circumstances. It really didn't matter.

"Sarah, I've tried to talk to the police and the doctors, both of whom were unwilling to give me a lot of information. I'm here to let you know that the consulate is ready to help you with any issue related to this accident. And yes, since you might ask, normally the consulate would not send someone like me to visit a banged-up US citizen, but since we had met and chatted, I volunteered."

Sarah looked at him in disbelief. "How on earth did you know I was here?"

"I can fill you in later about that," he said.

"Well, actually, you can fill me in right now as I am finding this a little strange. And I have nowhere else to go at the moment."

"OK, sure, it's not that complicated. I have a long-standing relationship with the management at Le Royal because I've always been a swimmer, and when I first came to Phnom Penh, I wanted to find a pool. I inquired at Le Royal, and the management was happy to let me swim there in the mornings before most of the guests were up. I got my pool—and they got a contact at the US embassy. Worked for everyone."

It seemed a little creepy to Sarah, but she let him go on.

"The staff there appears to know you pretty well too. I guess you've stayed there a few times? The front desk manager told me the hotel is also sponsoring your exhibition's opening events here, and you were supposed to have a meeting with the general manager this morning. When you didn't show—and they realized you didn't return last night either—they got worried. They seem very protective of you. It's kind of sweet."

Sarah had no idea the hotel was keeping close tabs on her, and she wasn't sure how she felt about all these people talking about her in her absence. Maybe it *was* just genuinely sweet.

"Anyway, they called the emergency number at the embassy early this morning, and I heard about their call, and now here I am."

"I hope they don't think I can't take care of myself, but I'm glad they called."

He commented on the spectacular bruise on her cheek and once again asked how she was feeling.

"Well, I'm not great and I feel pretty banged up and I'm a little worried that I'm here in a medical facility in a country that I suspect isn't as advanced as the US when it comes to health care." She wondered how this sounded, especially given that her injuries seemed rather minimal and they'd taken good care of her so far.

"The care at this hospital is generally good," he said, "and I'm sure they've done all they can for now."

Sarah didn't feel overly reassured by this but didn't say anything else. She hadn't really been in a position last night to make a decision about where to go.

James continued. "So can you tell me what actually happened? All I've heard is that a motorbike driver came at you and your friend and didn't take anything from you but grabbed your friend's bag. And heroically, it seemed, she hung on to it as if it were filled with gold." He glanced over at Jorani. "Seems her injuries are far worse than yours."

"You just missed Jorani. She was awake a little while ago and started to talk to me about what she thought may have incited the incident; she could probably tell you more than me. But apparently, she's fallen back asleep. So maybe *you* can answer a question for me: How do you know even that much? You seem to pretty much know everything I know about what happened. What's up with that?" He didn't answer her question, and although she studied him intently for the next several seconds, she couldn't decipher his poker face. Every fiber of her body screamed at her to just shut up. But she didn't listen. At that point she desperately needed to talk to someone. "James, this was not an accident or a random bag snatch. Jorani and I were deliberately targeted by that motorbike thief, who clearly wanted her bag."

James frowned as the gears seemed to spin in his brain. "Hmm, I wonder why. Did Jorani have anything of value in that bag—a wad of US dollars or euros, maybe, or some jewelry?"

Sarah hesitated and shook her head. She adjusted her position, wincing in pain, before she took the next leap. "Not that I know of, and I doubt strongly that she did. But here's the thing: Jorani is married to my friend and colleague Sam Heng, the curator at the national museum in Phnom Penh with whom I'm organizing the exhibition we discussed at your office yesterday."

"Along with Nigel Sanderson," James interjected.

She took a beat to wonder why he brought up Nigel's name. "Yes, with Nigel. Anyway, Heng seems to have disappeared. None of us has heard from him for two days. He was supposed to Zoom in to a meeting that Nigel and I had day before yesterday but was a no-show, which was not like him, not for something important like this. And Jorani has not heard from him or seen him, either, since Tuesday morning. She was pretty frantic last night."

Jorani stirred, and they both observed her for a minute. But she didn't wake up, so Sarah continued. "When Jorani came to see me at the hotel last night, she had brought along a small diary that she believed Heng had brought home from the national museum, although he hadn't said anything about it to her. She found it when she was searching through his desk at home looking for anything that might explain why he was gone. We left it locked in the safe in my room when we went out to dinner. Presumably it's still there."

"That's interesting," he said, his head cocked a bit to one side. "Why did you leave it locked up? Did you think it might be valuable?"

"I wanted to take it to dinner to look at it while we ate, but Jorani insisted that we put it in the room safe. That turned out to be psychic on her part. According to her, Heng had seemed disturbed and distant, acting strangely for the past few weeks. She didn't say this outright, but she seemed to think his behavior had something to do with this diary. It's certainly not financially valuable, but maybe there is something in it that's important. I don't know."

She waited for a response from him, though she wasn't sure what she hoped for. A revelation? Validation? But all he did was nod for her to go on with the story.

"Jorani hadn't finished reading through all of it, but the first pages detail life at the museum in the period just before and after the Khmer Rouge takeover in 1975. She thinks Heng was both shocked and distraught about what may be the most extraordinary part of the story— that it was written by his father, whom he never knew. But he did know his name, which is written on the inside cover of the notebook."

Sarah hesitated when she noticed James looking at her askance, as if this were too much of a coincidence to be real. Maybe she was telling him too much. She achingly reached for the water on her bedside table, but James lunged for it, beating her to the cup. He then handed it to her. She could have managed by herself. But it was a nice gesture.

"I know I'm digressing here, but Heng has an interesting, if tragic, backstory. After his pregnant mother was marched into the countryside and back to Siem Reap, his father continued his work at the national museum for an unknown period. He undoubtedly met a tragic end. Heng doesn't know that part of the story, and it's very likely he never will. He has told me that his mother died getting them to the Thai border, from which Nigel—the art connoisseur you have been inquiring about—rescued him all those years ago." James stiffened at the mention of Nigel, but she went on. "So you can see why, if the diary offers some additional insight into Heng's personal history, it would be important to him. His life story is one of the most compelling I have

ever heard. And the idea that he knew nothing about his parents, except their names, for so long—and then it turns out his father was also
an employee at the national museum—is remarkable. But I don't know
why Jorani thinks the diary could be valuable to anyone else."

Sarah stopped, exhausted both physically and emotionally. She fell
back onto the bed, and although it was probably inhospitable with a
visitor at her side, she closed her eyes. But when she heard James lift
himself up from his chair, she opened one eye and watched him walk
over to the window. She knew the basic layout of Phnom Penh, and
her window overlooked Monivong Boulevard, the main thoroughfare
of the chaotic metropolis. Its traffic patterns were insane. When she
had first come to Cambodia, she had been told that, long ago—after
both the Khmer Rouge and later the Vietnamese had been ousted—
the Vietnamese drove on the right side of the road, the Thais drove
on the left, and the Cambodians drove wherever they damned well
pleased. It was still sort of true. Watching the traffic never ceased to
amaze her. As James stared out the window, she wondered if he, a fellow American, might feel the same way. He turned around just then,
as if he knew she'd been watching him. She opened the other eye to
appear less weird.

"Sarah, there's a lot more going on here than I think you're aware
of," he said. "Probably more than I'm aware of. I don't know what the
motorbike thief was after, but your friend might be right. That diary
may hold answers to some questions that you and Jorani have. And
maybe even to some that I have. If you're willing, I'd like you both to
come to the consulate for a more formal debriefing. I think we can
help each other. However, for now, it might be best for you to stay here
and rest for another night."

Sarah wondered what he meant about *him* having questions. She
had thought his hospital visit was just to support an American in a bit
of distress. But his little interrogation, and his curious facial expres-
sions, had been hinting that there was more to his motivation than he
had let on.

"I know it may be difficult, under the circumstances, for you to
trust me," he said, as if reading her mind again. "But I would ask you
to, at least for the next day or so."

Sarah struggled to keep her expression neutral, given how this visit had grown increasingly mysterious. "I don't know. I'm not really sure why I should trust you or even what you are asking me to trust you about. I just met you yesterday, and honestly, you're beginning to seem more like a spook to me than a public affairs officer. But yes, I am quite sure that Jorani and I can both show up at the embassy when we're discharged. I assume my phone is somewhere with my other things, so please call me in the morning and we'll make a plan."

"Thank you. See you soon, maybe tomorrow. I'll keep my calendar flexible for you."

"Yes, until then." She paused, curious why an important government official would be so flexible to fit her into his undoubtedly busy day. "Thanks for coming."

Sarah closed her eyes again after he left. At first, she lay there wondering, once again, how she had found herself in this situation, which was way beyond anything that she had ever encountered in her life. She also tried to discern who this guy was and what he really wanted. She didn't have a clue. A nurse came into the room and added something to her IV bag, after which Sarah quickly began to feel drowsy. It must have been a sleeping aid. After a few minutes, she fell into a deep and needed sleep.

CHAPTER 17

Bangkok
Friday morning

"Sawasdee khrap."

"Good morning." The connection on the burner phone, which was operating on a sketchy and weak cellular network, was scratchy, but they could hear one another. Nigel reflected on how much this one technology had changed all their lives. The mechanics of business were easier now. It was far better than the paper trails, which had been almost unavoidable in the past. Though he was also sure that some of the ease of doing business today probably came from the fact that most of his clients now were private collectors, not museums. Museums required documentation and clean provenance. Many private collectors were not so scrupulous. "Where are we with the operation?" Nigel asked.

"We are good to go. The team will rest for the next two days, to be ready for Sunday night. We'll take three trucks to the site. We are ready."

"And you're sure the people you've chosen for this operation are good? Will they keep their mouths shut?"

"Yes, sir. We have used them in the past, and *they* think we will use them in the future. I have not told everyone this is our last job, just a couple of them. We pay better than anyone else and I trust all of them." He added, in a more sinister tone, "And, of course, they know *we* know where their families live."

Nigel chuckled at this response. A little intimidation never hurt when dealing with those who were on the front lines of his operations. And, of course, he knew that he held great power over his main operative on the front lines, with whom he was speaking, whose life had not turned out the way he had anticipated and whose need for money, to deal with family problems, seemed endless. But Nigel had no doubt that Anada's work and knowledge were first-rate. And, after this operation, there would be enough money for both of them to leave for whatever life they wanted.

"OK, remember, phones off after the operation starts. Do not call me until all the trucks and personnel are clear of the site and have arrived at the meeting point. From there, you will move the goods through the intermediaries over the border. The gallery in Bangkok that's handling the sale to the collectors is ready to receive everything. I'm not going to be there. You need to make this happen. Understood?"

"Yes."

"Then I will expect to hear from you Sunday night. Don't worry about waking me as I will be awaiting your call."

Before he hung up the phone, he decided to add one other request. "There is one more thing I need you to do for me. Last night's operation in Phnom Penh was unsuccessful, and I need you to investigate further in a different direction." As his field team leader listened, he described what he wanted done, and there was a quick assent indicating understanding.

Now, as he hung up the phone, he let out a big, tension-releasing sigh. This last operation would ensure him a secure financial future. He was eager for this to all be done, especially as he thought about how he had sensed some resistance and distraction on the part of Anada in recent conversations. Nigel wondered what was going on with that and whether it might affect this final operation.

But he put it out of his mind, at least for the moment.

CHAPTER 18

South Vietnam
1968

Afterward, even after the exoneration by the board of inquiry, Nigel was never completely clear about what had happened that night in the village near Tay Ninh. His guilt still overwhelmed him. His brain fogged when he thought of those minutes. What had happened in the blink of an eye had ended the life of one of his closest friends and changed the course of his life forever.

They had told him there was nothing he could have done and he was to return to full duty in the field. They had even given him a citation for valorous conduct under fire in the service of his country, or something like that. But he had long ago tossed out or lost the commendation. Had anyone asked him about the incident, he would have said that he felt wrecked and hollow.

No one ever asked.

He and his partner, Joseph Steptoe, had worked together for many months, collecting intelligence on possible enemy activity, work they saw as increasingly useless and futile. But both were young and new to the field. Neither had the life experience to understand the long-range consequences of much of what they were doing. They followed orders. They were commended for it.

He and Joe had come to one particularly silent village that afternoon. There were a few older women and small children around, mostly cooking or sweeping out the small huts that the Americans sometimes called *hooches*, but no younger women and no men. When asked, the villagers said they were working in the fields. They would be back that afternoon. So he and Joe had walked around, watching and waiting, until the men and women of the village returned.

Night fell fast in the Vietnamese countryside, as it did throughout the tropics. Without electricity, the cooking fires outside the thatched-roof huts provided the only illumination in the village after the sun had set. They were sitting just outside the village perimeter, smelling the wonderful spicy aroma of the Vietnamese food cooking close by, while eating the packaged and tasteless food they had brought with them.

Without warning, the forest exploded on three sides with gunfire and mortar shells, targeting them where they sat. They both grabbed their rifles and dived behind the large rock against which they had been sitting, leaving their food and their packs out in the open.

"Where's it coming from?"

"Mostly from the left, though some also from the right. At least three of them."

"Shit, someone in the village must have sent a warning out to the local VC. We're fucked. How much ammo do you have?"

"Ten rounds, so OK for now. Just don't waste bullets. I'm calling it in."

"We're in a small village five clicks south of Tay Ninh. We're taking heavy fire. Repeat, heavy fire. Please advise evacuation plan."

The radio crackled to life. "We copy. No evacuation possible now. Hold tight and we'll be there when possible."

Nigel and Joe looked at each other with raised eyebrows. It was worse than they had anticipated. The firing stopped momentarily, and they both took a deep breath. Their eyes met again.

"Fuck."

A few seconds later, a shot came from close range. At that moment,

Joe stiffened. Nigel would never forget those eyes. A second shot followed.

"I'm hit." Those were Joe's only words before he twisted and fell away from Nigel. The fire began again, and Nigel held them off as best he could. Between rounds, he could hear Joe's breathing slowing, until it finally stopped. He squeezed his eyes closed and tried not to think about it. He held his fire.

The barrage continued from both right and left until the enemy seemed convinced they were both either wounded or dead or not worthy of any more ammunition. They melted back into the forest. As dawn approached, Nigel cautiously crawled toward Joe's body. Soon the evacuation helicopter, which he had requested to no avail so many hours ago, arrived to take them back to Saigon. Joe would go home in a coffin, a twenty-six-year-old casualty of a futile and bloody war.

Nigel was absolved of responsibility, but he could not escape the remorse that accompanied the death of his friend and colleague, and he was paralyzed when he thought of visiting Joe's wife. He couldn't bear to think of her as a widow. She had been pregnant, and by now had given birth to a child who would never know their father. On his next home leave, he set out to visit her. He wanted to tell her what had happened. He had even driven past her small, neatly kept home once, but he hadn't been able to bring himself to stop. He continued driving, unable to find it in himself to meet her.

When he returned to Vietnam, he continued to grind out good work, and he received additional commendations both for bravery in the field and for the results he had achieved, but nothing was the same again. Ever.

His transfer from Saigon to Phnom Penh in 1973 had helped. As he'd boarded the military transport, he'd bid farewell to Saigon. He hoped he was leaving the insanity of war that he had seen, but the Paris Peace Accords, which had put an end to the bombing of the countryside of Vietnam, didn't bring relief to Cambodia. He found himself again enmeshed in the fog of war.

Later, when he looked back on his life and what it had become since that day in 1968, when Joe had died in a muddy and militarily unimportant village in South Vietnam, in a war that seemed endless, he couldn't pinpoint when or how everything had changed for him.

But he often thought it might have started that day he transferred to Phnom Penh and the time he had spent thereafter working with, and getting to know, both Khmer art and the people in the national museum who were so dedicated to its preservation. They were a balm for his soul. During his stay there, his opinion of Cambodia, which had been drawn into the morass of the regional conflict, evolved, and Nigel became increasingly enthralled with the history and art of the Khmer Empire, the gods and goddesses, the splendid temples. Everything else he had ever known about history and culture and art disappeared for him, replaced by admiration for what Henri Mouhot, the first to truly introduce the Khmer Empire to the West, had called a civilization "grander than anything left to us by Greece or Rome."

Nigel had not been able to save his friend Joe, and he ultimately had not been able to rescue the people whom he had come to know and love at the museum in Phnom Penh when he left. But rescuing Heng later had meant a lot to him. He understood it didn't begin to make up for all his sins in Southeast Asia and everything he had done wrong. But he hoped that saving and helping one little child would be better than nothing.

CHAPTER 19

Phnom Penh
Friday morning

Sarah awoke from a fitful but restoring sleep and stared up at the ceiling of the room, which she remembered a split second later was in a hospital in Phnom Penh. The events of what happened just two nights ago came back to her abruptly. She still felt weak, and her bruises and scrapes, and especially her head, still hurt, but she was definitely better and eager to leave the hospital and find Heng, who had now been missing for seventy-two hours.

It was still hard to twist, but she managed to turn enough to see if Jorani was awake and ask how she felt. Sarah's heart stopped. The bed was empty and unmade. Jorani's jeans, T-shirt, and scarf, which had previously been carefully folded and stacked, along with her sandals, on a small table on the opposite side of the room, were gone. In their place was a piece of folded paper.

Sarah could just make out her name, even without her glasses. She thrashed out of the bed, noticing in the process that someone had taken the IV out of her arm during the night. As she stood up, she felt lightheaded and had to grab onto the end rail of the bed to keep her balance. She sat down hard. Her heart pounded. After a few seconds of sitting with her eyes closed, she opened them, stood up slowly, and made her way over to the note.

She was at first confused, and then alarmed, by what she read. Sarah realized she had to get out of there now.

Her own clothing was still neatly piled on a table next to her bed, though it was much the worse for wear. Her pants were torn, as was her top, which also had a couple of smears of what she assumed was her blood. She didn't really want to put them on but had little choice, so she pulled off the hospital gown, stepped into her underpants, then pulled on her bra and hooked it closed. She was just pulling her T-shirt over her head when there was a sharp rap at the door.

"Just a minute," she said, pushing one leg and then the other into the baggy linen pants that she'd worn to dinner with Jorani. She stuffed the piece of paper into her pocket. Thinking that it must be a nurse who had come to take her vital signs first thing in the morning, she called out as brightly as she could. "Come in." She hadn't figured out how she would explain to the nurse why she was dressed and ready to go, or why Jorani wasn't there, or why she had to be discharged immediately. But it all proved unnecessary, as it was James Carlyle, once again, who walked through the door.

His expression suggested appraisal, making her feel uncomfortable in her own skin. "How are you feeling this morning? I must say, you're looking quite a bit better. And if I were to guess, I'd think you were about to be discharged, because unless you yanked it out yourself, it seems someone has removed the IV from your arm. Which is a good sign."

The room began to spin, and Sarah closed her eyes and bent over her knees. Maybe she wasn't as well as she'd thought. Her head was clearly still affected by the fall. James walked toward her, bent down, and asked in a concerned voice if she was OK. The dizziness subsided, but she sat down and took a deep breath.

"James, Jorani is gone." She pulled the note from her pocket and handed it to him.

He read it aloud.

Sarah, I am so sorry, but I am worried out of my mind and I need to find Heng. Please don't be concerned about me. I have my mobile phone, which was in my jeans pocket and not in my bag. I will be in touch. Much love, J.

"Jorani must have awakened in the middle of the night and slipped out of the hospital," Sarah said. "I'm no medical professional, but I don't think she's in good enough shape to be setting out in search of Heng herself. I can't believe I didn't wake up when she left. This is all my fault. I have to go and find her." She bit her lip, stopped talking, and looked at James.

Still crouched in front of her, James frowned, but there was more to his serious expression that unsettled her. "You're definitely not responsible for Jorani's actions. But I agree with you. She absolutely can't handle this situation on her own. We need to find her."

"What do you mean we need to find her?"

"You aren't in any shape to search the city of Phnom Penh solo for her."

Sarah said wearily, "Please don't tell me what I am or am not capable of doing at this point. Jorani and Heng are my friends. I need to do everything I can to find them. I am leaving this hospital right now. But if you want to come with me, I probably can't stop you."

James regarded her silently for a moment. "I'm in, but I need to make some calls to change up the rest of the day. I also insist that the doctors here officially release you, as I am not going to be party to illicitly taking an American citizen from a Cambodian hospital against medical advice. I'll find the doctor. In the meantime, you can finish getting ready to leave." He strode out the door into the corridor before she even had a chance to reply.

She looked around the room for her glasses, bag, phone, and sandals, momentarily worried that they'd been stolen or misplaced, but she found them inside the small cabinet on which her clothes had been stacked. Everything seemed to be there. She sat down and began to put on her sandals, when the door opened again. This time it was the doctor and the nurse from last night, followed by James.

The doctor addressed her sternly but kindly. James must have explained the situation about Jorani leaving. "I am releasing you. I am also telling you that you need to take it easy today. Do not exert yourself too much. You will be fine, but you had a pretty severe bump on the head. It's possible you will feel dizzy and weak for a couple more days. You will likely also be very sore. If you're still in Phnom Penh in a few days, I would like to see you again. If not, please see a doctor as soon as possible and explain the situation."

"Thank you. I appreciate this more than I can say. I'll do what I can to take your advice."

After the doctor walked out, the nurse nodded toward Jorani's bed. "Do you know where your friend has gone? I read that note she left you, around four this morning when I came to check on the two of you. She was already gone. Whatever you two are involved in here can't be good. I hope you'll be careful, as I am worried about both of you. And please, listen to what the doctor said. You have had a nasty knock to your head, and although you seem to be OK, you really do need to have it checked out at a better-resourced medical facility. We can only do so much here."

Sarah appreciated her kindness. "Thank you. I will be careful." Then, glancing at James, she said, "We will find her." The nurse walked out of the room, leaving Sarah with James.

Sarah punched the buttons for Jorani's number on her phone, but there was no answer. She left a message for Jorani to return the call as soon as she could and followed that up with a text in case Jorani wasn't inclined to listen to her voicemails regularly.

"I have a few ideas about how to proceed," James said, "but first I think that we both need a cup of strong coffee and some breakfast before we set out. I know a little café a few blocks from here. OK with you?"

She nodded as she realized she desperately needed caffeine. They walked slowly down the hall to the elevator. Though Sarah felt stronger with every step, and her head did feel a little better, she wasn't sure how far she could go or how long she would last. But he was right. Coffee and food were a good start.

At the café, they sat at a table toward the back of the room away from the window and ordered coffee, baguettes, fruit, and croissants. The French had done an alarmingly good job at extracting all they could from their Indochinese colonies without giving a lot back in re-turn. But they *had* taught the people of Vietnam, Laos, and Cambodia to make some of the best baked goods, particularly baguettes, that Sarah had ever had. The food at this small hole-in-the-wall café was no exception. She hadn't realized how hungry she was, after everything that had happened. It wasn't until she saw James watching her with an expression of controlled amusement as she wolfed down the baguette that she figured she must have looked like someone who hadn't eaten for weeks.

She swallowed and said, with a little chagrin, "Sorry. I guess I was hungry."

After some chitchat, the conversation turned serious as James asked her again to go through everything that had happened, begin-ning with Jorani arriving at Le Royal and ending with him showing up at her hospital room. She once again told him what she remembered but now realized there were many holes in her memory about the events, especially about what had happened between the moment the motorbike sped toward them and when she woke up in the hospital.

"Sarah, is there anything else you can remember? We have eyewit-ness reports from several of the locals who were there. Anything else that you can tell me is valuable. By the way, those bystanders may have saved your lives by sending you both to the hospital so quickly."

"Yes, others have told me that as well, and I am grateful, as I'm sure Jorani is too." She took another gulp of the excellent coffee, trying to remember, and shook her head slowly. "Look, there's no more that I can remember right now. Nothing. Sorry. Some of it is crystal clear to me. Some of it is a blur. Maybe with time, more memory will come back. I don't know. And James, not to put too fine a point on it, but I'm a curator of Southeast Asian art at a museum in the United States—not a spy. This kind of thing has never happened to me before. I'm not really sure what to make of it all."

As she said this, Sarah realized again that she wasn't sure what to make of *him* either. Come to think of it, he hadn't introduced himself with a title when they'd first met at the consulate. She'd assumed he was a public affairs officer, but he had never actually said that. She opened her mouth to ask him some questions, but realized that who-ever he was, he represented a level of official help on everything from finding Heng and Jorani to helping her with the exhibition, presuming this situation got resolved. She probably could not afford to ignore or reject his offer for assistance. But she definitely needed to understand more, and the sooner, the better.

He said he understood why her memory was shaky, and he sounded sincere. "To switch gears, should we try to find Jorani once we're finished here? She may also still be badly injured and shouldn't be looking for Heng by herself. You know her and I don't. Where would she go?"

Sarah replayed her last conversation with Jorani in her mind. "I told you last night about the diary and how Jorani was sure this was a targeted attack and the thief was probably after the diary. I assume she'd either go to her place, which is where I'd go for a nice warm shower after leaving a hospital, or somehow try to get to the diary in my hotel-room safe." Realizing she hadn't been back to the hotel in two nights, she wondered aloud if the staff was even more concerned about her now. "Do you think that room is still mine? Would they have moved everything out and opened the safe?"

"Taken care of. I extended your reservation for two more nights in case it was necessary. And I think it will be. But the hotel staff were very gracious and said you can have the room for as long as you need it. It's in large part due to their observation skills and extraordinary service that I found you. It's really quite remarkable in this day that a hotel would pay that much attention. They are anxious to have you back." When he shifted his gaze away from her and toward the window, she could tell he had something else on his mind. "I also alerted my contacts in the police department here in Phnom Penh about Heng's disappearance. Jorani had apparently reported it already, and there's not much they can do right now, but they will help when they can, if and when we get more information or evidence of a kidnapping. It helps that Heng is well known around Phnom Penh and is highly respected as a curator at the national museum."

Although she still wondered who this person sitting across the table really was, and why she was of such importance to him right now, she couldn't help but feel grateful for all his help. "Thank you," she said. "And I need to be sure to express my gratitude to Le Royal too. The staff has certainly gone above and beyond."

She nibbled on the final chunk of baguette and washed it down with her coffee. "Now, to go back to your question about finding Jorani. Yes, I think we should do that soon. But I'd also like to move forward with the mystery of the diary, assuming it's still safe at Le Royal. I think we should get someone to translate parts of it to figure out if this is actually what everyone is after. I'd like to at least understand why it's valuable enough to land Jorani and me in the hospital. And possibly be the cause for Heng's disappearance. So I suggest we go back to my room now, to check for sure that it's still there. I also wouldn't mind taking a shower and changing my clothes. Could we please make that a first stop?"

"Yes, of course." As he paid the bill, he asked, one more time, where Jorani might go.

"I'm still thinking that although it might present some danger, she would probably go home first to see if there was anything else that Heng had left which might be helpful in trying to find him. But also, it dawned on me that if she didn't go home or to Le Royal, she might retreat into her studio to think. As odd as that sounds, she's an artist, and her studio is where she works and thinks best. So I wouldn't be surprised to find her there. On the other hand, she might go to the museum. Or she might at least call some of Heng's colleagues there. I would suggest, after we make that quick stop at my hotel, we head over to Heng and Jorani's apartment, which isn't far from the hotel. I haven't been there for a while, but I think I can find it. We can figure out the next steps after that." It felt good to take charge. Maybe her injuries weren't as severe as the doctor had implied.

Sarah pulled out her phone to call Jorani again. Still no answer. "OK, let's go," she said.

When she stood, she did indeed feel a bit better after the food and coffee, though still a little unstable on her feet. James took her arm as they left the restaurant and steered her toward where he had parked his car.

CHAPTER 20

Phnom Penh
Friday morning

Jorani sat on the floor, surrounded by chaos, at the home she shared with Heng. As if it wasn't bad enough that her entire body was racked with pain, her private space was destroyed. Their three-story apartment building was located behind a large gate at the far end of a small, neat courtyard filled with tropical flowers and hidden by two small fruit trees. Though the front gate was normally locked, the fact that it had been unlocked and ajar hadn't bothered her at first because her neighbors frequently left it that way if they were only going out for a few minutes. What had caught her attention, and alerted her to the possibility that something was wrong, was the broken lock on the door leading to the stairway—and the door itself hanging askew, with a broken lower hinge. She'd walked up the stairs, through a second broken door, and into the apartment.

Inside, the scene had been even worse. Every drawer and cabinet in her normally tidy home had been opened. The contents now lay ankle deep throughout the kitchen, living, and dining spaces and the bedroom. Even the contents of the small bathroom cabinet had been strewn across the tile floor, and the liquid contents of some of the broken bottles had spread and were mixing together. The sliding door to the balcony was also wide open, and her pots of herbs out there had been smashed, and dirt had been scattered all over the balcony. The intruders had even, inexplicably, used a knife or similar instrument to destroy the apartment walls. The shock of the destruction, combined with the lingering effects of the motorbike incident, had left her numb and confused. Jorani stood and righted one of the overturned but unbroken chairs with her good arm and sat down again to survey the damage. She knew that crying would do little, but it was hard to keep in the tears. In addition to the overwhelming sadness she felt from the destruction of this place that she and Heng had worked so hard to make their own, she was still feeling woozy and unstable. She was not herself. Most importantly, there was still no sign of Heng.

She heard two people walking up the staircase and then a knock on the doorframe. Two of her neighbors called to her. She answered, and they came into the apartment and stared at the mess around them.

"What happened?" asked one of them in rapid-fire Khmer. "Are you OK? We heard a lot of noise coming from here a couple of hours ago, but it was early, and we were afraid to come over because it was still dark. It sounded bad, and we didn't know what might be going on here in the house. We had noticed that neither you nor Heng had been here for a couple of days. Are you here by yourself, or is Heng here also? What can we do to help you? Who could have done this?"

As they looked more closely at her, the other asked, "And what happened to you? Were you in an accident? Shouldn't you be in the hospital?"

Jorani replied, not quite truthfully, that Heng was out of town and that yes, she was alone and had been in a little accident a couple of days ago. It looked worse than it was, and she was almost recovered. But their obvious neighborly concern, though it was just short of nosiness, uncorked the flood of tears she had been holding back.

"I don't know who did this or why. It seems as if they were looking for something in particular to have caused such damage. Nothing seems to be missing, but I won't know until I have a chance to look at all of this more closely. Neither Heng nor I have much of value.

It's hard to imagine they were looking for gold or jewelry here." She paused before emphasizing again that she had no idea what they had been looking for.

After a few moments of silence from the neighbors, she blew her nose and dried her tears. She assured them she was fine and appreciated their concern, but needed to be alone to figure out what her next steps would be. After asking her, once again, if there was anything they could do, they both nodded and reluctantly left her to the mess that lay strewn throughout the place. Jorani realized she would be the subject of neighborhood gossip and conversation for the next few days but let it go. There was nothing she could do about it, and if she thought about it, she didn't really care. Gossip was just a fact of life in the building. She had other priorities, and she was in more and more pain with every passing minute. She wasn't sure she would last much longer.

After looking around further, and especially in the area where Heng kept his papers and work, she was sure nothing was missing. Could whoever have done this been looking for the diary? Was the diary really the key to Heng's disappearance, as she had suspected? Damn that diary. What could possibly be in it that was so critical? Those first few entries had been disturbing, but only, she thought, for Heng. What else could it possibly mean? She did hope that it was still safe in Sarah's hotel room, though. She was normally an organized and methodical person, but Jorani realized that right now, nothing was settled or clear about what she should do. She found that fact, in addition to the physical pain and household destruction, upsetting in the extreme. She had to find Heng.

She wandered around the mess and then sat down on the bed to think through her options. Should she go to the police again? She'd already been to them about Heng. They would probably start to think she was a little off. But her neighborhood officer had been very kind and helpful to her and her neighbors in the past. Maybe that would be an option? Should she tell Heng's colleagues at the museum? Should she send out an email or text or WhatsApp to her circle of friends and colleagues explaining the issue and asking for assistance? She decided that all these actions made sense. After surveying her belongings, dispersed everywhere, one more time, and becoming increasingly overwhelmed by the thought of what needed to be done to clean it all up, she started to compose an email on her phone. It was awkward with one arm in a cast.

Another knock on the doorframe interrupted her. "Who's there?" she called from the bedroom. There was no answer. She stood up and moved toward the living area, where she heard heavy steps and then saw a tall figure rushing toward her. He grabbed her, and a cry of pain erupted from somewhere inside her core. She struggled but, in her weakened state, was unable to resist. A heavy hand clamped a rag over her mouth, and another jabbed her good arm with a needle just before she passed out.

CHAPTER 21

Southeast Asia
1970s to present day

When Nigel left Phnom Penh under orders on that fateful morning in April of 1975, he knew he would spend the remainder of his life dedicated to art of the region, particularly the art of the Khmer Empire, and to its preservation, whatever that would take. Its monumentality and quality, the sensation he felt when he touched it, the overwhelming feeling of being in the presence of an empire ruled by god-kings who had created a vast and remarkable civilization, about which the world knew very little—all this captured him in a way that nothing before ever had. He began to feel as if this might be his way of honoring the cultures to which he had contributed some small measure of destruction. He had seen this pathway for his life the moment he left the museum for the last time before the evacuation, when he had taken the head of Uma. This was going to be his destiny, though he also recognized the irony in taking something away from a culture that he was sure he would spend the rest of his life trying to protect.

As he thought about it in the days following, he couldn't explain or justify to himself why he had taken the head. It had been an impulsive act that he never could have foreseen. Over the subsequent decades, this sculpture had come to mean so much to Nigel—its elegance and artistic merit, its connection to his friend Sokha, and even the story of Uma and Shiva from Hindu mythology, which seemed to embody for him virtues that he once valued but might have lost. Uma's undying love for Shiva, even when he rejected her. Shiva's strength and intelligence. It all spoke to him. But he also realized, years later, that it had been his first step down a slippery slope and a sharp descent through much of the remainder of his life.

Another turning point may have come when he began to visit some of the almost-abandoned Khmer temples in northeast Thailand. There was no security at these temples. The local population didn't seem to care one way or another about them and what happened to them. He wondered more than once what would happen if he just took some of those sculptures, but initially he refrained from doing so.

In the late 1970s—he could no longer remember the exact year—he had finally made his home in Bangkok, which was, at that point, the city around which the region turned. At first, there was little to no interest in any of the region's art on the part of rich collectors or most of the major museums around the world. He was able to satisfy his need for objects by purchasing works through the dealers in River City and in some of the small galleries and shops that catered to foreign tourists in the neighborhood of the Mandarin Oriental Hotel. The art was reasonably priced, and all his purchases were legitimate.

While Nigel was amassing his own collection, he also worked to convince the regional ministries of the value of their patrimony and collections. He emphasized that they should do all they could to keep the works in the country of origin, and he gradually became noted around the world as an expert on what was then viewed as strange and exotic art. Museum experts, as well as governments and rich collectors in Europe, North America, Australia, and even the more prosperous parts of Southeast Asia, consulted him.

And slowly the world began to wake up to the wonders of Khmer art. Demand grew. Supply remained meager. Primitive pipelines were developed to hack sculptures from temples and bring them out of Cambodia to dealers in Bangkok. Prices increased. Despite his low cost of living, he could no longer afford to continue to acquire the art that he had played a role in bringing to the world. He made the decision to change his methods. He could care for the art better than the authorities. He would just take it.

When Nigel revisited the temples of northeast Thailand, he took some of the beautiful pieces he'd so admired years ago. He began to branch out then and removed art from other temples and sites in the region. In Laos, he managed to obtain some marvelous life-size Buddha figures from the Tam Ting caves on the Mekong River, north of Luang Prabang. There was little security at the caves, which were only accessible from the river, and it proved simple to work with local people interested in making a little money to remove the Buddhas. He also had some success in taking sculptures from the temple at Vat Phu, set up on a hill well above the Mekong and just north of the border with Cambodia. Nigel figured all these sites would probably be guarded in the future, but they had been open then.

Myanmar had been incredibly simple. All it had taken were some well-placed bribes and gifts to the senior officials of the military, known as the Tatmadaw, and he had been able to cart truckloads of antiquities and prized antiques across the Thai border into Chiang Mai, where they were restored and cleaned before being shipped to galleries and dealers in Bangkok. Burmese Buddhas had become one of his best-selling items. Something about the material heritage of what was viewed as one of the most "exotic" of the Asian countries appealed to Westerners, especially the British, who had colonized the country more than a century earlier.

Ironically, Cambodia, the source of his obsession, had proved to be more of a challenge. By the early 1990s, there was a greater international presence, better organization, and far more security at the main Angkor site. There had been less at some of the outlying Angkor temples and at the sites that were farther away, like Banteay Chhmar, near the Thai border—where he had tried and failed—and even Preah Vihear, the beautiful temple set at the top of the escarpment that marked the border between Thailand and Cambodia, from which he had taken a small relief sculpture.

In the end, though, taking priceless Khmer and other world-class works of art had proved much easier than he would have anticipated.

He made a lot of money by supplying collectors and museums, who were either eager or ignorant, through dealers who were greedy and unscrupulous. He also filled his own apartment and expanded his collection with the works that he and his band of thieves had taken. Throughout all the years, he always kept the head of the goddess Uma, his first and most valued and beloved acquisition.

Setting up the network for all these transactions might have seemed daunting to others tempted to participate in this market-place, but it had in fact proved easier than Nigel had anticipated. Of course, he had worked hard at it, recruiting collaborators at several levels on both sides of the Thai-Cambodian border and ensuring they found reliable Cambodians to perform the delicate work of removing the sculptures from the temples. After his first few operations, he de-cided he also needed someone who was knowledgeable on the ground in Cambodia, and he found the perfect person, a disenchanted scholar in the field who was desperate for money. It had worked out well for ev-eryone. The Cambodians working at the temple sites were able to sup-port their families. The middlemen on both sides of the border made money on each transaction. The dealers in Bangkok got world-class art to sell to their clients. Nigel fed his bank accounts with signifi-cant commissions from intermediaries on both sides of the border and from dealers in Bangkok. And his field supervisor, Anada, earned the income he needed to take care of his family. Everyone was happy.

At first, Nigel had seen his role as being the savior of this art. He loved the region and had made it his home because it was a cultur-ally rich area infused with Buddhism and life moved at a slower pace than he would have found back in the US. But he also realized and took advantage of the fact that while it was culturally rich, the region was politically unstable, poor, and struggling in virtually all ways. Any values—religious, historical, artistic, community based—that the sto-len objects might have represented were quickly overcome by their economic value, and with every passing year, as the world discovered the wonders of the culture, their economic value rose.

When he thought about it in retrospect, which he rarely did any-more, his transformation from being an individual collector, pas-sionate and knowledgeable about the civilizations from which these objects had come, to being a looter and smuggler of these same objects had happened gradually, and then suddenly. By the 1990s, his meta-morphosis was complete. He was no longer an altruistic friend and defender of Southeast Asian culture and heritage, and Khmer heritage in particular. He was now a high-end looter. He took not only what did not belong to him but what belonged to an entire culture, ripping it out of its context and robbing the local population of something that was more important than most of them realized.

Ironically, this was the moment at which his stature in the field was highest. Universities all over the world had asked him to teach. He had been connected to major excavation projects.

He had even been one of the first professionals to return to Angkor after the departure of the Vietnamese in 1989 to see what had hap-pened to his beloved temples. They were overgrown with lush vegeta-tion, and because many of the sites still had active land mines, he had a couple of close calls while climbing around the architectural ruins. But this period had been a highlight of his life. And of course, he had met Sarah during the height of his career, and she still remained a prized colleague.

On some level, he acknowledged all his flaws, and there had come a tipping point a few years ago when he realized he was past caring what anyone thought. The thrill of the chase, and the ecstasy of own-ership, had completely drowned out his remaining doubts about what he was doing.

But now the world had changed. The ground had shifted since he had started collecting, and what had been tolerated was no longer tolerated. Both public opinion and the laws had changed over the de-cades. International treaties were enforced. Nigel resisted change for as long as he could. And finally, under a good deal of pressure from others in the field, he had agreed to return everything in his collection to the countries of origin upon his death. This gesture had been met with great fanfare by embassies and ministries of culture, as well as the national museums that stood to benefit. The hitch was that they didn't understand he had retained little of the art that he had taken. He, and an unwitting Sarah, had created impeccable, if false, prov-enance documents that had proved to be acceptable to a number of major museums and wealthy collectors over the years. She had done the research, and he had created the false records based on her work.

She never knew. But it seemed to him now that perhaps she had recently figured out that he had manipulated her work and she had actually been party to creating records that were not completely accurate.

All this would need to be sorted after he was gone.

He was old now, and he was done. Soon he could retire to read and study and keep in contact with his friends and colleagues. Surely everyone would be able to see that what he had done was good? Surely they would ultimately praise him for the role he had played in bringing this brilliant culture to the world? He was certain that, when they thought about it, they would see. Given all he had done, it may not have been a decent life's work in the eyes of many. But he had made a difference.

CHAPTER 22

Phnom Penh
Friday afternoon

James and Sarah parked in front of Jorani and Heng's place and climbed out of the car. As they walked through the open gate, they observed the tall wire-topped fence around the apartment courtyard. They also saw the broken door swinging slightly on its upper hinge.

Two apartment residents were sitting in the courtyard. One of them spoke in broken English. "Looking Jorani? No here. Was here. Now gone."

Sarah felt like she'd been sucker punched and ran toward the staircase. James grabbed her arm.

"We don't know what's up there," he said. "Wait here while I go in to look."

"Don't be fucking ridiculous. We're both going in right now."

He raised his eyebrows at her but nodded and released her arm. They carefully walked up the staircase and entered the apartment through another broken door, at the top of the stairs. Wordlessly, they explored the torn-up living room and surveyed the damage. As they went into the disheveled bedroom, James commented that Jorani would likely have freaked out if she'd seen this. He then pointed to the floor near a table in the corner. "Sarah, I know that Heng and Jorani are your friends, but does either one of them have a drug problem?" With the toe of his shoe, he kicked a syringe lying on the floor.

Sarah rolled her eyes. "The strongest thing I have ever seen either one of them drink is a beer. No, neither of them has a drug habit. Oh my God."

"Sorry, but I had to ask. Either someone was here when Jorani got back, or she discovered that someone had broken in and was here when they returned." He whipped a latex glove from his jacket pocket, slipped it on, and picked up the syringe to sniff it. "I'm guessing it was the latter and they drugged her and took her away."

Sarah's heart sank. Together, they slowly searched the rest of the apartment and the balcony. No one else was there. Back in the living room, she spotted a torn scarf on the floor and picked it up.

"This is the scarf that Jorani was wearing two nights ago when the motorbike came at us. I'm pretty sure it was in the pile of her clothing at the hospital. Proof that she was here this morning, then maybe drugged and snatched from here?" She reached down to pick up a pile of papers on the floor but paused when James held a hand out to stop her.

"Don't touch anything else."

She was surprised by the commanding tone of his voice but said nothing and did as she was told. Moving toward the center of the room, she once again felt wobbly, so she sat down on a chair, closed her eyes, and reminded herself to breathe.

"OK," she said after a few minutes. "I'm kind of analytical, and I have no idea what's going on here. Let's review what we know. Jorani and Heng have both disappeared now, and Jorani hinted that the key to why Heng was kidnapped revolved around some damn diary that was written by Heng's father decades ago. Could that diary really be so important? It didn't seem to me that there was anything earth-shattering for anyone but Heng in the sections that Jorani read to me. I understand that Heng would have been overwhelmed because it was written by his father, but there must be something more to it."

Her head still hurt a little, and even more so as she tried to think.

"Unless it had something to do with the passage about the theft of the goddess head from the national museum. Jorani only read a small portion of the diary to me, but I did gather that Heng's father, Sokha, may have witnessed the theft. It's one of the most famous—or infamous, I guess—thefts in the history of Khmer art. If I'm remembering correctly, Heng's father doesn't name the thief, but he refers to him as 'the American.'"

The sense that she was missing a connection came back. She shook her head as if to shake loose a missing link and then checked to see if James was even listening to her. He was.

"We have no idea where Heng and Jorani are," Sarah continued, "and we don't really have a plan about what to do next. It seems as if these people who took them, whoever they are, are serious and well organized. They will apparently stop at almost nothing to achieve whatever it is that they want to do, but we don't really know what that is, do we?" She stopped when she noticed what appeared to be a grin on his face. "Unless you know more than you're letting on." But whatever smile she had seen had disappeared. In just a quick moment, he had returned to wearing a poker face.

"In addition," she went on, "and clearly of lesser importance but still a really big deal both for me and many other people, as well as for the diplomatic relations between the United States and Cambodia, I would assume, is the exhibition on which I have worked with my colleagues for so long. Somehow it could be a complicating factor in all this. Of course, Heng is one of the colleagues working with me on that. But then there's Nigel, about whom you seem so curious." She waited for a response but received nothing. "We've all been working on this for many years, and all that effort seems to be on the verge of imploding because someone, or some group, is engaged in some activity that inadvertently has caused problems for us. Or maybe they don't want it to happen at all. I don't know why that would be. But I'll be honest: While Nigel's international reputation is established and not endangered, failure to pull the exhibition together could very well be a career-ending event for me, and frankly, at this point it seems as if it may also be a life-threatening moment for my friends Heng and Jorani."

Her analytical persona had weakened as she processed these

thoughts, and now she was no longer able to maintain a calm demeanor. She heard the shaky despair in her own voice. "Does that about sum it up?"

James had taken a seat beside her somewhere during her monologue, and now he sat back and crossed one leg over the other, hands linked behind his head. But still he didn't answer.

"Answer me, please. I want to know what is going on here. And I need to hear your thoughts."

"I'm not exactly sure what you want me to say."

"Fine." Sarah pulled out her phone. "I'm calling Nigel. He said he had ideas when I saw him in Bangkok about what he might do to try to find Heng, and I want to see what he's doing."

James placed his hand on her arm. "Sarah, please don't do that. Please."

"Why? If you won't tell me what's going on, or even what you think we should do, why should I pay any attention to anything you say? I am confused and frustrated beyond belief here. Scared too. I've spent a lot of time in my life dealing with people who aren't telling the whole story about something—collectors, dealers, even people in my own museum who don't want to deliver bad news. Right now, that seems to be you. So, what's the story here? If you're not going to tell me, please take me back to the hotel so I can get on with my day."

"OK." He rubbed his hands across his face.

"'OK' you're going to tell me something? Or 'OK' you'll take me back to the hotel?"

When he stood and pressed out the wrinkles from his khakis, apparently a habit of his, she understood what his answer was. Nothing. Nada. She would remain in the dark. So she tucked her phone into her pocket, put her sunglasses on, and left the disheveled apartment without another word. He followed. As he reached out to open the car door for her, she grabbed his arm. He stared down at her hand and then up at her face through his dark sunglasses, his lips set in a firm line. It was only ten thirty in the morning, and the air under the white-hot sun was already suffocating. Perspiration was already forming in her bra. "What in God's name is going on here?" she asked. "You're not a consular public affairs officer, are you!"

He proceeded to open the car door and gestured for her to get in.

She did, slamming the door behind her. James walked around to the driver's side of the car, sat down, turned the key in the ignition, and cranked up the air-conditioning. But when he made no move to drive away, she took that as an invitation to try one more time. Clearly he wanted to tell her something.

"I asked you a question," she said. "Did you hear me?"

"I know. And yes, I heard you. Actually, you asked two questions."

His humor wasn't funny. "Well, are you going to answer me?"

As he took off his sunglasses, she thought maybe now she could see if he was telling the truth. But that action gave her a front-row view of his eyes. She'd thought they were brown, but that wasn't quite right. Today they were dark hazel, with a stunning amber rim around the pupil. Magnetic, almost.

"The answer to your first question," he finally said, "is that I can't tell you right now. And the answer to your second question is no, I'm not a public affairs officer, nor did I claim to be when we met."

"Then . . . what are you?"

"This is not the right time for me to explain. As I said before, there's more going on here than you and even I know. I'm trying to put together the missing and jumbled pieces to see the whole picture so we can do something about it."

She noticed how he used the word *we.*

"I'm going to request the Phnom Penh police department to seal this apartment, and then I'm going to send in an expert team to check it out. I'm truly sorry about what has happened to Heng and Jorani. I'm trying to help, but I need more information."

"The whole picture of what? You keep talking in generalizations. I don't understand. What on earth is going on? And when will be the right time for you to explain all of this to me?"

"I can't tell you about a lot of it right now, but Heng's disappearance has complicated the situation."

All of a sudden, Sarah couldn't control herself any longer. She was in a foreign country about whose history she knew a lot. But she knew very little about how things worked in the present day, which meant she had no idea what was going on or what would happen next. She had almost been run over by a motorbike two nights ago. She hurt everywhere and should probably still be in the hospital. Heng and Jorani were both missing. Her exhibition plan was in shambles, and quite possibly dead. And she didn't know what to do about any of it. As the last straw, James had referred to Heng's and Jorani's disappearances as a *complication*.

She stared straight ahead at the windshield and, in a voice thick with anger, said, "Take me to the hotel."

"Sarah . . ."

"Don't say anything. Just leave me alone. I may not understand the entire picture right now, but I do understand enough of it to know that you aren't telling me everything that *I* need to know. You are deliberately withholding information from me. You are treating me as if I can't handle anything. If you'll tell me what's going on, great. If not, take me back to the hotel and I will take the diary to the museum and approach them and the Cambodian authorities to ask for their help. I'm also going to call Nigel because he needs to pull in his significant resources. I don't know who else I will approach, but I'll figure it out. I've got to do something."

"Sarah, that would be a mistake."

"Honestly, at this moment, I feel as if sitting in a car with a man whom I barely know, who is not telling me the whole truth about anything, is the mistake. I think it's time for me to leave you. I need to finish my business here."

She turned toward James, who was still staring at her, his face now more grim than smug. "Hotel. Now. Please."

Now it was his turn to stare out the windshield, avoiding her gaze. "Sarah, the diary in your room safe may be important for locating Heng and Jorani. But I believe their disappearance is also tied closely to a major case I'm working on, which probably has greater ramifications for us than the diary. I can't promise you anything, but if you'll work with me for the next few days—and trust me—I think we can find them. And I'll be able to get to the bottom of a major criminal network. And you'll hopefully be able to get your exhibition back on track."

Sarah snorted. "Case? What case? I'll admit that's a nice little speech. Sounds like a movie script. Considering that you won't even tell me who you really are, I have my doubts." He owed her more and she knew that he knew that. She stayed silent as he pulled out of his parking spot and made a U-turn to head back to Le Royal.

Neither had spoken by the time they arrived at the hotel. When the car stopped, Sarah said, "I don't trust you, and I want some answers that make sense to me. Think about what you want to do, and maybe you can call me tonight."

And with that, she got out, slammed the car door, and walked into the lobby of Le Royal, holding her head high despite the lingering headache. The women at the key desk welcomed her back and offered her a bottle of cold water.

Later that day, Sarah preemptively texted James to say she was flying back to Bangkok that night and would be in touch if there was anything they needed to discuss further. She told him there was no need for him to contact her. He didn't respond. As she packed up at the hotel before checking out, she removed the diary from the safe and wrapped it carefully in a scarf before packing it in the center of her suitcase. She wanted to be sure it was well cushioned by her clothes.

She had wondered about taking it in her carry-on bag but decided it would probably be safer to check it. She didn't want to risk her carry-on bag being searched and having the diary confiscated by the authorities, though she realized that the odds of anyone understanding what it was were slim. There was always the possibility it could get lost in transit, but she tried to put that out of her mind. She felt uncomfortable taking the diary out of the country; it didn't belong to her, and in a very real sense it was part of the history and documentation of a country whose past she treasured. And on top of all that, she couldn't read it, knowing few Khmer words despite her extensive study of the region's art and history, so she had absolutely no idea what was in it. But she didn't feel safe leaving it with anyone at either the museum or the consulate and certainly not with James. She would turn it over to some authority as soon as she could responsibly do so. For now, she was confident she was taking the appropriate course of action.

Though as she walked out of the room, she looked back ruefully. Maybe next time she would actually be able to sleep in her room at this beautiful hotel.

CHAPTER 23

Bangkok
Friday afternoon

The burner phone rang, and Nigel answered after one ring.

"They've picked her up, but no notebook. It wasn't in the apartment and she didn't have it with her. Did you want us to deliver her to the safe house to keep her with him?"

"Well done, and yes. Same place. We have a change of plans for the operation. Both our guests will be delivered to just outside Banteay Srei tomorrow, and then they'll be escorted to the temple on Sunday. We need to lay blame on them, and you somehow need to make it look as if they were the ones organizing everything that happens at the temple. I don't care how you do it, but remember that they are not expendable and are not to be harmed. They need to be at the temple in good shape. Safe. Is that clear?"

Anada grunted an acknowledgment that he understood.

Nigel went on. "Was there any indication at all of where the notebook might be? Did you find files related to Heng's work anywhere in the apartment?"

"Yes, we found files, but there was nothing that might be a diary or a notebook with handwriting in it. It was mostly computer-generated documents, mostly entries and essays for the exhibition."

"OK, thanks. Keep alert."

"Yes, Nigel."

"And one more thing. The reliefs and other sculptures must absolutely be on those trucks well before morning, when the doped-up heritage police will wake up and alert their supervisors. The authorities will send in more enforcement. You know what to do. Be careful, and good luck. You know when and how to contact me."

"OK."

As he hung up the phone, Nigel felt uneasy. He had just made yet another major change in the plan, and he didn't like last-minute changes one bit. He was not a spontaneous kind of guy.

CHAPTER 24

Phnom Penh
Friday night

Jorani slowly came to consciousness. She was tied up with plastic tape over her mouth, lying on a bed in a dark room, facing the wall. Her entire body still hurt from the motorbike accident, and probably from all that manhandling in her apartment too. She still wasn't thinking completely clearly. She rolled onto her stomach and then to her other side, awkwardly with hands tied behind her back and one arm in a cast. The room was small. A window up near the ceiling offered a little illumination into the space, but as it was clearly dark outside, the room was still fairly dim. She spotted a small table in one of the corners. The walls, painted light yellow, were peeling from the humidity. There was one door.

As her eyes adjusted, she realized another person was in the room, slumped against the wall in another corner. Also bound at wrists and ankles and taped at the mouth, the figure was motionless, which she surmised meant the person was asleep—or worse. She couldn't make out any features but watched warily as she tried to boost herself up on the bed without dislocating a shoulder.

After a number of bounces and sit-ups, she managed to pull herself to an upright position, wondering how much all that jostling would impede her arm's healing process. Her legs were short, so her bound feet dangled over the side of the bed. She peered more closely at the other figure. A man, it seemed. But no movement. *Is he . . . dead?* But then she detected shallow breathing. What a relief.

Her eyes continued to adjust to the dim light as she studied him, trying to make out some features. Then she couldn't help but shriek, although the sound was muffled by the plastic tape over her mouth. It was Heng, unconscious or sleeping. He was here. He was alive. They were together.

She scooted herself off the edge of the bed. The short drop to the floor exacerbated the currents of pain flowing throughout her arm and the rest of her body, but she managed an agonizing crab walk, on one elbow and two heels with ankles tied together, across the room to her husband. She nudged him with her foot. She pushed up against him with her hip. She gently headbutted him. Anything to try to bring him back to consciousness.

Slowly, he rolled his head. He opened his eyes, which were unfocused and directed up at the ceiling. He was clearly seeing nothing. She nudged him again, this time with her shoulder, and he jerked away as if to avoid contact. Jorani felt deflated, and slightly panicked, when he closed his eyes again. But then he reopened them. And this time he looked right at her. This time, his eyes opened wide. Tears immediately began to stream down his face and the plastic tape over his mouth. She maneuvered her face next to his, and they both silently cried, their salty tears mingling.

Jorani knew that despite her pain and a barrage of emotions, her relief, fear, and anger, she had to take control of the situation. She turned away from him and scooted backward to position her bound hands near his so she could try to work his wrists free of the cloth bindings. Whoever had put them on Heng must have been in a hurry, or ignorant, because it didn't take long for her to slip them off his wrists. She couldn't see him behind her but imagined him shaking out his arms, rolling his neck, massaging his wrists. What she did clearly hear was the plastic tape being abruptly torn off his mouth. He quickly untied her hands and helped her move her broken arm back into the position where it belonged. Then, after gently peeling the tape from her mouth, he squeezed her in the tightest embrace she could remember. The pressure against the cast hurt, but it was worth it for a moment. Then, knowing they had to act fast to find a way out, she started to extricate herself from his arms.

"Jorani. Jorani, no, please don't let go," he said, tightening his hold on her.

She couldn't tell if his plea was laden with fear or sorrow or remorse, but she needed him to calm down. "Shh."

"I didn't think I would ever see you again." His tone was frantic, his pitch higher than normal. "I was also worried. You and Sarah and Nigel . . . What would you think of me? How concerned you would be. I was more worried about that than I was scared for myself. Though I admit I was scared shitless. But how did you end up here with me? Where are we? One minute, I was in front of the museum. Then something happened, and I was somewhere else. But I think that whoever has done this keeps drugging me. My head is foggy." His voice sounded so vulnerable and scared, almost childlike, as tears ran from his eyes and snot from his nose. "What's going on here, Jorani? Why is this happening?" He paused for a bit, his head cocked like a dog listening for a cue from its owner, and sniffled. "What day is it today?"

Jorani had never seen him so upset like this, and she took his face in her hands. "I'll explain in greater detail later, but for now, I'm here, and we need to figure out how to get out of here. I'm pretty sure we're still somewhere in Phnom Penh. I'm not sure what's going on, but I can tell you a little bit about what has happened since you disappeared. I can also tell you that I think you have information that is key to figuring out what's going on, and you need to tell me everything, and I mean *everything*, that you know about that diary you brought home from the museum." She paused. "Yes, I know about the diary, even though you didn't talk to me about it." She paused again before adding, "Oh, and I think it's Friday night. But frankly, I'm not sure, either, because a lot has happened to me too." She lifted the arm in the cast, and he leaned down to kiss it.

Heng quickly untied his feet and proceeded to untie hers while she gave him a synopsis of what had happened in the past few days. She began with the call from Sarah and then moved through all that had happened since: discovering the diary, having dinner with Sarah, being run down by a motorbike, leaving the hospital without being discharged, returning to their ransacked home, and then being kidnapped herself and brought here.

He looked at her in disbelief and then dropped his head into his hands. "Oh, no, I can't believe this. All my fault. I should have told you about the diary when I found it. I shouldn't have tried to think this through on my own. I was in such shock when I found it, and it was just too hard for me to talk about it. Did you read it? And where is the diary now?"

Jorani rubbed Heng's neck and shoulders. "As far as I know, the diary is still in the safe in Sarah's room at Le Royal. If there is anyone we can trust, it's Sarah. While I need to know everything you know about that diary, I think it's a higher priority that we get out of here now. But one thing I do know is this: As it was written by your father, I know what a shock that must have been for you." She patted him to signify the little back rub needed to end. "I'll give you more of that when we get to a safe space. But for now, we need to get going. Quickly, before someone comes back."

They crept to the door, and Jorani carefully pulled on the doorknob a little, unsure what or who they would find on the other side. It seemed to give way a bit, almost as if it wasn't firmly latched shut. She gently twisted the knob. The door opened.

"It wasn't even locked!" Jorani whispered, astounded that these guys seemed to have no clue what they were doing. "But they're probably nearby. Let's be quiet. And careful." She put her finger to her lips to emphasize her point. Heng, standing behind her, nuzzled his chin into her shoulder as acknowledgment.

Jorani scanned the area just beyond the door. It seemed safe, so they tiptoed single file down the short, dark corridor. Because there was no ambient light seeping in from the closed rooms on either side, they slid their fingertips along the wall as guides. There were light switches, but they didn't dare flip them on for fear of attracting attention. When they reached the door at the end of the corridor, Jorani put her ear to it.

"Nothing," she whispered to Heng. The door made no sound as she quietly turned the knob and cautiously pushed until it was open wide enough that they were able to see what lay ahead: a large warehouse-like area with a number of stacked crates, and forklifts to move them around, all organized in an orderly fashion. No one was in sight. On the far side of the large expanse of floor, Jorani identified another door. This one looked as if it led to the outside. "Come on, let's go," she said quietly, urgently, as she stepped through the door into the warehouse.

They crept close to the floor, keeping in the shadows of the forklifts and crates, until they nearly reached the exterior door. It didn't fit squarely in its frame, and through the cracks at the top and bottom, she could see the fluorescent light found all around Phnom Penh. Jorani's heart pounded.

They were no more than ten feet from freedom when all the fluorescent lights inside the warehouse space flickered on. Jorani and Heng spun around. Two menacing, bulky figures blocked their exit path.

Without saying anything, the two men, disguised behind black balaclava masks, came forward and grabbed both Jorani and Heng. Again, they tied their feet and hands, and, this time, they blindfolded them too. Even in her surprise and despair, Jorani realized these guys didn't know what they were doing—or maybe they were being compassionate because of her cast. Either way, her hands were loosely tied, this time in front of her. Escape might still be possible, but for now she and Heng needed to do as they were told. These two guys might not have guns, but they were big and in better condition than either her or Heng.

But as she was carried out the door into the warm, humid Phnom Penh night, noticing the smell of the river, she wiggled and kicked a little. *It never hurts to try to fight back!* Unfortunately, their grip on her tightened, and whatever empathy they'd felt for her had disappeared, because now they practically threw her into the back seat of a vehicle. It wasn't exactly comfortable, but it was roomy enough that she thought it might be an SUV. It would be OK, she thought—until she felt a needle jab her good arm. She nodded off as the car sped away.

CHAPTER 25

Bangkok
Saturday morning

James was already calling Sarah. Sarah had only arrived in Bangkok the night before and was now back at the Shangri-La Hotel feeling disoriented, beaten up, and not a little helpless. When she'd entered her room last night, she'd locked the diary in the room safe. Then she had gone out for a night walk along Charoen Krung Road, up toward the Mandarin Oriental Hotel and then over to the Royal Orchid Sheraton and the River City Shopping Mall.

When she had first started coming to Bangkok, River City had been one of the hubs for the legal and illegal antiquities trade in the region, teeming with shops that were filled with antiques and objects from all over Southeast Asia. She had seen rare and priceless Lao Buddhas praying for rain, exquisite antique textiles from the hill tribes of northern Thailand, and sculptures from Cambodia that she had been sure, even early in her career, were authentic, not copies. But it had also been here that scholars of Angkor had found sculptures that had been looted from Cambodia, and items of heritage that had been either stolen or obtained for a pittance were blatantly on sale by shop owners and dealers openly selling the loot. Some of these prized treasures were subsequently seized by the Thai police, and in recent years they weren't as openly traded. Even though the works of art were still displayed in shop and gallery windows, the businesses themselves were closed and appointments were required for entrance.

And now James was calling her, before she'd even greeted the day properly, to say that he, too, had just flown in from Phnom Penh and wanted to see her and Nigel that afternoon. How annoying. "I thought I asked you not to contact me and said I'd be in touch if we had anything to discuss or act on."

James sounded a little tired. "Yes, I believe you did say that, but I don't take my orders from you." His words may have been rude, but his tone not so much. "There's a lot that needs to be sorted out here. I think we can help each other if you'll just let me explain why we should visit Nigel this afternoon. Together."

Sarah wondered if she'd regret this. "OK, tell me."

After he explained in detail what he wanted to do, she reluctantly agreed to go to Nigel's apartment with him. She wasn't sure why James insisted that they *not* tell Nigel ahead of time that they were coming. Nigel didn't like surprises. But James would not offer her a reason, and it seemed he knew what he was doing, so without another plan and with no ideas of her own, Sarah agreed. Besides, Nigel rarely left his apartment these days, so she was pretty sure he'd be there if they showed up unannounced. They arranged to meet in two hours in the lobby of the Shangri-La, and a short while later they were standing outside the apartment building in the heat. She rang the bell, and Ahmi came on the intercom.

"Yes, may I help you?"

"Ahmi, it's Sarah. Is Nigel home? I need to speak with him."

The intercom was silent for a minute and then crackled back to life. "Yes, Khun Sarah, Khun Nigel is home. He can see you." The door buzzed open.

Sarah and James entered the cool lobby and took the elevator up. Ahmi opened the door to Nigel's foyer, and this time, unlike previous times Sarah had visited him, there was no cheerful and affectionate greeting from Nigel upon her arrival. Ahmi stood alone in the foyer and looked at them nervously, and perhaps a little sadly, as she led them silently inside. But she didn't escort them to Nigel's office, as Sarah had expected and hoped, but instead brought them to the formal living room with its uncomfortable traditional Thai furniture covered in the highest-quality Thai silk. Sarah had been to many social events in this room over the years and always felt as if it were a room in a historical home. Beautiful and understated and elegant. With extraordinary art. But she never felt as if anyone lived there. She had always ended up with a backache after sitting on the furniture for long periods, and she much preferred Nigel's crowded and chaotic office with its piles of books and papers, the detritus of a long lifetime, and some comfortable seating.

"Khun Nigel will be with you in a minute," Ahmi said, retreating from the room without making eye contact or even offering tea or water. Clearly, the dynamic in Sarah's relationship with the household had changed since the last time she was here. She nevertheless tried to make herself comfortable on the sofa while James looked around with interest at the various objects in the room.

"In case you're interested, none of them is a copy," she said. "They are all originals, and many of them came into his collection long ago, though he openly acknowledges that some of them were later acquisitions from other private collectors, mostly here in Bangkok but also from Singapore and Hong Kong. More than you wanted to know, I'm sure."

When he didn't reply, Sarah continued. "Nigel's collection of Southeast Asian antiquities is one of the finest still in private hands, and I played a role years ago in helping him grow the collection by researching individual pieces and their provenance. It's not a period of my career about which I am particularly proud, but I learned a tremendous amount, and it paid the bills." She was sure James would question why she wasn't proud of that work, but still he perused the displays around the room without any reaction to her commentary. "Nigel knows his collection could pose a problem, though perhaps less so because he lives here and these objects have never left Southeast Asia. And neither Thailand nor Singapore ever signed on to the 1970 UNESCO Convention about illicit trafficking of antiquities, so the legality of his having some of these objects is a little murky."

Finally, James ended his self-guided tour and appeared mildly interested in something she'd said. But just as he opened his mouth to speak, Nigel entered. He addressed Sarah, blatantly ignoring James.

"Hello, Sarah. To what do I owe the honor of your unscheduled and unannounced visit today? I was not expecting to see you and am not sure what you're doing here." He seemed stiff and more formal than usual to Sarah, but not overtly rude. "I can't recall a time, in all these years, when you just dropped by." Still, he ignored James.

Sarah thanked Nigel for seeing her on such short notice and gestured toward James. "This is James Carlyle from the US embassy in Phnom Penh. He has been helping me to—"

Nigel's demeanor changed. Whereas he was merely businesslike a minute ago, he now seemed impatient and put off. He sat down with authority in his usual chair—the only furniture Sarah had frequently noted was not traditionally Thai, but a high-quality American armchair covered in beautiful Thai silk—and interrupted her. "Sarah, Mr. Carlyle and I have never met, but I am more than familiar with his work and role at the embassy. I consider him to be intrusive and his work to be useless. He is not helpful in any way to scholarship or the study of Khmer art."

So, it wasn't just that James was familiar with Nigel. The door swung both ways. Nigel knew about James Carlyle, and she suspected he knew more about this embassy representative than she did. She found this intensely irritating.

"Please, forgive my poor manners," Nigel said, nodding and gesturing at the other end of the sofa for James to take a seat. "Do tell me why you are both here."

James fixed his gaze on Nigel. "Thank you, but I'd prefer to remain standing."

The tension in the room was already thick, and they had barely made it past the salutation phase, when Sarah noticed James clench his jaw and ball his hands into fists. She hoped he wouldn't be too confrontational with Nigel. He had previously assured her he would be civil.

"I asked Sarah to come with me to your apartment today because you and I have never met and I'd like to talk with you about some rumors I keep hearing from my Cambodian contacts in the heritage

field. They've been speculating about a major theft of Khmer antiquities being planned at this very moment, and I wondered if you've heard
anything from anyone you know about it. I am well aware that you are
the best-connected scholar and collector in the region, and it's also my
understanding that you are concerned about the state of looting at the
archaeological sites in Cambodia. Is any of this sounding familiar to
you?"

Sarah sat nervously on the edge of her chair, looking back and
forth between Nigel and James as if she were at a tennis match. She
had been pretty successful in navigating the politics and cultural
niceties of Southeast Asia because she had mastered, or at least understood, the need for nonconfrontation—and even silence, at times—
though this indirect approach to managing difficult conversations
almost always grated on her. Couching questions in a nonthreatening
manner. Gauging nonverbal clues. While James had told her what he
was hoping to accomplish in this conversation, she wasn't sure that
he was going about it in the right way, and she was already becoming
alarmed at his confrontational tone. She hoped he wasn't going to try
to play both bad cop and good cop here.

Nigel, though, also had a way of looking right through you with
cold, sharp eyes when he was upset, and today the glare he returned
toward James was particularly icy. "I don't know why you'd think I
would have any kind of knowledge about a potential major theft from
an archaeological site."

Sarah noticed that James had not mentioned whether this planned
theft would be at a field site or somewhere else. She didn't see him
flinch, however.

"That is not my world," Nigel said. "So, the answer to your question is no. I have no idea what you are talking about. I also resent you
walking into my home and asking me questions like this." He switched
his cold gaze to Sarah, even as he continued to speak to James. "To be
clear, it sounds as though you're implying that I'm a criminal. And you
seem to have co-opted my dear Sarah into working with you, which
is a problem for our exhibition—not to mention our friendship—
especially since our collaborator Heng seems to have curiously abandoned us at this very moment. What am I to say?"

For once, James almost seemed flustered, casting a quick glance over at Sarah while removing his hands from his pockets and crossing his arms across his chest. Sarah was almost tempted to let out a cheer for the points Nigel had just scored. But then Nigel abruptly changed gears.

"Isn't your job to protect people in your jurisdiction and their properties? Maybe I should be asking what *you* are doing to try to find Heng. It would seem to me that that would be in keeping with your line of work, perhaps more than worrying about some ancient sculptures or whatnot. Do you have any updates? Who is searching for him and where? In Phnom Penh? Angkor? Even here in Thailand?"

Sarah waited for James's next move. She knew he had expected Nigel to parry with him but didn't know what his next line of questioning might be, and she was having a hard time reading the dynamics of the room. Nigel was angry. James appeared reserved, but she knew, deep down, he would be persistent. Wouldn't he? She had no idea where they were going. And how did *she* fit into what was happening here? She had decades of association with Nigel and great admiration and affection for him. He was in large part responsible for where she was today, though at this instant she was wondering exactly where that was. She had zero history with James, who might actually be headed for the losing end of this conversation. She didn't know what to make of him. Or his clear distrust of Nigel. Her anxiety level was rising faster than the express elevator at the Shangri-La, and she was clearly not going to be able to mediate this confrontational discussion as she'd initially thought she would. Though she didn't even know if that was supposed to be her role.

"Thank you for your time, Mr. Sanderson," James said abruptly, placing his palms in prayer position as a sign of gratitude and respect, though whether the move was sincere was up for debate. "I have come to you because of your expertise and connections, and I would never *accuse* you of anything related to the illicit trafficking of antiquities or theft from archaeological sites. In a situation like this, I need to bring in all the resources I can, and I am merely doing due diligence. I am simply trying to figure out what might be happening, and when it might happen, to avoid an international incident and the further desecration of the temples of the Khmer Empire. You are the foremost expert in the area, but as it seems you haven't heard chatter about this through the local grapevines, we'll be leaving now."

Nigel's shoulders relaxed a bit. "May I ask what temple your sources are telling you might be the focus of this looting attempt? Or when might it be happening?"

"I'm told that it will be Preah Vihear and that it will be happening sometime in the next few nights. As I'm sure you know, access to that temple is simple from the Thai side but difficult from the Cambodian side. We are bringing in both the Thai and Cambodian authorities. Any theft from that temple might cause an international incident like the one in 2003, when the Thai embassy in Phnom Penh was burned to the ground. I wasn't here then, but certainly an actual theft would create more ill will than false rumors on the internet might, and all I am doing is trying to prevent this."

Sarah had been following the international tensions surrounding Preah Vihear for much of her career. It was terrifying to think what sort of chaos might evolve if a theft were to occur there. But it was also, admittedly, exhilarating to think she might somehow be able to stop it.

Nigel grunted. "Tough temple to try to take anything from. The road on the Cambodian side is terrible, and they will probably destroy their truck suspensions before they even arrive. Plus, the presence of so many Thai and Cambodian police on each side doesn't exactly mean they'll be working in isolation." Then, as if seeming to realize what he had said, he smiled to himself and added, "It's a fool's errand. They'll never make it."

"Thank you for your time, Mr. Sanderson. Sarah, do you have anything to add?" Without waiting for her answer, he started for the door.

"Yes, as a matter of fact, I do."

James stopped in his tracks and then slowly turned around. The fact that she had surprised him with her assertion was a bit gratifying.

"Nigel, I apologize if this intrusion was above and beyond for you," she said. "I believe we are all working toward the same ends. I hope that Mr. Carlyle has not been too insulting. But I would expect that you, of all people, would be interested in helping to prevent a theft from a temple. I would think this is important to you." Of course, she was thinking of the diary, and she paused for effect. She wanted to ask him about being in Phnom Penh in April of 1975. If he knew anything about what may have happened at the museum in those days right before the Khmer Rouge arrived. And about the head on his upper shelf. But there was enough tension in the air, and she did not.

The way that Nigel and James both stared at her made it clear that neither of the men had expected her to say anything. James seemed speechless, and Nigel seemed uncharacteristically intimidated. She wasn't sure if what she'd said helped either of them. But she'd had to say her piece. She pivoted and hurried toward the door before losing whatever confidence had prompted her little rant.

"I do care about this, Sarah," Nigel said.

She felt his eyes on her back and turned to look at him. He seemed confused and stressed. He looked more like an old man than he had when they'd first arrived. Emotions were doing battle in her heart, and at that moment it seemed compassion might win. "I'll be back tomorrow so we can finish up the work we had planned for my visit here," she said. "I guess we'll have to proceed without Heng."

When she and James walked out of the living room and into the foyer, she found Ahmi waiting there nervously for them.

"Khun Sarah, be careful" was all she said before letting them out the door.

Sarah and James followed the small soi, or side street, that led back to Rama I Road and the shopping district of Siam Square. As they walked, she grabbed his arm. "What the hell was going on in there? You don't seem to think you owe me an explanation, but you do. Big-time. This was not the kind of meeting we had discussed."

"Will you come back to the embassy with me so we can talk about this?"

Reluctantly, Sarah nodded. She really wanted to be rid of James Carlyle once and for all, but she also desperately needed to understand.

They found a taxi at the next corner, and James directed it to the US embassy on Wireless Road. As the taxi progressed toward the embassy, Sarah decided she couldn't wait any longer and demanded an explanation of what had happened at Nigel's apartment. When James didn't reply, just as he hadn't previously, she refused to accept his dismissal.

"I'm talking to you and would appreciate the courtesy of a reply. What was going on between you and Nigel? I've known him for decades, and I've never seen him so agitated or uncomfortable. I'm going no further with whatever you are involved in here until I get some answers."

Still no response from him, and she felt her face reddening. Before she had a chance to say anything more, he held up both hands in a truce.

"Sarah, stop. We're in a taxi. We will be at the embassy in a few minutes. Cool your jets."

Still fuming, especially about his condescending tone, she followed James through the gate into the compound after they reached the embassy a few minutes later. He registered her with the Marine guard on duty before leading her up to a borrowed office. He indicated that she should sit down at the table in the office. She sat. He closed the door.

CHAPTER 26

**On the road to the Angkor Archaeological Park, Cambodia
Saturday afternoon**

Heng woke to find himself in a vehicle moving slowly over typical Cambodian roads—bumpy. He tried to open his eyes but found he was blindfolded and gagged and also realized that his hands and feet were bound. For the first time since that morning outside the national museum, he couldn't see what was going on around him. It made him even more scared. Given the space around him, he surmised he was in an SUV with the rear seats folded down. Whoever had put him here must have taken the time to spread out something soft for him to lie on, as it was not as uncomfortable as he would have imagined. He rolled slightly and realized that someone was lying next to him. From the familiar scent, he knew it was Jorani. He breathed a sigh of relief. They might not know what was happening, where they were, or where they were going, but he was grateful they were together. He could also sense and hear the two men in the front of the car. He had no idea how long he had been unconscious, and they didn't sound like the same two masked men with guns. Somewhere along the route, the drivers must have switched out. These two sounded a little smarter.

"How much farther?" The one in the passenger seat asked the driver.

The driver grunted. "Another few hours. We're more than halfway to the site on Highway 6, and we'll be entering from the back side up Routes 66 and 67, not from the main site entrance. Better chance of avoiding detection. But we're making good time, and we should be there on schedule."

"I don't like this. I know the boss has said this is the last job, but it seems to me he's bitten off more than we can chew with this one. I'm a little worried about how we're going to pull this off. I know we have the people and the equipment and the vehicles, but it's a lot to attempt overnight. Plus, even though Banteay Srei is a long way from the center of the main site, the authorities have been watching it lately and posting patrols on a random basis for the past few years, just like they have elsewhere. But it's the last job and the payout is going to be high, or so he's told us. I just hope everything goes OK. Plus, once we deliver them, we're out of it and the group on the ground takes over."

Heng groaned, then heard a swishing sound. He guessed it was the sound of one of the men turning around to look at them.

"Shut up. I think he's awake."

"Yeah, so what? He's tied up. He can't see what's going on. We need to keep moving to deliver both of them on time. You have to hand it to the boss—kidnapping a curator from the national museum to help out?" He chuckled. "This could end up being a very interesting evening."

"Interesting? No! I don't like this shit. I just want it to be over."

Heng listened to this and wondered what they were talking about. What were he and Jorani supposed to be helping with?

"They need water. We at least need to stop and give them some. They probably need food as well, and to take a piss. Remember, the boss wants them well and fully functional when we get there."

"OK, we'll stop. Next crossroads market."

Heng felt a nudge in his side. Jorani was awake and had also been listening to the conversation. He rolled up against her to let her know that he knew she was awake.

A few minutes later, the car began to slow, and the driver pulled off the road. The vehicle stopped. One of the doors opened, and the man in the passenger seat got out. Next, the back hatch opened, and Heng was pulled up to a sitting position. His tape gag was ripped off. He heard the man helping Jorani to a sitting position as well, and it seemed he was being surprisingly gentle with her. He wondered if her tape would be removed with more care than his had been.

These guys didn't really seem to be professionals at whatever they were doing here, which, when Heng thought about it, was probably kidnapping, although he hadn't heard any mention of ransom. At the very least, they were being abducted, and he suspected these men had been co-opted into doing this. And he also guessed that whoever was overseeing this operation, as they called it, was not a professional criminal.

"Not a word out of either of you, understand?" one of the men said, his voice calm and almost friendly, rather than mean or rough. "We're not going to hurt you, but you need to keep quiet. Understand? We're going to take off your blindfolds and untie your feet and hands for a few minutes, but don't give us any trouble. Please."

Jorani murmured assent. Heng nodded wearily. When one of the men took off their blindfolds and undid the loose cloth ties on their feet and hands, he glanced at Jorani to be sure she was OK. She nodded. After they each gratefully drank water from the single plastic bottle offered, they were escorted, one by one, to the primitive toilet at the small thatch-covered convenience market. The driver brought them some rice with chicken and some slices of papaya. As Heng was directed back to the car, he glanced around, trying to get his bearings, and he realized they were far from Phnom Penh, apparently on the highway en route to Angkor. If what the driver said could be believed, they were on the way to Banteay Srei. But why?

He tried to remember what he knew about the temple. He had once known a lot about it but had forgotten most of it. Brilliant example of early Khmer art and architecture. Small scale, so comprehensible. Good visitor center. Tourist favorite. Target of Malraux back in the 1920s, when André, his wife Clara, and a friend had hacked sculptures off the temple and returned with them to Phnom Penh, where they were promptly arrested and later tried, though none of them served any time for their attempted theft.

One of Heng's first projects, years ago, had been to help plan the work that was going to be done out at Banteay Srei. He had relied a lot on Anada and his knowledge of the temple and its sculpture, and the two had worked together across borders to create a viable work plan. For some reason, it always fell to the bottom of the priority list, though the Swiss had done a lot of work in the past decade, and the site was already beautiful. But it was the major temples, at the main Angkor site, that had always been the priority. Size mattered at Angkor. Though stunning, Banteay Srei was not as grand, or as visible, as many other sites.

Heng was still not thinking completely clearly, but the events of the past few days were beginning to coalesce. He thought he might be starting to understand what was going to happen. And what played out in his brain was not good.

It was time to interact with his captors, starting with the one who had given him the water. "Why are you taking me and my wife to Banteay Srei? What operation have you been referring to? It can't possibly be anything official, or we wouldn't be taped up and riding in the back of an SUV. What's going on?"

The water man looked at him curiously, as if Heng's questions had been stupid. "Think about it. If you're as smart as people say you are, you'll figure it out. And don't think you can escape or get out of this. You're now in the thick of the action."

Jorani said nothing, instead gratefully accepting the bottle of water when it was offered again. While sipping, she side-eyed Heng. He frowned at her and shook his head slightly. *Don't say a word.* She nodded.

The afternoon was beginning to fade. Their mouths were retaped and the blindfolds replaced. They were instructed to lie down again in the back of the car, and they spooned, as best they could with her broken arm, as their hands and feet were retied. The driver pulled back onto the road.

Heng was now fully awake, and his mind was racing. They obviously knew who he was, and they were taking him to the Banteay Srei temple. Whatever they were planning was clearly illegal—and definitely not official. He also realized that they—like the two men who had initially kidnapped him—were working as part of a group under the direction of someone they called "the boss," who was clearly in charge of whatever was happening.

Many of the sculptures of Banteay Srei had been removed from the site years ago and brought either to the national museum in Phnom Penh or to Conservation d'Angkor for safekeeping. They had been replaced by copies. With growing unease, Heng realized this group of criminals wasn't stupid. They weren't going to steal the reproductions. Instead, they were probably planning to carve some of the remaining original sculptures off the building and take them away.

They were going to loot the temple.

And somehow they were going to make it seem as if he and Jorani were responsible.

Heng thought about this with growing anxiety. He'd had multiple run-ins with the authorities in the ministry of culture in the past because he felt they were slow and always seemed to be more interested in bureaucracy and paperwork than in protecting the heritage of Cambodia's past. He and the present minister of culture, in particular, had repeatedly clashed over the past few years, and Heng had usually failed to win the arguments. There was no love lost and little respect between them. He was beginning to understand the precariousness of his position.

He inferred from the conversation in the front seat that he was going to be implicated as responsible for the theft of the temple sculptures. But even given their rocky relationship, could the ministry possibly believe he could do this? If the theft was being organized, it had to be by someone with wide reach and knowledge of the area and a coordinated group of helpers. Heng had been in his position for years and knew all the major players, both ethical and shady, in the world of Southeast Asian antiquities. He ran through all of them in his brain, trying to figure out why and how and by whom this was going to be done. And he kept circling back to one person.

He tried to push that idea out of his mind.

But to no avail. Because there was only one person in the entire region, probably in the world, who had the connections, and the resources, to pull off a heist like this. Heng just couldn't believe Nigel would actually do something this dodgy, especially just as they were about to finalize the exhibition of a lifetime. But no matter how he thought it through, he kept coming back to Nigel—well-funded, knowledgeable, and a collector and adviser to other collectors. But then again, Nigel rarely left his apartment these days and almost never left Bangkok. There was no way he could be directing the thefts on the ground, and as far as Heng knew, none of the shady characters he had crossed paths with over the years possessed the knowledge, or even the intelligence, to know what to do at a site. There had to be a different explanation. If Nigel was responsible, there must be an intermediary, someone who could direct activities in the field. Someone who was trusted and handpicked by Nigel. While he wasn't completely convinced this was the situation, he found himself returning to this scenario, over and over, and processing how it might work.

If Nigel were the mastermind of this theft, it might partly explain some of what had happened when Heng had been in Bangkok the week before. Nigel had, as always, been hospitable. His apartment and staff were at Heng's disposal for the entire time he was there. But Nigel had been distant, a little preoccupied, and had not been available to Heng for their usual lively talks about the past over a glass of beer, or a gin and tonic for Nigel, in the early evening before dinner.

Instead, Heng had eaten by himself at the apartment, or had gone out with Anada and other friends, while Nigel sequestered himself in his office behind a closed door. Heng had thought it odd at the time but had let it go; the man *was* getting old, after all. The only time that Nigel had been interested in talking to Heng was when he had brought up the diary. And Nigel had been uncharacteristically disappointed that Heng had not brought it with him to Bangkok.

There was one passage in particular that popped up in Heng's mind when he recalled Nigel's reaction to the diary, and that was the reference to an American who had come to say goodbye to his colleagues at the museum and who, according to his father's eyewitness account, had taken the head of Uma from the tenth-century sculpture. That sculpture had, long before that, been relocated from the temple of Banteay Srei to the museum, and during the planning stage for the upcoming exhibition, he and Sarah had wildly hoped that the head, missing since the 1970s, would somehow surface during their extensive research. The diary clearly gave some clue about its disappearance, but up until now, Heng had not known where that clue led. But now he also recalled Nigel's expression when Heng had mentioned the passage about the theft and Nigel's mention of knowing people who had been in Phnom Penh back then.

Could Nigel have been *the* American?

With a start, Heng saw this all coming together. Nigel didn't want it to get out that he had stolen something from the national museum. *No*, he thought. *That's just not possible.* It was ludicrous to even think that, after everything Nigel had done for him throughout his childhood and even as an adult when he entered the field of Khmer studies. But what if it were true?

And then another thought blasted him. One far more painful than the image of Nigel stealing Uma's head: What if Nigel had known what was about to happen under the Khmer Rouge regime and had not done anything to save Heng's father or any of his colleagues at the museum?

Heng tried to shake those suppositions from his head. He was not thinking clearly. He forced his mind to pivot and to think about his immediate issue, which was that they would soon be arriving at Banteay Srei. Whoever was orchestrating this heist planned to frame him and Jorani to make it look as if the two of them had planned the theft. He had no doubt now that whoever was planning this would take care to execute the theft in a sophisticated and subtle enough manner that the ministry, as well as APSARA and the police, might believe them—or at least believe them for long enough to allow the thieves to cross the border into Thailand with the sculptures. *And then who knows what would happen and what charges might be brought against us?* He needed to come up with a contingency plan for what to do. He knew many people, and had many friends, in the area around Banteay Srei and especially in Siem Reap. They could certainly be helpful to him if he could get in contact with them, but he had no phone and no other means of communication.

Jorani was a complicating factor, though she was clever and fearless. She could be an asset in whatever might happen. All this thinking was exhausting him, however, and he decided he should try to sleep, to gather his strength for whatever might happen once they arrived at Angkor.

But he could not. As the SUV continued northwest up Highway

6 and toward the Angkor Archaeological Park, Heng lay there, wide awake, haunted by thoughts about Nigel Sanderson, his mentor, father figure, and friend, who was most probably a thief—and had been one for a very long time.

CHAPTER 27

Bangkok
Saturday afternoon

Sarah stared across the table at James. She was furious.

"I'm going to repeat some questions I've already asked you more than once. This time, I would like some answers. First, I had asked to see a public affairs officer at the embassy, and you showed up, but you are clearly not a public affairs officer. So who are you? *What* are you? And secondly, what was going on with Nigel back there? I felt as if I were at Wimbledon, watching the two of you strategize, volley, and occasionally serve an ace. You'd told me that you didn't know him, that you'd wanted to come with me to 'meet' him. You *lied* to me. And now I want to know what is happening. Is James Carlyle even your real name?" She was nearly out of breath. "Who the hell are you?"

James drummed his fingers on the table for a long while, and, true to his poker face form, said nothing. Sarah was tempted to stand up and tip the damn table over onto him, except that it was probably too heavy for her and she'd look like an idiot. Finally, thankfully, he rubbed his chin between his forefinger and thumb, grinned mirthlessly, and then spoke.

"Sarah, how much do you know about the illegal antiquities trade in Southeast Asia?"

"Don't try to answer my questions with a question. I won't fall for a diversion like that. But since you asked, I'll give you the courtesy of a reply, and in return, I expect a full explanation from you about what is going on. On all fronts. OK?"

"Fair enough," he said, leaning back in his chair and crossing his arms as if settling in for an entertaining show. As much as this irked her, she already felt the dopamine surging, as it always did whenever she was invited to talk about her field of expertise, a passion she couldn't control.

"First of all, I have a damned *doctorate* in the field of Southeast Asian art. Which means I have probably forgotten more about illicit trafficking in the region than the staff at your embassy collectively ever knew. Dealing with it, parsing out the details, figuring out what's going on in this field of study—it's critical for my job, and the profession, and the functioning of museums today." She leaned forward, elbows on the table, in reply to his relaxed pose. She just might have been regaining the upper hand.

"Second, I am well aware that many countries which are rich in archaeological materials and sites are economically poor and politically unstable these days. That, in and of itself, presents problems for the conservation of cultural heritage. When you combine this with the insatiable and rapacious desire of private collectors—and yes, some museums—it creates a flow of illicitly obtained objects from the poorer countries into the richer ones.

"Many important archaeological sites have been looted to such a degree that they are no longer valuable records of history. The Tam Ting caves near Luang Prabang, in Laos, lost priceless and spiritually valuable Buddha figures over the past thirty years when they were stolen out of the caves. The pots from the archaeological site at Ban Chiang, in northeast Thailand, are scattered around the world, while they really should be in museums in Thailand."

She paused, realizing how talking about her passion somehow

both triggered and moderated anxiety. She could have used a cup of herbal tea.

"This story repeats itself thousands of times throughout the region. Vietnam, Myanmar, and especially Cambodia have also lost so much. Given the war-torn history of Southeast Asia in the second half of the twentieth century, and its important history and archaeology, the region has become the source of a tremendous amount of cultural material—art objects—now held in private collections. And in museums as well. Most museums today do try to determine the provenance of objects before purchase, but many objects were donated or purchased before the UNESCO Convention on illicit trafficking of 1970 came into effect. But the fact that the US didn't sign it until 1983 and neither Thailand nor Singapore ever signed on to the convention has further complicated the situation. Bangkok and Singapore have therefore become the most important transit cities for objects from this region, and some items do remain in local collections, though they are inaccessible to the public. Many, however, have wound up being shipped abroad to waiting collectors.

"Cambodia has been particularly hard hit by this problem even though they have agreements about this with the US. Years ago, there were rumors that one could go to a gallery in River City in Bangkok and peruse catalogs of objects still in situ, which would then be procured—for the right price. I never saw these catalogs, and I don't know if they actually existed, but just the rumor was bad enough. At the very least, it is an indication of the enormity of the criminal activity involved."

She stopped to search his face for some sign of interest or recognition. "Is this more than you wanted to know?"

"As a matter of fact, I find this fascinating. I probably knew most of this already, but you are definitely assuring me that you're quite the expert. Please go on."

She got up and walked around the small office, looking out over the traffic on Wireless Road but not really seeing the view. In her mind, she had wandered off to Angkor.

"The situation at Angkor has improved immeasurably in the past decades, with the strong work of APSARA, and the heritage protection police, and the improved protection of sites. But all in all, it's still a slimy and dangerous business due to the amount of money involved. In addition to the rumors about catalogs and commissioned thefts, I've also heard stories about how the networks operate and who's in charge. For years, nothing was ever substantiated. But lately, there has been solid, published research on the looting teams and how they operate. Some are scouts. Others are gatherers. All are managed by a level of overseer, who frequently makes the contact with the galleries in Bangkok. You're right, it is fascinating. And it's tragic."

"So your knowledge of these operations is pretty much hearsay? You don't get involved?"

"Of course I don't get involved. Not directly, anyway. At the museum, we are sometimes offered objects with dubious provenance and little or no documentation, and if that's the case, we decline further contact with the potential donor or dealer. If there's enough suspicion and evidence, we sometimes report them to the respective authorities, and given that we are an American institution, we may even contact a Homeland Security Investigations office. But we see only a fraction of what goes on. Sometimes, it's just a single object at a time. But sometimes it's a flood."

She circled back toward the table but wasn't sure she was ready to sit down. Standing was empowering, especially with James still seated. He had to swivel around to see her behind him. "And Nigel?" he asked.

Sarah had hoped his name wouldn't surface. Sure, he was a collector of items with questionable provenance. But he didn't seem to fit into this part of the discussion. She returned to her seat, across from James. "I am fully aware that Nigel's methods and history of collecting have not always been completely aboveboard, but the ground has shifted and the rules have changed since he began collecting in the 1970s. You have to admit that many of the objects in his collection have been saved from destruction because he has kept them. Bear in mind also that he has promised his works will return to the countries of origin when he dies. He doesn't plan to open a museum with his name on it or have the art sent to a major museum elsewhere. He's doing the right thing by returning them to governments for transfer to their own national museums. He may be doing it too late for many people, but he is doing it."

She felt his eyes on her. "I know what you're thinking. But there's no way he can control what will happen with all the works that have passed through his hands and are now scattered all over the world. That is a lot of objects."

Had his gaze intensified? She'd been feeling on top of the world with her little lecture but now started to feel uncomfortable. Did he ever even blink? Well, she wasn't done with what she had to say. And then she had to get him back to disclosing whoever he really was.

"But setting Nigel aside for a minute, all of what I have been talking about is just the surface. Things may be improving, but the trafficking over the years has been, and continues to be, much more insidious and cuts more deeply into society, and into the national interests of the countries here, than what I've conveyed. Also, although the region still struggles economically and politically, the quality of life *is* improving, and these important cultural objects which people have collected are critical signposts for the cultural identity of the people. So Nigel, and whatever he may have done, is small potatoes. Getting back to your question about what I know about the illegal antiquities trade of Southeast Asia, let me sum it up like this: There are individual collectors who are doing something they shouldn't be doing, and there are also much larger looting and smuggling rings that are well established and organized and that are robbing the people of the region of their heritage and identity. They are also robbing them of many of the reasons why tourists travel here. Do you think anyone would visit Cambodia just to see the Killing Fields? They come to see Angkor."

She felt like an attorney who had just delivered a critical closing argument. The proverbial pin could certainly have been dropped on the tile floor and clearly heard. She knew she had impressed him with her knowledge. But now came the moment of truth. Would he tell her what she needed to know?

After an extremely long minute, those remarkable eyes locked onto hers.

"You are right. These smuggling and looting groups are very well organized throughout the ASEAN nations," he said with a quiet yet firm voice. "And they *are* robbing the people of their culture and so much more. But I think there's something you've missed. For several of the key countries of the association—Vietnam, Laos, Cambodia, Thailand, Myanmar, Singapore, and to a lesser degree Malaysia—your friend and mentor Nigel isn't exactly small potatoes. Indeed, he is *the* mastermind behind the largest remaining organized group."

Now the silence mushroomed as Sarah froze, stunned. She did not know what to say. Or think. She wasn't even sure she knew how to breathe. How do you possibly react when someone has made a preposterous allegation that you know, without a doubt, is entirely false—but could also be utterly true? She shook her head, emphatically, angrily. "No. You're wrong. I refuse to believe that. My Nigel? He was certainly a dealer, but he's not a thief. You've got the wrong guy."

James looked hard at her, his teeth grinding during another interminable silence.

"No," she said again. "Can't be true." Sarah glanced at the door and momentarily envisioned dashing out of the room. But what purpose that would serve was unclear. All she knew was that she somehow felt as if she was being accused, and whether it was accusation of a crime or of stupidity almost didn't matter. Both would be intolerable.

Nodding, James spread his hands flat on the table. "Sarah, I know it's hard to believe. We, and local authorities, have been working on this for a long time. We have thus far been unable to catch anyone above the lowest level of diggers and smugglers, and those aren't the people we want to catch. Honestly, they're just trying to feed their families, and we understand that. But some of these frontline diggers are starting to come forward now with information. It's extremely difficult to apprehend those at a higher level, but now we have some evidence that Nigel was the client for the attempted theft, way back in the 1990s, of the reliefs at the Banteay Chhmar temple on the Thai-Cambodian border. That attempt was, of course, partially foiled by the Thai police, and at least some of the panels were returned to the national museum in Phnom Penh, but Nigel had foreign buyers lined up for all of them. You know better than I that the loss of those reliefs would have been devastating. You may not believe that Nigel was responsible for this, but all the evidence points to him."

James paused, and for once she was grateful for his silence. This was a lot to digest. "The sheer scale of the smuggling in which he is involved is mind-numbing. Khmer art began to flood the market in the late 1970s, and especially in the 1980s, during the occupation of Cambodia by the Vietnamese. We don't think Nigel was originally part of the trafficking world, but as far as we can tell, he seems to have moved into it sometime during the 1980s. That someone could have such disdain for the culture and heritage of the countries which have taken him in, and trusted him for decades, is truly sickening. I don't know what more to say." He shook his head and waved a hand as if waving away a disgusting thought.

Meanwhile, Sarah's brain was firing in way too many directions. *Could what James is saying possibly be true? And why and how does he know about all of this?* She knew Nigel's methods had not always been completely aboveboard, especially in the early years, but all of this was really incomprehensible to her. If James was right, it meant that when Nigel was teaching her—and when she was working for him—he was already involved in this world. And by association, she had unwittingly been as well.

And how would this square up with everything, literally *everything*, that Nigel had told her about his objects? And the exhibition? Sarah groaned inwardly, thinking about the exhibition—*her* exhibition—which was on the road to becoming a train wreck. She gradually became aware that James was speaking again.

"We thought that once we had stopped one of the major pipelines, it would be the end of most of the large, organized, and illegal trade activities. But as it turned out, Nigel had an even bigger piece of the pie than we had imagined. He's a smart guy and has been more under the radar than other players. He's not as flamboyant or social as the others, which made him less visible. He also has the respect of many in the international community."

Again, he paused, which gave her a fighting chance of keeping up with the unfolding story. But her thoughts couldn't coagulate, and her concentration was overtaken by the noisy rattle of the consulate's air-conditioning and the muted street noise from outside.

"Now, to circle back to your original question," James said. "You are partially correct about me. My name *is* James Carlyle. But I am not a public affairs officer. I am an agent of HSI, which you seem to be familiar with already. Originally based in New York in the Cultural Property, Arts, and Antiquities Unit, I have been conducting a long-term investigation on cultural property crimes in Cambodia and have been posted in Phnom Penh for several years now. As much as I miss aspects of home, I have no plans to return to the US, at least for now, until this investigation is finished. I'll probably end my career here, as mandatory retirement looms for me in a few years. We've been trying for some time to catch Nigel, but he is elusive and clever, and his well-organized network is nimble and devoted to him. We've come up empty-handed every time. It is also rumored that he pays better than others in the business."

He was going on, but Sarah had stopped listening. Holy shit! Homeland Security Investigations. She recalled a chat she'd had years ago with a Homeland Security investigator who had been at the same conference as she had. She hadn't been able to figure out at the time if he had been flirting with her or trying to recruit her, but the selection process, training, and work schedule and rotation that he had described for investigators was formidable. Also, there was the gun part. She remembered the serious and dedicated investigators with whom she'd had brief contact through the museum. She had thought her education and career path had been complicated, but it was nothing compared to what someone like James had likely been through. Wow. James was HSI. Maybe he *did* know what he was talking about.

Maybe he was right about Nigel.

"Why in God's name didn't you tell me you were HSI? I've spent the last couple of days wondering what exactly you were doing, why you were being so cagey, and I feel as if I have wasted time worrying about that when I have other, more immediate things, like an exhibition and a couple of disappeared friends, to think about."

"Sarah, I've been wanting to give you the entire picture of what I'm attempting to do here. Our meeting with Nigel today gave me an opportunity to observe how he would respond to certain questions. I was honest when I told you that Nigel and I had never met; what I didn't tell you was how we knew *about* each other. My informant has been passing a great deal of information to me about how Nigel operates. And, as he is well connected in the ex-pat community in Bangkok, people there have also told him about me. It has been a game of cat and mouse, and we're at stalemate." He drummed his fingers on the table. "Even though we have loads of evidence, I still feel, at this minute, as if I'm losing."

Sarah understood how someone could devote their entire career to a project and feel unsuccessful in its completion. A part of her felt sorry for James. And she was still trying to figure out how she felt about Nigel. But she had the feeling there was still more to this story than what James was telling her. On the interminable flight across the Pacific, when she should have been trying to sleep a little, she'd watched one of those classic cop movies about a miserable detective who'd been chasing a bad guy for years. As with any such movie or book, there's always a backstory that drives the detective more than the simple fact that a crime has been committed. And right now, those wrinkles on James's forehead, and the bags beneath his otherwise stunning eyes, hinted that this could very well be the case for James too. But she would need to tread lightly to get to the rest of the truth, the way a conservator would use soft brushes and microfiber cloths to work with a delicate, ancient object. She could be direct but not demanding. A gentle tone, a slight smile.

"I sense there's still more to your story. I'd love to hear it." She was pretty sure he wouldn't take the bait, but it never hurt to try.

Surprisingly, James took a deep breath and said that yes, indeed, there was more. Again he set his palms on the table, almost as if bracing himself before unburdening.

"In the 1960s, Nigel and my father were stationed together in Saigon as intelligence officers as part of CORDS, the Civil Operations and Revolutionary Development Support program. My father died under circumstances that were never fully explained. Nigel was there, so I know he knows what happened to my father, and I want to know what he knows. More to the point, I want to know if he killed my father or if he could have prevented his death."

Wow, Sarah thought again. She hadn't seen that coming. This story was getting much better than that dumb in-flight movie she'd watched.

"There's at least one thing Nigel doesn't know about me: that his field partner back then, Joseph Steptoe, was my father. When my mother remarried after my father's death, my stepfather adopted me, and I took his last name."

She wasn't sure if she should tread on this fragile ground, but she decided to go for it. "Do you want to tell me what happened to your father?"

Now it was his turn to stroll over to the window, as if looking out on the landscape would conjure the right image for him. "I don't think my mother was ever completely clear about what happened, and I'm not either. She was pregnant with me when he came home in a military coffin." He stopped in front of the window but didn't turn around. "The official story was that my father and Nigel were out in the field just south of the city of Tay Ninh, working on pacification and intelligence gathering, and they were talking to some of their Vietnamese assets. There was an attack on the village. Nigel survived, and my father did not. The report said my father had been killed by North Vietnamese or Viet Cong fire, but who knows? There could have been a lot that never made it into the document. So, officially: enemy fire. I've never been convinced that's entirely accurate, though."

"Nigel?" she asked, incredulous.

"I am speculating, and I don't know for sure. What I do know is that Nigel left Saigon years after the incident. It's unclear if this was his choice or if he was forced out of Vietnam. I had a friend from college, career military, who had access to the records, but they were spotty. Nigel was sent to Phnom Penh, where he worked at the embassy until April of 1975, when he was evacuated with the rest of the remaining Americans before the Khmer Rouge marched into the city. It's not clear to me what he did in Phnom Penh, though I do know that he got involved for a while with some of the staff at the national museum. He had probably been told to scope out their Khmer Rouge sympathies, and he may have taken it to the next step and spent more time there than necessary for his job."

Sarah joined him at the window, hoping the gesture would demonstrate the compassion she truly felt. "That's a very compelling story, and one which unfortunately played out way too many times during the various wars in Southeast Asia. It's also one that seems to transcend national boundaries. Do you understand how parallel your story is to Heng's? He also lost his father in times of war, and until very recently knew nothing about what had happened to him. You, of all people, must be able to understand how he felt when he read that diary's first entry and how motivated he was to pursue it and learn more. I freely admit that I'm having a hard time processing all of this."

Gently, but trying to remain professional, she took hold of his arm. A sign of support but nothing more. "I'm not saying that I believe all this, but if it is true, if Nigel is the mastermind of a massive smuggling ring *and* if he may have played a role in your father's death, *and* if he may even have been at the national museum in Phnom Penh when Heng's father was there, this is way above my pay grade. What's your plan? What are you going to do?"

She awaited a reply. There was none. How could James know what to do? How could anyone?

Something else occurred to her. "And I guess I'd like to know how much of your investigation is being done under the auspices of the government of the United States and how much of it is a rogue operation. Will you share that with me?"

James looked startled. "Rogue operation?"

"Well, yeah—how much of this are you just doing on your own? I doubt the US government is aware that you're investigating the US military's historical records from more than fifty years ago."

"Everything related to Nigel's trafficking ring is official and known to my colleagues in HSI and ICE, as well as the senior-level staff at the embassies in Phnom Penh and Bangkok, the higher-ups at State in DC, and the authorities in both Thailand and Cambodia. It is the primary reason that I'm stationed here. My quest to understand what happened to my father, and to know if Nigel had anything to do with his death, is a little less official."

"Hmm."

He looked uncomfortable, which wasn't exactly her intent. "OK," he said. "My need to understand what happened to my father is completely off the record. No one in any of the organizations with which I am affiliated knows anything about it. My mother and stepfather are dead, and my half siblings aren't aware of what I'm doing, though I'm sure they would be supportive. You're the only one who knows about this. I would appreciate it if we could keep it that way."

Neither said anything for a minute. So much to process.

"James, I'm still frankly disbelieving, unconvinced, dubious—I don't even know what the right word is—about what you've told me about Nigel being the linchpin of a Southeast Asian smuggling operation, but if what you have said is true, there is something I should tell you that's been bothering me for the past few days. I was in his apartment in Bangkok a few days ago, working on the exhibition details.

Heng was supposed to be there as well, on Zoom, but he never called in. Nigel seemed worried about the fact that he wasn't there, as he did when you and I just met with him. And I admit I was the one who insisted, at least at first, that everything must be OK. Heng was just being Heng. I had put his absence down to Heng's independent nature and figured he would show up at some point." She shook her head and said bitterly, "How wrong I was about that. But my point is that Nigel never really did anything about it, and that bothers me. He said he wasn't sure what to do, even though he has connections all over the region. He should have been able to figure something out."

"I can see why that would be upsetting, and puzzling. Let me assure you that many people are working as hard as possible to find Heng. We will find him, wherever he is."

"Who? Who is working to find Heng? And what exactly are they doing?"

"The police in Phnom Penh and other national authorities in Cambodia," James said.

"I hope so. I will never forgive myself if anything happens because I was too wrapped up in a stupid exhibition to realize the seriousness of his disappearance." Sarah took a deep breath and went on. "But I also wanted to mention that something else caught my attention that day. When Nigel left the room for a few minutes, I was scanning the shelves for a book and saw a group of small Khmer stone heads, mostly of relatively poor quality and maybe even later Cambodian copies of antiquities, on the top shelf in his office. They were partially hidden by piles of books. But in the midst of this group was a small dark-gray, high-quality sandstone sculpture that looked, at least at first glance, as if it dated to the Koh Ker period."

"Sorry, but what century are we talking about here?"

"Probably tenth. It looked familiar to me, but I couldn't tell from a distance what it was and had pulled the library ladder over to get a better look at it, when Nigel came back in the room."

"I'm guessing he wasn't pleased."

"No, he wasn't. For some reason that I can't understand, and certainly can't explain to you or myself even now, I lied to him and told him that I was just looking for that book, which was partially true. But he must have seen me looking at the heads because his glare suggested

I had done something I shouldn't have done, or seen something I shouldn't have seen. Later, as I was leaving, I looked up again at the sculpture but couldn't figure out what it was. I was jet-lagged. I wanted to go back to the hotel and take a nap. Even if I had wanted to pursue it with him, I don't know what I would've said. But I knew it was something."

"And this has been bothering you ever since that day because . . . why, exactly?"

"Because I have realized that it was the head of the goddess Uma, which disappeared sometime in the 1970s from the national museum's sculpture of Uma and Shiva from the Banteay Srei temple. If Nigel was in Phnom Penh just before the Khmer Rouge took the city in April of 1975, he may have taken the head from the museum. And kept it all this time. Of all the hundreds of objects that have disappeared from Cambodia over the decades, it's one of the most famous, with the means of its disappearance being one of the most legendary and mysterious. Heng and I had even joked about finding Uma's head and being able to reunite it with her body, and the figure of Shiva, for this exhibition.

"Now I wonder if Heng also saw the head in Nigel's office. If he did, and if he read the first section of the diary, which describes an American stealing the head in April of 1975, he may have made the connection. But surely no one could do anything as stupid or insane as to kidnap an internationally known curator because he had found a sculpture that had been stolen in the 1970s—right? Any penalties Nigel may have faced for having it would be minuscule after all these years, and at any rate, it's all going back after his death. Honestly, Heng and I might even have been convinced to change our rules related to ownership attributions and exhibit it and label it "anonymous private collection" rather than have Nigel face the consequences of having it in his apartment. But now I'm beginning to think that not only did Nigel steal the head of Uma, he also kidnapped Heng. The last few days, and my—our—interactions with him may have just been elaborate theater."

Sarah stopped suddenly. "Oh, shit. I'm making your case for you, aren't I? That one individual head is a relatively small, though very famous, matter. It's just one example of what has disappeared, but what it represents to Nigel and his associates may be immeasurable as it

would mark the beginning of a long slide, steeper and more dangerous than some of those trails on Doi Inthanon." She substituted the
name of Thailand's highest mountain for an otherwise overused cliché
to test him. When he laughed and said he'd hiked those trails numerous times, and acknowledged how slippery they could be, indeed—
especially the trail to Mae Pan Waterfall—she decided he'd passed.
"Anyway, now I feel stupid. Heng must have figured all this out. So
what should we do about this?"

Sarah and James batted ideas back and forth, and James came up
with a plan. All she would need to do right now, to which she unhes-
itatingly agreed, was to send an email from her phone to Nigel and
ask if she and James could return to talk to him again tomorrow. The
whole situation was making her increasingly uncomfortable, but she
owed it to Heng and Jorani to do what she could.

CHAPTER 28

Bangkok
Saturday afternoon

The phone connection, for once, was crystal clear.

Anada started to speak, but Nigel cut him off. "Are you ready to go?"

"Everything is in place, and yes, we are ready," Anada said. "We have both of them and a plan. Regarding our other issue, however, there is still no sign of a diary."

"OK. No more communication now until the operation is over."

"Understood."

As they ended the call, Nigel thought about Heng and Jorani and wondered how this whole operation would end for the two of them. He didn't wish any harm to either of them, and he knew Anada didn't either. But he could not know how the events of the next forty-eight hours would play out.

After this was all over, he would be done, and so would Anada. He sensed unease and sadness in Anada about the finality of it all. But he also sensed that Anada was not telling him everything about what was going on. Had there been problems within the group, which was now operating in ways that it had never had to in the past? Anada would never admit anything about that, and there would be no point in asking. Nigel decided to focus on the comfort he and Anada would both gain when this last arrangement was finished.

CHAPTER 29

Banteay Srei, Angkor Archaeological Park
Saturday evening

Heng and Jorani's captors had removed the blindfolds and the tape over their mouths again and left them locked up and alone in the car, although Heng suspected they were nearby. As he peered through the window, he recognized immediately where they had stopped: near the temple of Banteay Srei.

He had great affection for the people who lived in the small township of Banteay Srei. They had been very kind to him over the years whenever he returned to the site, first as a wide-eyed university student with his friend Anada and just discovering his cultural heritage and roots. Later, he had come back as an American graduate student, and he and Anada had looked at the temple with much more experienced eyes. Finally, the pair had returned as curators at their respective national museums, Heng in Phnom Penh and Anada in Bangkok. They had both made friends with some of the people who worked at the site, including the heritage protection police staff. Enjoying beers together had helped cement their friendships with their security colleagues over the years.

Heng and Anada had helped the local population understand more about their neighborhood temple. When Anada decided to write his doctoral dissertation on the freestanding sculptures of the temple, the knowledge of the local population had proved invaluable. The two friends were vested in the temple and its preservation and future. They respected it. To Heng's knowledge and relief, there had been no looting of the site in the recent past, despite its distance from the main Angkor Park, and he had hoped that both he and Anada, along with Jorani, would continue to enjoy more time at the temple in the future.

He looked over at his wife now. Her eyes were open, but she had not moved from her position in the back of the vehicle. Her body language was indecipherable in the gathering dusk, with the soft tropical light filtering through the trees into the car. Heng also could not read her expression. He tapped his foot against hers.

She sat up, blinked a few times, and looked around. "Banteay Srei?"

"Yes, we're at Banteay Srei," he whispered. "I can see the parking lot in the distance, and there are not many cars or buses. I can't believe this group thinks they'll be able to loot this site. And how do they know what to do? What about the heritage protection police?"

"But why are *we* here? What use could we possibly be to them? You know a lot about this temple, but nothing that would be helpful in looting its sculpture and architectural elements. Right?"

"I've had time to think about this over the past hours. I'm not sure, but I think we may be here for two reasons and neither of them is good. First, I think Nigel had me kidnapped because he thought he could get hold of the diary. I had mentioned it to him and told him about references to Americans in Phnom Penh. He seemed to find that interesting and said he knew some of the people who were there at the time. I didn't think much about it then, but deep down I probably figured he himself had been there during those years. But more specifically, there's a passage in the diary that describes an American coming to the museum to say goodbye to his friends just before the Khmer Rouge arrived in Phnom Penh."

"Yes!" Jorani said. "That was the first entry, and I read it and gave a quick translation to Sarah, including the part about Uma's head. She didn't say anything about it, but she clearly also found it interesting."

"So you read the part about the American taking the head of the goddess Uma from the sculpture of Uma and Shiva?"

"I did," Jorani said, "but I didn't know what to make of it."

"Neither did I. And I'm not a hundred percent sure even now. But what I do know is that the sculpture originally came from this temple, and it had been in the national museum since the early twentieth century." Heng paused before going on. Jorani watched out the window. It was getting darker, and the diminishing light seemed to match her mood. She was probably wondering the same thing he was: *How are we going to get out of this situation?*

"I think the American was Nigel," Heng said. "And I think he must have thought I would figure this out and realize he had stolen the head."

Jorani didn't act surprised. "I think you're right. So, somehow, that's one of the reasons we're here. What's the other reason?"

"Jorani, I have tried to deny the logic of this, but I think that theft was just the beginning of Nigel's criminal activity. I'm starting to believe he has been deep in the world of illicit trafficking of antiquities for years now. He may have, in fact, been behind many of the large-scale thefts that have taken place at important sites for decades. He is the only one I know who has the broad knowledge and networks that might allow him to do something like this."

"Are you serious?" Jorani asked. "I can accept the idea that he might have taken a sculpture or two back in the day, when he was young and maybe not aware of the seriousness of his crime. But look at him now. He's a world-class expert in this field. Why would he do this?"

"Good question. I haven't worked out his motivation. But what I do know is that he couldn't have done all this alone. Or even with a bunch of locals. I suspect there is someone else, someone knowledgeable, who is helping him with all of this."

Even in the waning twilight, Jorani looked as if she'd seen a ghost. "I know who it is." But then they both heard people approaching the car. "Shh. They're back."

The car doors opened, and the two men got back into the front seat. They drove a short distance from the site and stopped again.

They then carefully took Heng and Jorani out of the car, untied their feet and hands, and allowed them to stand for a few minutes before walking them into a small house on the outskirts of the township of Banteay Srei. The men left them in a room that was furnished with worn but comfortable furniture and a table with a thermos and three cups. Heng was walking toward the door to see if it was locked when one of the guards stuck his head back in to tell them there was a toilet and sink in the adjacent room. He pulled the door closed, and Heng could see through the window that both men were standing guard outside.

He recognized the place from the times he had spent there in the past. It was near a house where friends lived, with whom he and Anada had stayed when they came to Banteay Srei decades ago. He wondered if those friends still lived there and if they would be able to help him and Jorani.

Meanwhile, she wandered around their surroundings and then stopped at the table, opened the thermos, and sniffed. "Someone is coming to see us."

"How can you tell that?"

"We've been left hot tea and three clean cups. Also, they have untied us and left the door unlocked. They want us to be as relaxed as possible whenever whoever is coming arrives. And I know who it is."

"Who?"

"Anada."

"What?" He shook his head and dismissed her with a wave of his hand. Had Jorani lost her mind? "No, that can't be. Why would Anada be here?" But then he saw the little grimace on her face, as if she'd eaten something rotten. "You can't be suggesting that he has anything to do with all of this. *Can* you?" His stomach churned. "He's my best friend. Why would you think this?"

"You were unbelievably moody and out of sorts when you came back from Bangkok," Jorani said. "And even though you wouldn't tell me anything, you did mention that both Nigel and Anada had been a little distant and not like themselves. It was only the second time I could remember that you had ever said anything like that about either one of them. The first had been a time long ago when Anada's sister was seriously ill and they didn't think she would make it. I didn't think much of it at the time, but in retrospect, they must have both been worried about you. Nigel was certainly worried about the diary, but both of them were probably also worried about the theft they were planning and how it would affect you, especially if you figured out what the situation was. I'm guessing it was Nigel who decided the only way to deal with you would be to try to pin the blame for this theft on you. It sounds like madness, but I couldn't think of any other explanation. And you have to admit that Anada would be the perfect team leader in the field, given his knowledge of the art. Plus, he always needs money for his family." She sat at the table and began to pour the tea into three cups.

Heng shook his head. "I don't know what to make of your theory. Part of me thinks it's insane. But the other part of me thinks we shouldn't touch the tea until someone else drinks it first. I've had enough of being drugged for the rest of my life."

She set down the thermos, stood from her chair, and linked her arm in his. Together, they circled the room as a couple might stroll through a park. Heng needed to get the kinks out of his muscles and the bad thoughts out of his head. As they passed the table and teacups for the third time, the door creaked open.

Heng gasped.

Sure enough, there stood Anada, his arms opened wide, the way he normally would when greeting his old friend, as if there was nothing strange about the present situation. But when Heng froze where he was, Anada dropped his arms and laughed sheepishly. "I guess you weren't expecting to see me here."

Jorani spat out "I was."

Anada stepped all the way in, and the two guards followed. He motioned to them and they stayed by the door, one on either side, like sentinels. The last time Heng had seen Anada was that dinner a couple of weeks ago when he had stayed with Nigel in Bangkok. That had seemed almost like old times, though Anada had not looked at ease even then. Now he looked completely different, all business and no warm smiles or friendly fist bumps. Heng released Jorani's arm from his. "Anada, what are you doing here?"

Anada seemed surprised that the tea had already been poured. Again, he laughed, and as if understanding Heng's misgivings, he took the first sip. "It's a little hot, but it's perfectly safe to drink. You could probably use the caffeine after your long drive here." He slid one of the chairs away from the table. "Please, sit down and we can talk."

Both Heng and Jorani remained standing, he with his arms hanging limply and she with hers across her chest. Heng didn't know what Jorani was thinking, but he was still wondering if they could somehow get away past the guards and make it to his old friends' house.

Anada seemed to be settling in, however, as he crossed his right leg over his left and jiggled his foot. He took another sip of the tea and nodded at Jorani's arm. "So sorry about that. I hope it doesn't hurt too badly."

She grunted. And although Heng appreciated Anada's supposed concern about his wife's well-being, there was still something about Anada's mannerisms that Heng had never seen before. It was bewildering. "Anada, what is going on here?"

"Heng, surely you must have figured everything out by now? If you have not, you are not as smart as I—or anyone else—thought." Anada nodded at the guards as if they were in on the joke.

Angry heat rushed through Heng. "Explain yourself!"

"Calm down, my friend. You see, my team and I are planning to take some of the small remaining sculptures from this beautiful temple at Banteay Srei, about which I probably know more than anyone on planet earth. We already have a buyer for them. The artifacts will be out of the country and on their way to their new homes within forty-eight hours."

Jorani exploded. "Don't tell us to calm down! What the hell do you think you're doing? Turning on your best friend and me, his wife? Looting the very same site that served as the basis of your doctoral research? You won't get away with this, and you'll end up in prison somewhere for a very long time. I should have known when you didn't answer my phone calls that something was wrong."

It took a moment for Heng to process Jorani's reaction, and he was proud of her for standing up for him and all their work over the years. He felt the same way she probably did: angry, afraid, and betrayed. But he knew they needed to avoid escalation, so he decided to follow Anada's advice and try to remain calm.

"Anada, I am trying to be rational here, but I don't understand. Are you saying you're part of an international trafficking operation? How? Why? I think you owe me an explanation of what you are doing."

"Of course, dear Heng," said Anada, his tone having devolved into uncharacteristic sarcasm, which fit him about as well as a pair of shoes three sizes too large. "I am always happy to explain myself to the exalted and brilliant curator of the national museum in Phnom Penh."

Heng closed his eyes tightly. He could barely believe this was happening.

Anada continued. "You and I started out at the same point in university, and we were sure we would be friends forever. We had such a tight bond! But I have never understood why you have become an internationally known curator of Southeast Asian art, feted in Paris and New York and the capitals of the region, while I toil with detailed provenance records and write labels for objects in the collection of the National Museum of Thailand. Visitors read them, look at the objects, and then walk on to the next one without really absorbing all the work I have done. I don't think that I am paid enough. And I don't believe I have ever been recognized for my knowledge of the field or been given a challenge that could raise my profile in the museum world. Even with this upcoming exhibition, which I admit is exciting and intellectually stimulating, it is now clear to me that I will never be recognized for my work. I'm not sure why this has happened, but it has."

Heng began to speak, though unsure what he would say. "Anada, why—"

Anada cut him off. "I also have financial obligations to my family that are overwhelming. You know my family story—father dead in a construction accident, mother and sister ill. Their care and medication are expensive. They have no money, and I cannot afford to pay for what they both require. When a wealthy collector and expert in the field proposed a different path to financial security, I debated with myself for quite a while before I said yes, because I have an obligation to my family above all. I just direct the operation on the ground and tell the workers what to cut and take. They do all the work. I don't have to do any of the manual labor. The boss of the operation treats me well and pays me well. Cambodia has enough treasures. They won't miss the few that we are taking. And anyway, this is our last job." Again he nodded toward the guards. "We can all retire from this line of work and be financially set for the future."

Jorani picked up a cup of tea, sniffed it, and set it back down. "Nigel?"

Anada laughed, although the side glance he cast toward the guards suggested that he'd have preferred to keep Nigel's name out of it. He replied in a whisper. "Who is the one person in the region with the resources and knowledge to pull off this kind of operation? Yes, of course it's Nigel."

A wave of nausea washed over Heng, and bile rose into his throat. His heart began to race. He grabbed for the chair and dropped into it, having trouble focusing on the figure sitting across from him. He had denied what he had known all along to be true. His mentor and friend Nigel was the mastermind of a major smuggling operation of extraordinary scope and complexity, and it had all most probably begun with the theft of Uma's head from his national museum in 1975. Heng took a deep breath and nodded at Anada to acknowledge that he understood. But still this was his lifelong friend Anada. *How could he?*

Jorani shook her head at Anada like an adult disappointed with a child's behavior. "This may solve some of your problems, but it is creating a host of new ones that could very easily spin out of control. Your network may have worked for a while, but do you really think you'll get away with this now that Heng and I know what you're doing? These guys you've hired"—she gestured toward the sentinels—"may be good at temple thefts, but they're crap at kidnapping. People are looking for us, and we know everything now." She took Heng's hands into hers but remained focused on Anada. "You won't get away with it."

"What you must appreciate," Anada said to Heng, ignoring Jorani, "is the brilliance of Nigel's most recent idea, which is a deviation from the normal process, but which became necessary when you discovered your father's diary in the museum files. Nigel told me that he suspected your father had written about him taking the head of the goddess Uma, but because you didn't have the diary with you when you visited him in Bangkok, he couldn't be sure. He also wasn't certain if he was specifically named in the diary or if your father protected him and left his name out. These uncertainties threw a little spanner into the works. We have had to make some adjustments."

"Adjustments?" Jorani asked with a disgusted look on her face. Heng was again proud of her and how she refused to be left out of the conversation. When Anada didn't even consider her question, Heng began to fume again.

"Usually our method of operation involves getting in and out quickly so that no one knows who has been here," Anada said. "But this time, you're going to help us. We're going to disable a truck to make it seem as if you were unable to leave the site after your workers have left. And then you'll be here for the heritage protection police when they show up the next morning. Given the number of run-ins you've had with the Cambodian authorities over the years, and your arrogance in dealing with them, I think they will have no problem holding you two responsible for organizing the theft. It's unfortunate, but you both have become a cost of doing business for us."

Heng found it ironic that Anada wouldn't acknowledge Jorani's involvement in the discussion but planned to implicate her in the crime, especially with one arm in a cast. "Leave Jorani out of this." She squeezed his hands. "She knows nothing and is not involved in any way in this mess."

"She's here now," Anada said, laughing. "And she certainly knows what's going on. That means she's what we call *a liability*. In fact, she seems to be smarter than you at figuring some things out and accepting the situation. So she is a big problem, actually."

"That's where you're wrong," she said. "I am not fucking accepting the situation. You need to let us go right now."

Despite the gravity of their plight, Heng was startled. He had never heard Jorani use that word before.

Anada stood up and stretched. "Sorry, but that's not possible, Jorani. Sorry. Well, Heng, I've been honest about what is going on here. I also would like you to know that we have no intention of killing or harming either of you, but I am confident you'll both be spending the next years of your life in separate prison cells up-country." He sneered. "Lots of time for you to write about Khmer art there and to think about the end of your ascent through the museum world." As he approached the door, his guards opened it for him. "And don't bother trying to escape," he said, half turning toward Heng and Jorani one more time. "Security may have been lax in Phnom Penh, as we'd had no time to plan, but it's excellent here. My guards will be right outside. Goodbye for now, Heng and Jorani. I'll see you both later."

Jorani looked at Heng as the door latch clicked. "I wonder what he means by that?"

CHAPTER 30

Bangkok
Sunday morning

Sarah awoke after a night of fitful sleep and readied herself mentally for the visit to Nigel's apartment. James had told her he would be at the hotel by one o'clock. She drew the curtains open and looked out over the Chao Phraya River, which seemed less agitated this morning. It was going to be another hot and sunny day. While she preferred living in the moderate climate of Southern California, Sarah also loved the heat and humidity of Southeast Asia. She often joked with her colleagues who traveled to countries with colder climates for their work that she never had to pack moisturizer in her luggage and that her skin always looked amazing all the time when she was there. No longer sure this was true, now that she was almost fifty, she still loved the soft feel of the air and the smells of a Bangkok day and night. It was so different from the quasi-desert air of Southern California.

She had showered and dressed and was now thinking through her approach to Nigel and the day's visit. How was she going to handle seeing him after yesterday's testy meeting? Her phone rang. It was James. He got right to the point.

"Good morning, Sarah. Are you ready? You're still planning to go with me to talk to Nigel again today, I presume?"

"Well, good morning to you also, James. Yes, I slept fine. Thank you for asking. And how are you this morning?"

There was silence at the end of the line for a moment. "Sorry to be so terse. We may be approaching the end of what has been a very long road for me. I'm just anxious that things go well today. And the more I've been thinking about it, the more worried I am about bringing you into this situation. It's not too late to back out if you're concerned or think something might not go well. I feel responsible for your safety."

"Nonsense. I have known Nigel for decades. If he had anything to do with anything that we talked about, I will never forgive him. But I need to be part of the solution. So, to answer your question, yes, I'm concerned. As I told you before, I am a curator, not a spy. I don't know that I can do this, but I need to try. Imagine how I would feel if much of my past thirty years in the field had been based on the advice and guidance of a crook and I didn't do anything to help stop him. And I'm ready to go whenever you get here."

"OK, I just wanted to check and give you a last way out. You don't have to do this if you don't want to."

"Stop asking me about this. I'm in."

He confirmed he was still planning to arrive around one, and they'd go directly from the hotel to Nigel's place. Sarah hung up the phone and now needed to put her own plans into motion. Her stomach was tied in so many knots that she, for once, was going to skip breakfast. On her way out of the hotel, she left a note for James at the front desk.

The deep heat of the day had not yet set in, and the walk to the BTS station was pleasant. She rode the aboveground metro, surveying the skyscrapers, hotels, and skeletons of half-finished buildings for which ground had been broken during flush financial times. The variety and density of life here never failed to astonish her. She doubted there was another country in the world whose life was so dominated by one city, one that was brash and chaotic but with an underlying Buddhist heart.

After changing trains at Siam Square, she exited the National

Stadium station and walked quickly down Rama I Road and turned right into the soi. At Nigel's apartment building, she rang the bell with some trepidation. Her last encounter with Nigel had not gone well, and she was sure it was going to color their relationship going forward.

"Yes?" came Ahmi's disembodied voice from the box on the wall.

"Ahmi, it's me," said Sarah. The door buzzed open, and Sarah took the elevator up. Ahmi met her at the front door of the apartment and, thankfully, escorted her into Nigel's office instead of the stiff living room. He was seated at his desk going through what seemed to be a bottomless pile of paper documentation. Good old Nigel.

"Sarah, my dear, please come in. I need you to help me go through all of these papers to make sure I'm giving you everything you need for the final loan paperwork. Come! Sit here with me and we'll figure it out together. I thought your colleague James was coming also, but I'm glad you left him behind, as I, for one, find him incredibly annoying and self-righteous. And you are earlier than I had expected you."

Sarah felt both relieved and confused. This was indeed the old Nigel, her mentor and friend, asking her to work with him to solve a problem. This was the Nigel she knew and loved. There was no sign of the hostility he had shown her and James yesterday afternoon, and he seemed eager to get back to work with her on everything she would need to take with her back to the museum in a couple of days. But she was confused. It didn't seem possible he could have pivoted so quickly. Maybe he just needed a good night's sleep. Goodness knows they all, including her, could use one at this point. She sat down next to him, certain she had made the right decision to come by herself. She hoped James would understand.

"OK, Sarah, here's the documentation about the lintel from the temple at Koh Ker that is going to be set into one of the first galleries. Do you need more information than is here in these papers?"

The next few hours continued in this manner. He questioned her about what she needed. Was it enough? Did she need more? How was she planning to install this object and what would she say about it? They took a break for another excellent lunch, during which Sarah thought once again that she could probably be happy eating Thai food every meal of every day for the rest of her life. Shortly after they finished eating, Nigel told her he was feeling a bit tired. "I need to take a little rest, but I'd like to finish up this work in an hour or so. Could I leave you here in the office by yourself for a bit?"

Sarah tried to conceal her surprise. This was certainly odd, as Nigel was noted for being able to work for long periods of time without resting. But she remembered that he had also taken a rest at their earlier meeting, and he wasn't getting any younger.

"Of course. No problem. I'll just catch up on my emails and organize some of these papers. Please take your time. It's been stressful over the past few days, with Heng disappearing and leaving the two of us to get all this work done." She had expected him to react to this. He didn't. That was also odd.

He left the room, and she listened to his footsteps climbing the stairs. Alone now, she could look around his office. As many times as Sarah had been in the apartment, she'd never been above the first floor, though she knew Heng had spent the night in Nigel's guest bedroom upstairs many times. But first she scrolled through her emails and texts to give Nigel time to drift off. There wasn't much to respond to; one advantage of being fifteen time zones ahead of everyone at home was that most emails were sitting in her inbox first thing in the morning, and she had already dealt with them at the hotel. Everyone at home was probably eating dinner now. As many times as she had crossed the International Date Line, she could never come to grips with the time differences around the globe.

When she was finally sure that Nigel would be gone for a while, she closed her computer and put it into her computer bag, next to her tote bag on the floor. She stood up and studied Nigel's vast library, housed in wall-to-wall, floor-to-ceiling shelves on two sides of the room. She drew her gaze up toward the row of stone heads, which she had seen a few days ago on the top shelf. Her eyes narrowed. The head that she thought she'd seen was still up there with the other heads. None of them were planned to be part of the upcoming exhibition, so there would have been no reason for it to move. After pausing to listen and make sure no one was around, she found the library ladder and moved it across the floor. She briefly wondered if there might be cameras installed in the room but decided that the household wasn't tech savvy enough to pull that off.

She climbed up the ladder with trepidation and felt her stomach sink. When she reached the top and was able to look at the head in more detail, she closed her eyes and took a deep breath. She hadn't been wrong about what she had seen a couple of days ago. She hadn't been wrong to tell James about it either. She knew she should text him right now. But she felt paralyzed.

It was indeed the head of Uma from the tenth-century sculpture of Shiva and Uma. Documentation had noted it was taken from the temple of Banteay Srei in 1914 and exhibited in what would become the National Museum of Cambodia. She knew—every historian of Southeast Asian art knew—that the head of Uma had disappeared in the 1970s and that no one knew what had happened to it. She also knew from the passage in the diary, which Jorani had translated for her, that an American had taken the head in 1975.

James had been right about Nigel being involved in the illegal antiquities trade in Southeast Asia. She hadn't wanted to believe him. She had wanted to hold on to a part of her past. But although she had been right about so many things, she'd been wrong about Nigel, and now she was certain he was the American in Heng's father's diary.

Was he a different person from what she had imagined him to be all along? How could it be possible he had done this? Sarah shook her head to clear her raging thoughts. She lifted the ancient artifact, carried it down the ladder, and put it on the desk to study it more closely. It was dusty but showed no signs of deterioration and was in good condition. She carefully put it into her tote bag, which she put back on the floor next to her computer bag. She then went back to working on the paperwork that Nigel had left with her. But she was unable to concentrate on anything. One part of her wanted to flee the apartment with the head, but she also wanted to confront Nigel and ask why he'd done what he'd done. She had to hear it directly from him. She had to have him explain it to her. She needed to understand.

About fifteen minutes later, Nigel came back into his office, his eyes glancing around the room and up to where the heads were displayed. He walked slowly toward his desk, sat down, pulled in his chair, and looked at her intently. "Oh, Sarah," he said. "How could you?"

Sarah went cold. He hadn't been tired. He hadn't needed a rest.

He had set a trap for her, and she had walked right into it. He had expected her to take the head.

Sarah stared back at him. She doubted she had ever been this confused and angry in her life. She picked up the bag with Uma's head and walked around to his side of the desk. "Nigel, please tell me what is going on here. Please tell me that James is wrong about you and your role in the illicit trafficking world. I have followed your lead. I've trusted you. And now, this." She raised the bag in her hand. "You were the American that Heng's father wrote about. You were the American who took the goddess Uma's head from the museum in April of 1975. Yes, Heng's father wrote about you in his diary. And you were worried that, as soon as Heng had translated the whole thing, you would be exposed. So you used me, just like you have for decades. How could you? And how could I have been so stupid?"

Nigel laughed and shook his head, playing the role of disappointed mentor. "My dear Sarah, there is so much that you do not understand about Asia. You think that because you have degrees and work at a reputable museum, you are knowledgeable. But you are not. Where do you think those beautiful sculptures, which I have helped you and many others—so many other greedy curators and collectors—acquire over the years, have come from? You didn't seriously believe the provenance and history documentation that came with them, did you? 'Private Swiss collection.' 'Hong Kong gallery.' Really, how naive are you? If you didn't know those works had been clandestinely excavated or hacked off their temples, you should have."

At that moment, Sarah felt like one of those sculptures being chiseled off its base. His tone and his words were beyond hurtful. They were devastating.

"Your research and work many years ago created the documentation for objects like these," Nigel said, "so you yourself have some culpability in this whole enterprise." He stopped and looked at her. He was eerily calm.

Meanwhile, she felt blood draining from her face. She was terrified. All those pre-internet months of painstaking research through books and auction or exhibition catalogs. All those letters she had sent to museums and archaeologists and ministries, asking for information.

While she had certainly never knowingly falsified or created information, she had on occasion left out evidence that might have pointed in an unfavorable direction. She hadn't committed, but she may have omitted. He was right about that.

"Nigel, yes, you are probably right. I was naive. I should have understood more about what was going on than I did. But Cambodia was such a puzzle for many of us, even then, and you were key to helping all of us figure out how the pieces fit together." She paused for a second before adding, "For all of us. But look at what you're doing now. You are destroying and stealing the heritage of these people. You have denied, and you are still denying, the Cambodians the chance to understand their history and what it means. You are nothing but a common thief. You are actually worse than that because you didn't have to operate like this. You were respected by everyone. We all consulted with you on a regular basis about everything! You had it all. Why? Why did you do all of this?" She lifted the bag to shoulder height.

Nigel considered the bag for a moment. "I am far more than a sometime smuggler of antiquities, and you have little idea what I have done in pursuit of my passion. I could not have afforded a collection like this without more money than I had. I needed funds, and I got those funds by obtaining, through whatever means I deemed necessary, objects that ended up in the collections of rich people and museums in Southeast Asia and all over the world. People and museums—including yours, I might add—both before and after you arrived, paid me to be the dealer of these works. My work evolved gradually at first and then it became a torrent. I admit it."

"I have Uma's head in the bag here, and I am taking it to the authorities," she said.

"I don't care at this point who knows about it. Uma's head was my first acquisition—"

"You mean your first theft!" She clutched the bag to her chest.

He sighed as if the entire discussion was boring him. "I felt bad about it for a while, but it has been better off with me over the years, and yes, my estate will return even *this* head to the proper authorities upon my death. I might add that under your influence, I have decided to atone for the sins perceived by others.

"But I have done some good here too. The work that I provide the

Cambodians on-site helps them earn a fair wage to provide food and shelter and medicine to their families. They dig these works up and bring them to me, or my associates, and I pay them. They can live a decent life and rise above their grinding poverty. You can think about that over the next hours."

At his mention of time, she wondered what time it was just then. Would James be showing up here? She could use a little help right around now. "Nigel, you know that is a hackneyed argument. There are other organizations better equipped to deal with economic issues in these communities. Also, legitimate archaeology was just being re-vitalized after decades of chaos. Your diggers' skills could have been used there. I don't buy these arguments. You were teaching and en-couraging them to be criminals. Everyone who has worked in the re-gion is concerned about this. Most of us have tried to contribute in some way to the betterment of life here. But the answer is not to make everyone a low-level criminal."

Nigel rose from his desk, and Sarah took a step backward, and then another and another. The atmosphere felt thick with menace as she backed away from him toward the door to the foyer.

"But sadly, I'm afraid that you now know too much about too much, Sarah. You were an asset to me and my associates. Perhaps you were an unwitting asset, but you were an asset nonetheless. Now you have become a liability. We have no room for liabilities. But, my dear Sarah, I want you to know that I am and always have been fond of you. I'm sorry."

Sarah's knees shook as she heard the threat in Nigel's voice. James had been right, and she hadn't believed him. She had made a terrible mistake in not waiting for him and coming here on her own. Nigel was at best a thief. And at worst—who knew?

She abruptly turned and ran toward the apartment door. Her exit was blocked by a grimly smiling Bona moving toward her with a scarf in one hand and a syringe in the other. She swung the tote bag by its straps at him, with Uma's head inside, and he flinched as it hit him on the shoulder. He tore the bag from her hands. He grabbed her and held the scarf over her nose and mouth while jabbing the needle of the syringe into her arm. As she lost consciousness, she thought she heard Nigel say, "You know what to do, Bona."

When Sarah came to, she was surrounded by what first looked like a forest of sticks, but as she blinked and cleared her mind, she discovered it was a collection of brooms and mops. She was in a closet filled with miscellaneous tools for keeping a house clean. She boosted herself upright and groggily shook her head, trying to come to her senses. She tried to figure out why she couldn't move or even feel her limbs, and then she also realized that her mouth was taped shut. As she twisted around to look for a door, she recognized the flooring pattern, which was the same as the floor onto which she had dripped sweat just a couple of days before. It now seemed like a century ago. She was still in Nigel's apartment.

She had no idea how long she had been there, and her heart began to beat wildly as she remembered the events that had transpired. Bona must have tied her up and carried—or, judging by how she felt, dragged—her up the stairs to this closet and locked her in. Her head ached. Her stomach rumbled.

She could not believe what had happened in Nigel's office. He had betrayed everything he had taught her over the years. She closed her eyes and tried to forget the wild-eyed look on his face as he ordered Bona to deal with her. He had looked out of control, as if he would shoot her if only he'd had a gun, which she knew he did not. When he'd spoken, his tone was that of someone who didn't know her, even if the words suggested he did. She felt crushed, and she felt afraid. But mostly, she felt very, very angry.

Sarah turned her attention to trying to free herself. Her hands were tied together behind her. Her feet were bound. But she didn't seem to be tied *to* anything. She scooched along the floor to the small free space in the center of the closet, envisioning how she might untangle herself. She didn't think she could raise her arms over her head given how they were tied together behind her back. She feared her legs were too long for her to work them through the circle of her arms even if she was able to bring them to her front, but she decided that was preferable to a shoulder dislocation. With great effort, she lifted herself off the floor with her bound hands and feet and pulled her tied hands part way under her. She paused and caught her breath and lifted herself up again so that her hands were now in front of her, though under her legs. She was bent forward over her knees. She had thought this would improve her situation but was now not sure. She tried to think.

From what seemed like a long way away, she heard a doorbell ring, stop, and then ring again for a long period, as if someone were leaning on the button. She strained to hear what was happening. The bell abruptly stopped and was followed by the soft sound of a well-oiled and maintained door opening and closing. Sarah heard muffled voices: a man's, and then a woman's, whom she was sure was Ahmi. The man was speaking in a loud, angry voice, and the woman was speaking in a quiet and hesitant manner, which indicated to Sarah that she was either ignorant of what was maddening the man, or she was terrified. The voices abruptly stopped. She strained to hear, but there was only silence.

Sarah now sat leaning forward in the middle of the closet with her legs bound in front of her and her hands under her thighs. The muscles in her legs were beginning to kink, and her rear end felt asleep. As she was thinking about how ridiculous she must look, and what she should do next, she heard steps approaching. Had Nigel—or worse, Bona—come back? Where were they going to take her? What would they do to her? She breathed deeply to try to slow down her pounding heart. It felt as if it were going to explode.

The door opened. Ahmi, who looked terrified, and James, who appeared vastly relieved, peered down at her on the floor.

Speechless, Sarah just looked back up at them. She thought she might never have been so glad to see any two people in her entire life. And, once again, she wondered how she must look at this moment.

"Oh my God, Sarah. Are you OK?" James said.

"Yes, thank you," she tried to mutter even though her mouth was taped shut. He carefully removed the tape and then, after untying and untangling her, offered a hand to stand up. "Easy does it."

She stood up a little unsteadily and shook out her legs and arms. The three of them walked down the stairs, Sarah more slowly than the other two. She held tightly to the railing as she descended. She and James took a seat at the table in Nigel's kitchen, where Ahmi made coffee for them. Sarah massaged her wrists and ankles.

"Ahmi, we need your help," James said. "Can you tell me what Nigel is doing? What has been going on here? I know you're not involved. I promise nothing will happen to you. But I also know you see everything that goes on in this house. Please help us."

Ahmi sat quietly for another minute. She glanced toward the foyer and then looked at James and then Sarah.

"He thinks I do not see anything. He thinks I am stupid. But I know he is doing something very wrong. It makes me afraid sometimes that I work in a house where things like this are happening. I don't want any trouble with the police." Again, she glanced at the doorway to the foyer.

"Go on," James said. "You're safe with us."

"It wasn't always like this. When I first came to work with Khun Nigel many years ago, he seemed to be a good man, a kind man, and I was lucky that I had found such a place to work. As you know, Sarah, my husband has problems and cannot work, and my boss has always paid me well. I have been able to support my family while my husband has stayed at home with the children. I have learned English, and I have met interesting people. This is a very uncommon arrangement in Thailand, but it worked for us. Khun Sarah, you know that it is sometimes hard for people from the north in Bangkok. But Khun Nigel has always been good to me.

"But over the years, he has changed. Bona has changed also. He has always been rough, but in the past few years, he has become mean and difficult to have around. There have been men coming to the house on a regular basis who frighten me, though I do not know what they are talking about. Sometimes I will catch a glimpse of them talking in Khun Nigel's office, and they stop until I have walked past and then they close the door. I do not like this, and I have not known what to do. I do not know what has happened to him."

She stopped for a moment, then repeated, "I don't know what to do. Please help me."

"Ahmi, we can help you, but you need to help us also. You have already been very observant. Sarah and I are going to go find Khun Nigel and talk to him. I would like you to leave the house. Go home. We will call you later after we have spoken with Khun Nigel. But first, Sarah and I need to talk privately. You can leave before we do. I promise nothing will happen to the house and you will be safe. Are you alone here today?"

Ahmi nodded. "Yes, now that Bona and Khun Nigel have left." She looked simultaneously relieved and dubious, but after exchanging phone numbers with Sarah, she went to collect her things, and Sarah walked her to the door of the apartment. Ahmi disappeared into the elevator.

"Poor Ahmi," said Sarah as she walked back into the kitchen. "I remember when she came to work for Nigel many years ago. She had only arrived in Bangkok a short while before then and was still overwhelmed by everything. She had lived for a little bit in Chiang Mai up north, but she had spent a lot of her life before this in a small village with no electricity and a communal water source. He saw something in her, employed her, and paid her well. She learned English and has probably had a more interesting life than she ever could have imagined. I do suspect, though, that she has put up with a great deal from Nigel over the recent years. He is frequently wrapped up in his work and his world and can be unintentionally short with people, though I do think that he was very fond of Ahmi." She sat and sadly said, "Just as he was fond of me. Or so I thought."

James looked at her. "Sarah, now that Ahmi is gone, can we have a little chat?" He pulled the note she had written him, which was now crumpled and damp, from his pocket and read it back to her.

> James, sorry but it's better if I visit Nigel by myself to get answers. I'm heading over there now (eight thirty). I'm sure that he will open up to me more easily if you're not there. If you're reading this, it means I'm not back by one. But don't worry. I know how to deal with Nigel.

Listening to her note made her uncomfortable, like wearing a wool sweater in a tropical climate—tight and suffocating. She knew he was upset with her, and with good reason. She was upset with herself too.

"WTF, Sarah? What on earth made you decide this was a good idea? I will probably never be allowed back in the Shangri-La Hotel after my outburst in the lobby. I'm surprised the desk attendant didn't call the manager—or worse, the police. I had to run in the baking heat and humidity of midday Bangkok to the BTS station, grab a train, change to another train, and then run here from the National Stadium station. Do you have any idea what an idiotic idea this was? We had a plan. You ignored it." He paused, fuming. "I'm aware of your academic credentials in the field, and your relationship with Nigel, and your familiarity with a lot of what goes on in Southeast Asia. But could you please, for the rest of the time we are tossed together in this situation, please, please let me take the lead on what we do? Luckily, Ahmi recognized me. I suspect she knew that you had been put into that cleaning closet upstairs and saw me as someone who might be able to help her, both in this immediate situation and maybe even in the future."

Sarah rubbed her brows. This whole situation had gone from stupid to terrifying to humiliating.

He went on ranting. "I have spent a lot of the past hour trying to get a grip. I'm the professional in this situation, and that means it would be useful if you paid a little more attention to me and what I think is best." With that, he removed a gun from a holster he'd been wearing under his jacket and put it on the table. "Don't worry. This is a nine-millimeter Glock, the gun carried by most Homeland Security investigators. I'm not going to shoot you, but I am so hot and sweaty that it's uncomfortable for me to have to lug this around."

Now Sarah was freaked out. She stared at the gun on the table, which seemed to underscore every word he'd just said. "Yes, I was wrong. I'm sorry, you have every right to be furious with me. But I need you to understand that I can bring a lot more to the party here than you seem to think I can, and I need you to stop treating me like baggage rather than an intelligent and resourceful woman!"

James paused and stared at her. The he shook his head, grinned, and nodded. "OK. I accept your apology and hope you'll accept mine. I'm well aware you are both intelligent and resourceful. I'm sorry."

"I will confess," she said, "that I am also more grateful to you than I can ever express for showing up when you did. I feel as if a great, crippling anxiety that I've always harbored about myself, and my life and my career, has been lifted. At the same time, I'm in the most unnerving situation I have ever faced. And what about Heng? And what about Jorani?

"If you had told me my father was a serial killer, I would not have been more surprised than I am about what you have told me and what I have learned over the past few days about Nigel. I know that something has happened to him, but I can't explain it. We were once so close, and it's as if I don't know him anymore. I thought I knew him. But now I don't know. I just don't know much of anything except that I am angry. Angrier than I can ever remember being. And to top this all off, he made off with my tote bag with Uma's head in it, and we—I— need to try to recover this, as it will make a smashing addition to the exhibition."

James looked at her, first in disbelief but then slowly nodding as his face softened into a warm grin.

"But I need to see this through to the end, whatever that may be," she said. "So what are we going to do?"

CHAPTER 31

Banteay Srei
Sunday afternoon

Heng and Jorani had awakened that morning as the door to their room opened. A meal consisting of a large thermos of coffee, fruit, eggs, and bread and butter was pushed through the opening in the door before it was closed again and locked. After devouring the food, they spent most of the day thinking about ways to escape and how they might go about it. They came up with no answers. Overwhelmed with exhaustion and despair, Jorani lamented to Heng, "We're not spies or thieves. We are arts professionals, and this situation is way out of our league."

They had run through every potential outcome and scenario they could imagine with no clear answer or approach. Anada had acknowledged that a theft at the site was planned for that evening, and Heng seemed paralyzed, while Jorani was becoming increasingly enraged about the situation. She paced around the room.

"How can this be happening? What can we do? We should be able to figure how to get out of here. Heng, do you still know people who live around the temple? You and Anada spent so much time here when you were in school. People here don't tend to move on that quickly, especially with the economy so strong with tourism these days. Do you still have contacts here?"

Heng frowned. "Jorani, I don't remember. I need time to think."

Jorani, almost shouting, said, "Heng, we have no more time to think. We need to get out of here and inform the authorities now." She slumped on one of the chairs and covered her face with her hands. She needed Heng to come up with an answer for her, but he had nothing to say. It was getting later in the afternoon, and the sun's rays were slanting into the room, creating a pattern of bright boxes on the floor as they shone through the windows. Her despair was interrupted by the door opening again.

It was Anada, carrying a new tray, this time with a thermos of tea and clean cups. "I trust that you found your accommodations accept-able last night and have passed a pleasant day so far?" This time, he was alone. No guards.

Jorani exploded, not caring how Heng would feel about her loss of control. "How can you do this to us? How can you do this to people whom you have known for decades and with whom you have worked? We trusted you. I see now that we were wrong to trust you, but it is incomprehensible to me that you think you can get away with this." She had worked herself up into such a frenzy that now she choked up. Unable to flee the room, she did the next best thing and rushed over to the far window overlooking the forest landscape outside. It was the closest thing she could find to an escape.

Heng picked up her narrative. "Anada, if your family needs money or food or medical help, we can figure out how to do that. We both have friends who would be happy to help you out. This is not the way. Please rethink what you are doing. I don't know how deep you are into this whole mess, but it's never too late to figure how to get out."

Anada said, "At this point, Heng, I'm afraid it is too late. But I assure you this is the last operation. We will all come out of it with enough cash to put ourselves out of business."

Still facing the world outside, where twittering parakeets hadn't a care in the world, Jorani observed Anada's voice. He didn't seem as brash as he had during his previous visit. She also noted Heng's pause and imagined him studying his old friend's face.

"Anada," Heng said, "I am going to ask you one last time to stop, and I would appreciate it if you, for old times' sake, could hear me through without interruption."

She pivoted to see Anada's expression and body language. He seemed both exhausted and puzzled, but he nodded and sat down in the available chair. He was clearly trying to appear relaxed, but Jorani thought he was in fact uneasy. She also wondered where this could possibly be going but did not interrupt Heng.

"When we first met at Chulalongkorn so many years ago," her husband said, "I was in complete awe of you and your intellect and ability to synthesize problems and solutions. You were also the most extraordinary connoisseur of Khmer sculpture I had ever met, even when we were just starting and only at university. Honestly, I believe that today you are still the most perceptive judge of the style in the world. Your catalog entries made me rethink my approach to the early sculpture of the Khmer Empire. I don't think that any of the rest of us would have made the connection between the two halves of the lintel from Phimai that were in the private collection in Dallas and the national museum in Bangkok, but you did. And now the joined lintel is a highlight of our exhibition. Your brain is amazing and operates in a manner that is light-years ahead of other curators we know."

Anada looked at Heng in disbelief. As normally a humble man, he may have never heard such accolades. "And what has that gotten me but a mediocre rental apartment in Bangkok and not enough money to help my family, which is everything to me? I haven't even been able to afford to get married. I don't have children. I work long hours. I'm almost fifty years old. I'm poor and exhausted."

Jorani interjected, "This was a life that you chose, Anada."

Anada looked at her for a minute and started to respond. But instead he shook his head and turned to Heng. "Unlike you two, Nigel saw how difficult my life was becoming. He helped me get back on my feet again by asking me to take on a high level of responsibility in his operation. And honestly, the government of Cambodia doesn't do that great a job taking care of its antiquities. It's better now than it was twenty years ago, but it's still not good. The overcrowding at Angkor, and the not-so-gradual degradation of the water table and environment around Siem Reap, are enormous problems that need solving which no one is tackling and which are probably deemed more important, at least to some bureaucrats, than a bunch of sculptures. For the sake of the survival of this art and the Khmer sites, maybe more of it *should* be in private collections or in museums that have higher standards of care. It could actually be preventive conservation."

"I can't deny that we, at the museum and at other agencies, aren't perfect at what we do," Heng said. "There are definite holes in our strategy, and I myself get enormously frustrated at the waste that I see of the funds coming into the museum. We have received resources—technical, financial, and human—for years now, and in some ways, I'm convinced that nothing ever gets any better. But that doesn't mean we don't keep trying to make it better."

He paused before continuing. Anada appeared to be inspecting his fingernails, but Jorani could tell he was listening. And feeling guilty. Good for Heng.

"I can't begin to understand your familial pressures, Anada, but I know your mother and sister mean everything to you. Even back in the days when we were in school together, you had the best relationship with your mother and sister of anyone that I knew. As someone who had no family, I was jealous of your tight relationships with them. I hoped someday to be able to create that kind of family for myself, which I have been able to do with Jorani and with my work colleagues."

He shot a look at Jorani, still standing at the window, that urged her to bear with him. He seemed to have a plan. Meanwhile, Anada continued to act uninterested, although Jorani didn't believe this could be true.

"We—you and I—have done a lot together," Heng said, "and I thought we were happy doing it. What happened to your idealism and need to ensure the role of Southeast Asian art in the art history of the world?"

Finally Anada sputtered to life as if unable to contain his neutral demeanor any longer. "You are living in a fantasy world if you think those kinds of things matter when compared to having enough money to make ends meet and provide for the people you care for. What am I supposed to do? Drive for Uber? Work part-time on the weekend at a convenience store? Those jobs would pay a fraction of what I am making here, and they'd be a lot duller as well. At least in this position working for Nigel, I am able to use what I know while making a kill-ing." He paused, his expression softening. "Well, not an actual killing. But a lot of money."

Jorani jumped in. "And if you don't plan to kill Heng and me, what do you plan to do after this theft? We know what you are doing, and we won't hesitate to tell the authorities. You are delusional if you think they'll believe we are involved in this crime. How do you expect to support your mother and sister if you are rotting in jail?"

Anada acknowledged her with a shrug. "Jorani, you presume that I'll be caught, and I don't plan to be. It will be your word against mine, and you'll be the one who will be discovered at the site with incrim-inating evidence on your person. They will know you yourself didn't take the art, but they'll see you both as the instigators of the theft. I wouldn't be too sure that the authorities won't blame you. Given Heng's multiple run-ins with the ministry staff and the art establishment in Phnom Penh, I personally know of a number of higher-ups who would be only too happy to have him out of the picture for a number of years. And disgraced."

Heng's shoulders dropped, and he bit his lip. "Anada, I am truly sorry you feel this way about me. I think I have always tried to give credit where it is due and to help you and others as you have helped me over the years. You were my best friend. I guess I don't know what to say anymore. But you will not get away with this. And you will have destroyed a career and the lives of a number of people—Jorani and me, your mother and your sister, and you yourself. Think about it, Anada. You are better than this."

Anada looked hard at Heng. Jorani could tell Anada wanted to say something. He even hesitated and opened his mouth before he shook his head, stood up, and walked slowly toward the door. As he grasped the doorknob, he turned and said, "I, too, wish that this could have been different. Those times with you in Bangkok at university were the best times of my life, and I will never forget them. But I need to do what I need to do."

And with that, he opened the door and walked out. Jorani caught a glimpse of the two guards at the door. They had clearly overheard the conversation and peered in at Heng with what seemed to be a combi-nation of disdain and pity before the door slammed shut. It was also clear those two were going nowhere until she and Heng were hauled off to the temple. Jorani felt drained and helpless, unable to offer any comfort or solace to her husband.

CHAPTER 32

Bangkok
Sunday afternoon

Sarah walked slowly on the uneven pavement as she followed James along the quiet and deserted soi away from Nigel's apartment and toward Rama I Road, which they could see was full of traffic and people. Sarah thought the wisest option would probably be to go straight to Suvarnabhumi Airport and get on a plane out of the country. But she didn't have her passport or her credit cards with her, which made that impossible. And anyway, she was angry and wanted to confront Nigel yet again.

"Stop, James," she gasped as she put her hands on her knees and stooped over to catch her breath and stretch out her muscles.

"We can't stop," he said. "I know Nigel isn't home, but it may only be a matter of minutes before someone comes back to the house and discovers that you aren't there anymore and that Ahmi is gone. They will contact him."

"I'm sorry, but my legs are cramping. You're not the one who was tied up like a pretzel in that cleaning closet. We can keep going. I just need to walk slowly for the next block or so."

"I'm also not the one who went to Nigel's apartment alone to confront him."

Touché, thought Sarah. *Well played, Agent Carlyle.*

By the time they reached Rama I Road, Sarah's legs felt better, and she was able to walk as quickly as possible in the obstacle course that passed for a sidewalk in Bangkok. They rode the escalator up to the BTS station at Siam Square, and James bought both of them tickets.

"Where are we going?"

"Down to the Saphan Taksin station. I know that Nigel uses a warehouse near the station, and I suspect he may be there right now with some of his men, going over their plans. I've called my Bangkok-based HSI partner in this investigation and asked him to meet us there with the Royal Thai Police."

On the train, James pulled out his phone and opened his Google Maps app. "I saw some paperwork in Nigel's apartment indicating that the warehouse was located here." He pointed at the map. "Which jibes with information that we already had. I'm guessing, but I suspect that Nigel uses it to store art works that he's moving around the region to collectors and galleries or to sell through dealers here in Bangkok. According to our years of tracking his activity, his operation is international in scope. It also seems to be a stratified, four-level operation consisting of field operatives on-site, facilitators on both sides of the Thai-Cambodian border, well-known but corrupt dealers in Bangkok, and Nigel organizing the whole shebang from his apartment. We have eyes on most of the players, and we learned about a year ago that Nigel has a strong collaborator who can travel freely between Thailand and Cambodia, someone who is knowledgeable about the art. We were able to identify him, and while working with the Royal Thai Police, we approached him a few months ago. He has since become our informant.

"His information is invaluable and the source of much that I know about what's going on. It's how I know, for example, that there's going to be an attempt to take sculptures from the temple at Banteay Srei either tonight or in the near future."

"What? You said it was going to be at Preah Vihear."

He laughed. "That was to throw Nigel off. I didn't want him to know what we knew. Anyway, Nigel's operation is very professional. Our informant has told us that it's run with a small group of trusted associates who then have their own networks in the field. The operation is so tightly run and diffuse that no one knows more than their immediate area of responsibility. It's incredibly well organized and operated, if one can say such a thing about an illegal and immoral activity. It's certainly the best I have seen."

Sarah looked at James and then out at the city of Bangkok, which was unfolding in front of them on the elevated train. She almost wished she didn't know about what Nigel had been doing in this city.

"I don't know if Nigel is at the warehouse right now," James said. "But I hope so. There's no time like the present to pay him a visit."

The train sped along. "I want to thank you again for finding me in Nigel's house. I was wrong. I thought I could fix the situation by myself because there seems to be such hostility between you and Nigel. At this point, I don't care about the antiquities or the smuggling or anything else that Nigel may have done. I want my friends back alive as soon as possible, and I know you want to get to the bottom of the mystery about your father." She paused, not sure if what she was about to say next was true—or how it could be true. "I'm not even sure that I care about the exhibition anymore, though no one probably cares whether or not I do. I do care, though, that my computer is still at Nigel's house, and I'm going to need to retrieve it at some point."

James looked at her as if she'd lost her mind.

"Well, it was probably not the most intelligent move you've ever made, but you're safe now. And I think we'll be able to find Heng and Jorani, and break up Nigel's smuggling ring, in the next few days. If I can find out more about my father, that will be an added bonus. And the truth is that I need you and your knowledge of Khmer art with me when we do this, to validate what we find. So thank you for being willing to help me."

"How dangerous will this be?"

"We'll have backup soon, and you know what they say: There's safety in numbers." He watched passengers shuffling toward the exits as the train approached the next station. "And also, I'll do everything within my power to ensure your exhibition goes forward. You've worked too hard for too long to let everything implode."

A strong twinge of gratitude for his empathy coursed through her and prompted her to reiterate that despite her misgivings, she was willing and eager to help him too.

The train dropped them on the eastern bank of the Chao Phraya, just below the Taksin Bridge. They walked south past the grounds of Wat Yannawa and down an extension of trendy Charoen Krung Road to a group of older warehouses and other buildings fronting the river in an area which had not yet been gentrified. The beginnings of change were visible, though, with a few serviced apartments and a Pizza Hut nearby. The river here, south of the Taksin Bridge, seemed to smell more like the ocean than upstream, though Sarah knew they were still miles from where the river emptied out into the northern end of the Gulf of Thailand. The stench could just as easily be caused by algae overgrowth, dumped wastewater, and other pollutants.

James stopped abruptly and looked down a small deserted street to the right that led toward the river. "I want to look around a little bit here before the others arrive. Are you OK?"

"Do I look like I'm not OK?"

He laughed. "I guess I'm asking you for the last time if you're up for whatever may happen here in the next hour. It might not be pretty."

Sarah shrugged. "I don't know. But at this point, after having been abducted and held captive by someone who I thought cared about me, I feel as if I am in for a dime and in for a dollar, or a baht, or whatever, so let's go." Her eyes widened as he checked to make sure that his gun was secure in its holster.

"Thank you." James was all business now: His expression, his posture, and even the tone of his voice had shifted, as if he'd gone into a telephone booth and come out wearing a superhero cape. It was odd but comforting. "So here's the plan. We have known about this warehouse and its contents for several months now, but you and I won't go in until everyone else shows up. While I'm hoping this won't become violent, I need to be ready. Once inside the warehouse, I'll need you to identify any art works we find." He scanned the nearby landscape.

"We're lucky that it's late Sunday afternoon. There aren't a lot of people around, which would make things more difficult."

The area certainly was deserted. In fact, Sarah wasn't sure she had ever seen a part of Bangkok so empty. They turned toward the river and walked past boat slips, locked piers, warehouse entrances, and smaller alleys branching out on either side. James stopped at one warehouse door, which was covered with a steel grate, and glanced at his phone.

"This doesn't seem like the kind of neighborhood the United States government would encourage its staff to hang out in," she said, feeling a little nervous at her surroundings.

"Maybe not, but it's convenient to the river and to transportation, and not heavily populated a lot of the time. It's pretty much a light industrial and warehouse area. Perfect, in some ways, for Nigel's operation."

He gestured with his arm that they should keep walking. As they approached a beaten-up door in the middle of the next block of buildings, James stopped. His voice was low. "This is it, Sarah. Last chance to bail out."

His concern for her well-being was starting to annoy her. "That's at least the third time you've asked me that. I have no illusions that I can change Nigel's mind about anything at this point, but there may be some value to my being here in case he is here. Plus, as you already made clear, you're going to need someone who actually knows something about the art." She pointed at the holster. "I will fully admit that I am scared, though, especially with that thing. But let's go." She gave him a thumbs-up and moved behind him.

The steel grate across the door appeared relatively new and strong. She wondered what his plan was to get them inside. As if reading her thoughts, he motioned with his gun to the edge of the building. "Let's go around that corner and see if there are any windows. Maybe we can see what's going on in there while we wait for our backup." There were two windows at low street level in the small alley. Surprisingly, neither of them was protected by bars.

"Stay behind me and out of sightline," he said. "Just in case anyone is standing by those windows inside." He crouched beneath the window, then rose slowly to peer over the sill. He shook his head. "I don't see evidence of anyone being here. But now we wait." As they huddled in the shadow of the building, out of the direct sunlight, it seemed to Sarah that James was checking his phone every thirty seconds. She assumed he was waiting for some kind of communication from his colleagues, but he was tense, and she didn't want to interrupt his train of thought. She slowly sat down on the ground, leaned her head against the building, and closed her eyes. He crouched beside her for a few minutes until two figures came between them and the sun. She assumed they belonged to his team.

She was wrong. It was Nigel and Bona. Nigel had Sarah's tote bag over his shoulder.

"Well, well, well," Nigel said. It was clear to Sarah that he hadn't expected to see her again that day and that he really didn't want to see James either. Bona gestured with his gun for James to turn over his Glock, which he slowly removed from the holster and slid across the ground. Sarah didn't know a thing about guns, but Bona's looked bad.

"Time to get up," Nigel said. "And follow me." He unlocked the steel-grated door around the corner, and the clicking of their shoes echoed on the concrete floor as the four of them walked down a corridor. After passing rooms filled with desks, chairs, lamps, and file cabinets, they came to a large, unpartitioned space with a high ceiling. Though the room was dim, Sarah was able to see a number of open crates, various objects on pallets, and several large-scale sculptures sitting on the floor along one wall. Against the other wall were industrial shelves with hundreds of pieces—heads, which she was certain had been hacked off the walls of temples, and small freestanding sculptures which she assumed were stolen from smaller temples or side chapels. It seemed as though Nigel was taking them on a victory tour, and as they walked, she was able to see the objects more closely. She spotted several large-scale, footless works lying on the floor, including a Harihara figure representing Vishnu and Shiva, which had recently been reported missing from a newly discovered temple near the site at Koh Ker. She, Heng, and Nigel had planned to have it in the exhibition before it had disappeared less than a year ago. She shook her head as she thought about Nigel's role in all this. She simultaneously felt exhilarated and disgusted to see all these pieces—and miserable and angry at Nigel.

"This is unbelievable. Outside of the National Museum of

Cambodia and the Musée Guimet in Paris, and maybe a couple of other big museums, I don't think I have ever seen such a collection of high-quality works of Khmer art in one place," Sarah said. "I am astounded. But I also don't understand. I am sick."

Nigel offered a couple of chairs for James and her to sit in. "Well, Sarah, it seems as if I greatly underestimated you. I'm impressed that you somehow managed to escape the closet. But sadly, your freedom will be short-lived. Mr. Carlyle, please cooperate, or I will instruct my associate Bona, who is standing at the ready, to shoot both of you. I had vowed not to harm either of you, but you have sorely tried my patience. He won't kill you, but he could make you very uncomfortable. Also, put your hands where I can see them. Bona, let's move them farther into the interior, away from the door, so they won't even contemplate making another escape."

Upon Bona's direction, James and Sarah stood up so he could move the chairs away from the door toward the center of the space. When he waved his gun at them, they sat back down. Sarah had never felt so terrified. She saw that James's gun had been placed on a table against a third wall, too far for James or her to reach. She didn't know anything about guns, but she knew something about people, and she could tell that Nigel and Bona both meant business.

"So, Sarah and James, I am fascinated that the two of you figured out where this place is. How did you manage to get here? What was your plan? What was your logic in coming here today?"

She knew Nigel didn't really care about their answers to his questions. He was agitated and trying to fill the awkward time and space while, more importantly, trying to figure out what to do about yet another unexpected development. His lack of spontaneity could be helpful most of the time. But it could also be a concern, such as in times like these.

"Did you think I wouldn't be around and you could call the Thai authorities and they would come to the rescue? And why did you think that anyone would show up to help you? I have more friends in the Thai police than you can possibly imagine. Did you think you could call a few tuk-tuks and take some of this evidence away to whomever might be interested? Honestly, I don't understand what you planned to accomplish here. Please indulge me."

James moved to speak first, but Sarah cut him off. "Nigel, I don't understand what has happened to you. I do know that the Nigel whom I have known for so many decades seems to be gone. What's happened to you? What is wrong? I, for one, am speechless and sad and have nothing more to say unless you want to talk about stopping this right now—"

He interrupted her. "You're clearly not speechless, my dear."

James now cut in. "Nigel, you must know you are not going to get away with this any longer. We've had you under surveillance for months now. We have infiltrated your team, and we know about the operation you're currently planning. That's right—you may think your planned looting of Banteay Srei is a secret, but we know all about it—"

Sarah had been startled to hear that Nigel was planning a theft there when James had mentioned it on the train, not only because of its legendary significance in the art world, but also because that was where Uma's head—the one she'd found in Nigel's home—had originated. She wondered why Nigel had chosen that site.

"And as we speak, authorities are waiting for your operatives to show up at the site where they will be arrested. And regarding your captives, Heng and Jorani—wherever they are, you'd better hope they're OK. If not, you are going to be facing far more than charges of looting and illicit trafficking in antiquities."

Nigel rolled his eyes and chuckled. So he did have Jorani and Heng.

"You can laugh all you want," James said. "But be assured: Backup is on the way. And while you may think your Thai contacts trump mine, they don't. They will be here soon too."

"Oh, Mr. Carlyle, you talk a good game, but I have the utmost confidence in my team, and furthermore I believe you're bluffing. They have been with me for years. They are loyal. And well paid. As for Heng and Jorani, they are with my team at Banteay Srei right now and will be found at the site after the looting with enough evidence to convince the authorities that they are the masterminds of the theft. Not to worry, I do not intend to harm them. They should be fine. Unless, of course, they decide to be heroes and stop the operation. Then there may be a problem."

Sarah groaned. She knew that was exactly what Jorani might do. But she was grateful and relieved to learn that, thus far, they were both alive. And they were together. Or at least that was what Nigel was telling them.

As Nigel began to walk away from them, toward the back area of the warehouse, James stood as if to follow him. "There's another, more personal reason I'm interested in talking to you about the past, the more recent past. I want to know more about what happened in 1968 in South Vietnam when you and Joe Steptoe were attacked at the village outside Tay Ninh."

Nigel froze.

"Do you remember Joe? Or what happened? I suspect you do. I'd like you to tell me why he died—and why you lived. Nigel, what happened that night?"

Nigel did an about-face, and his expression suddenly appeared anguished. He almost looked faint, as if he might collapse. Sarah was stunned that James was bringing this topic up at this moment, and as angry as she was, she was afraid that Nigel was going to have a heart attack right there and then. He was unsteady on his feet. He was breathing shakily. He ambled back to the chair where James had been sitting, deposited himself into it, and cleared his throat.

"You are talking about something that happened over fifty years ago. How do you know about it? Why do you care?"

Sarah had already discovered that James had a skill of locking eye contact with other people, and now he was laser focused on Nigel. "Joseph Steptoe was my father."

Even Bona now appeared intrigued.

"And I want to know what happened to him that night. I don't believe the official report's version, given to my mother, was completely accurate. I believe you were there. And I think you know what happened. So now I want you to explain it to me. Tell me, Nigel. Did you kill him?"

Nigel furrowed his brow. "How can that be possible? I thought your last name was Carlyle, not Steptoe. Joe cannot have been your father. Although—" Nigel studied James's face.

"But he was. After my father died, my mother remarried two years later, when I was a toddler. My stepfather, Samuel Carlyle, adopted me. Joseph Steptoe was my father, though I never met him. So again, I ask you: What happened that night, Nigel?"

Nigel let out a deep sigh and, as if he were a balloon that had been popped by a pin, lost all his bravado in an instant. His entire being deflated; Sarah was more certain than ever that he was about to drop dead on the floor. Even Bona seemed concerned, moving forward toward his boss. But he kept his gun alternately trained on James and Sarah.

Nigel's voice was flat now, as though he were in a trance and mesmerized by thinking about past events. "Joe was my fellow officer and my colleague. And he was my best friend. I would never have done anything to hurt him. We worked together. There were times when we spent every waking hour with one another. We could almost finish one another's sentences. We both knew on some level that what we were doing in Vietnam was useless, and probably morally repugnant, but we were young, and we were doing our jobs—and we were damn good at them.

"That night, we had stopped at a village and were waiting for some of the villagers to come back from the fields so that we could talk to them. I remember vividly sitting outside the circle of hooches, leaning against a rock, when rapid fire came from several directions. Someone in the village must have tipped off the Viet Cong that we were there. We scrambled behind the rock with our weapons, leaving everything else out in front of the rock and in the line of fire."

James's gaze was glued on Nigel. Sarah watched James. Bona kept his ready stance. Nigel didn't pay attention to anyone present. He was connected to the ghosts of his past.

"A sniper got him with one shot and then nailed him with one more to finish the job. I listened to him lying on the ground, his breath becoming increasingly erratic and shallow, until it stopped. There was nothing I could have done for him. We had nothing beyond a basic first aid kit, which was in his pack in front of the rock. Had I tried to reach it, to help him, I would have been shot as well, although I doubt there was anything I could have done. Many minutes passed while I listened to my best friend die." Nigel paused with a pained and haunted expression on his face.

James studied the same floor that Nigel was fixated on.

Sarah didn't know what to do. Or say.

"They finally sent a helicopter to evacuate us the next morning,"

Nigel said, "and take Joe's body back to Saigon. It was something we all had become quite adept at doing. A few days later, I watched his coffin being loaded into the belly of a plane at Tan Son Nhut with many, many other coffins of America's youngest and bravest, all of whom had been sold a lie. When I was back in the US on leave, I did start out several times to visit your mother, but I could never bring myself to ring the doorbell. I have never forgiven myself for what happened that night."

Sarah glanced at James and then back at Nigel. "And then what happened?" she asked.

"I went back to Saigon and did pretty well there. I continued to be a productive team member. Ultimately, I was sent to Phnom Penh to work at the embassy there." He lifted his gaze toward James. "The US assigned me to check out some of the staff at the national museum, where they suspected there were Khmer Rouge sympathizers. It was there that I fell in love with Khmer art and culture." He paused as if lost to his memories. "Of course, there weren't any sympathizers. Actually, the staff was naive about the Khmer Rouge. Some even saw them as liberators. But there were no Khmer Rouge operatives or anyone even friendly to them.

"I was eventually assigned to other work at the embassy, and ultimately on April 12, 1975, we were all ordered out of the country. I still have nightmares about the fates of all those Cambodians with whom I worked in Phnom Penh, especially Sam Sokha, who I assume you know by now was Heng's father. I tried to get him to leave with his family, but he decided to stay. I never heard from any of them ever again, so I assumed they were killed in some barbaric manner."

Bona had slipped away for an instant, but at just the right moment in Nigel's story, when there was no chance James would make a move to escape. He now handed a bottle of water to Nigel after twisting it open for him. The old man drank greedily.

"Your father's death was the single most horrific event of my life," Nigel said. "I have never forgotten it. And never will. It changed everything." He drank more water. "Everything." After exhaling another big sigh, he smiled mirthlessly and sadly to himself. "I don't expect you to believe me when I say this, but I am truly sorry for what happened, and I am also grateful to have had the opportunity to tell you the whole true story, at least as I see it. By the way, I was honest in the inquest interview and told them exactly what had happened, and I was completely exonerated. But I have never let go of the guilt I hold because of that night."

He leaned back in the chair, sagging. It was a pitiful sight, and for a second, Sarah thought that maybe she and James could overpower him—and Bona, who was clearly distracted by his boss's account of what happened and his weakened condition. But Nigel soon pulled himself upright and stood up from the chair.

"None of this negates the fact that the two of you are meddling in a place that is very dangerous. I have no choice but to take action so that my final job can continue. I don't know how you found out about the operation at Banteay Srei, but I know you were bluffing when you told me that someone had infiltrated the ranks of my operatives and that the Royal Thai Police are on the way. As I said before, I am entirely certain that my staff and those I have in my pay are loyal."

When James had told Sarah that they had infiltrated the ranks of Nigel's gang and help was on the way, she had believed him. But now, everything Nigel had said seemed completely sincere, including his belief that his people would be loyal to *him* and he had the Royal Thai Police in his pocket. She was back on the seesaw, first believing one of these two men and then believing the other. If Nigel had been telling the truth, did that mean James had been lying about help being on the way? She felt a rising panic.

Nigel instructed Bona to tie them up. "Effectively this time, for God's sake. And stash them in the back room." He once again said he didn't plan to hurt or kill James or Sarah. "But I do need to have you both out of the way until tomorrow at dawn, when my final operation will be finished. I will be leaving you here until then. When I am gone, one of my associates will come and free you. What you do after that is your own business. But, Mr. Carlyle, we will of course be taking your gun with us."

With that, he walked out, clutching Sarah's tote bag, which presumably still held Uma's head.

Bona frisked James under his jacket, and checked his pants pockets. It was too bad James hadn't given her his gun, because Bona didn't seem to think it necessary to frisk her. But he did tie up her wrists and ankles and repeated the process for James. He grabbed James's gun but, contrary to Nigel's order, left the two of them on metal folding chairs in the middle of the warehouse rather than locking them in a back room.

After they left, Sarah breathed a sigh of relief. At least they were both still alive.

"Well, shit," James said with some wonder in his voice. "I can't believe I'm about to say this, but I believe what he told me about my father's death and what happened in Vietnam so many years ago. It was a different and difficult time, and they were just kids. Kids who were asked to take on an enormous responsibility in a confused and uncertain war. What he has said is essentially what appeared in the report, though parts had been redacted. I got the confirmation I was looking for." Sarah tried to discern whether his face reflected sorrow or relief. Maybe it was a bit of both.

"But I'm still deeply saddened over fifty years later," he said. "I am sad for my mother, who lost her husband at such a young age. I am sad for myself that I lost the father I never knew. And I am sad for a generation of military and intelligence professionals who were caught up in something that turned out so badly. I am even sad for Nigel, for whom my father's death was clearly a horrific and life-altering experience."

She knew he needed a few minutes to let this sit, so she gave him some time. Finally, she decided she needed to say something even if it wasn't exactly what he needed to hear right now. "OK, James. I understand and respect your need to process what you've heard from Nigel about your father. And if things were different, I might tell you to take all the time you need. But I don't think we have the luxury of time right now. We need to get out of here, and we need to stop him from whatever he's planning for tonight. Then, most importantly, we need to find out what's happening with Heng and Jorani. Do you have any suggestions? Because I admit I have no ideas. I am also still very scared."

"As a matter of fact," James said with a glimmer in his eyes, "Bona missed a small knife I have taped to my foot in my sock, down inside my shoe. He may be large and intimidating, but he's about as thick as the cloud cover over Bangkok in a monsoon. I guess he didn't think to check my shoes. Let's work through this together. Maybe you can lower yourself to the floor and turn around so that your hands are near my feet and you can try to pull it out of the sock on my right foot. Without stabbing me. It's small, but once you've got it in hand we should be able to saw through these ropes, which seem quite thin. I will say it's pretty clear that Nigel and his team aren't in the business of kidnapping and holding people. I guess that's something."

Sarah dropped to the floor with as much grace as she could muster and in a few minutes had maneuvered her position so she was sitting in front of him but facing away from him. Her hands, tied behind her back, fumbled with his left ankle and shoe.

"It's my other right foot, Sarah. Not that one."

It was a good thing he couldn't see her face, because she knew it had turned a little red. She groped for his other foot and clumsily untied the shoe.

"Now reach down inside my sock. It's in a sheath on the bottom of my foot. See if you can find it." He flinched a few times as her fingers explored his sweaty sole. He was definitely ticklish. What a strange situation to be in with a government agent she barely knew.

"Got it," she said, slipping a minuscule knife sheath out from his sock. She reached her arms up and back until she felt him remove the knife from her grip. He awkwardly began to saw through the rope around her wrists.

"Be careful with that. I do value my hands." She'd been trying to make light of the situation and hoped she hadn't insulted him.

"Mm-hmm." He methodically sawed with the tiny knife, and moments later she felt the rope loosen. With a twist of her wrists, she was able to break it. She briefly massaged her hands, untied the ropes around her ankles, and then untied his feet first and then his hands. As she sat on the floor looking up at him in his chair, he took her by the shoulders.

"Sarah, I never meant for all of this to happen. You have been amazing, but I completely understand if you want to walk out right now, go back to your hotel, collect your passport, and get on the first plane home."

She considered those hands on her shoulders and refrained from reminding him that he had already offered an opportunity to back out several times, and each time she'd refused his offer. "Not on your life," she said. "I need answers and I need my friends. You're not going any-where without me."

He gently squeezed her shoulders before pulling away. "That's what I was hoping you'd say. So, let's go. I don't know where Nigel and Bona may have gone, but we should track Nigel before Bona. Because we're so close to the river, I suspect he'll be trying to leave by boat from one of the nearby piers."

She stood up, feeling stiff, and twisted first to the right and then to the left while quickly surveying all those statues and other antiquities. Her back cracked with each direction, and she wondered if he felt as stiff as she did from being restrained like that.

"Oh, and Sarah—"

"Yes?" She untwisted herself. He took a step toward her.

"Never mind. Let's get out of here. They took my phone, and I need to find a way to figure out what happened to our backup."

She refused to admit to herself that she'd been hoping for him to say something else, something . . . personal. "Wait," she said. "I know we need to get going, but I need a few minutes to register what is in here for future reference. If you've been straight with me, there are ministries and governmental agencies all over the region that are going to want to know what's in this warehouse. I know there isn't time to inventory all of it now, and there will be much work to do later, but I'd like to have a sense of it before I walk out of here. It's why you brought me, isn't it?"

He acquiesced, and for the next few minutes, Sarah wandered through what she could only describe as a wonderland of Khmer sculp-ture. There were pieces that looked familiar to her and pieces about which she had no knowledge. It all took her breath away. The history of Angkorian sculpture could be written with the examples in this room, which very few people had seen for eight centuries. She would do all she could to ensure that the works here were returned to their proper places in Cambodia.

She heard James's footsteps echoing down the corridor and then returning a short while later. He had found a landline in the office and reported that their backup was stuck in Bangkok traffic and wouldn't be here for some time. Though she found it ironic that police per-sonnel couldn't somehow navigate bottlenecks and gridlock, she also understood how that might be possible in a metropolis like Bangkok. She followed James out the steel-gated door into the small soi. By now the sky was rapidly darkening.

James pointed toward the river. "I don't know which way to go, but I would suggest we head south. I don't think there are any ungated piers back the way we came, so Nigel wouldn't have been able to access a boat in that direction." He suggested they go back to Charoen Krung Road as there wasn't a continuous walkway along the river from their position. Their path first took them through a large, deserted open space and then back to the river again, where they emerged onto the bank at a small walkway and pier. The area smelled strongly of fish from the nearby Fish Marketing Organization. In the distance, the usual river traffic, which didn't stop even after dark, was moving in all directions. The nighttime illumination of the boats gave a surprisingly festive air to the scene, though Sarah felt only anxiety.

James checked out both directions along the river. "I suspect Nigel normally accesses the river from a pier around here where access isn't locked, and as far as I know, these are the closest ones to his warehouse with easy access." They walked out onto several piers, keeping their eyes open for anything, or anyone, of interest, but as twilight deepened, it became harder and harder to make out anything at all.

Sarah kept spotting boats and even large pieces of debris in the water, but her discoveries amounted to nothing. She was about to give up when she could just barely see one more pier. "Look," she said. "Maybe over there?"

"Lead the way."

They picked their way, side by side, down a rocky, narrow path that hugged some old buildings lining the waterway. As they neared their destination, they saw it was a small rotting pier. It looked both decrepit and abandoned. James placed his hand on the small of Sarah's back and put his finger to his lips. He pointed ahead.

Sarah could see him now, not more than fifteen yards away, standing on the riverbank and looking out over the water as if awaiting something or someone. Nigel had something strapped across his chest. Was it her tote bag? Whatever it was, he clutched it tightly as if he couldn't bear to lose it.

"What do we do?" whispered Sarah.

"I only see Nigel," James whispered back. "It looks like the two of them have split up and he's by himself. I can't sneak up on him from way out here, but I'll try to crawl low against the side of the building until I'm closer. It's dark enough that I should be well hidden. Stay here and stay low. Don't make a sound. And if the backup arrives, point them toward me."

She nodded understanding. But as he crept in Nigel's direction, she realized she didn't understand much of anything anymore and in fact was becoming increasingly unsettled about whatever Nigel was planning to do—although she had no idea what that might be. She held her hands to her mouth and called out. "Nigel! It's me, Sarah. Please stop this and let us help you."

Nigel startled and whipped around. James was still hidden in the shadows.

"Please, Nigel," Sarah said. "Whatever it is that you have done, we can help you with whatever is coming."

Nigel did not reply, and he did not move. But James abruptly stopped moving. Sarah moved directly toward the pier, circumventing the route James had taken. She was out of his reach but not out of earshot.

"Sarah, for God's sake, stop!" he whispered. "Let me handle this."

She ignored him, confident she had everything under control for the moment. In a few seconds, she was on the pier, only a few yards from Nigel. The boards were more dilapidated than she'd initially thought. The stench of the water was stronger here, nearly overwhelming. Nigel had moved farther out on the structure and was now standing directly over the water. She was close enough now to confirm it was indeed her tote bag in his arms.

Nigel, who had kept his eyes on Sarah and seemed temporarily paralyzed by uncertainty, suddenly glanced behind her, back toward the path and the shadows where she knew James had been hiding. Immediately aware of a moving presence behind her, she turned around. But it wasn't only James approaching.

Bona lunged from behind James and hit him, first in the stomach and then in the face, with fierce force. James fell on the riverbank near the start of the pier, where it began to jut out into the river. She tried to run back to James, but Bona blocked her exit. So she ran the other direction, farther out onto the crumbling pier, and Bona followed her. Just as he raised his arm to hit her, the board under her gave way, and the left side of her body fell through toward the water. She felt her forearm twist unnaturally underneath her as it caught on the board, and her leg jammed against one of the ancient rotting pylons below. She clung to the part of the board that was still connected to the pier, above water, and breathed heavily. The pain was immediate and tremendous. She didn't know how long she could hold on.

Sarah also wasn't sure if she had the strength to pull herself back up onto the pier with her one good arm. The flow of the river looked intensely rapid farther out, and the racing water just a few feet beneath her was loud. Bona stood over her and could certainly stomp on her hand. How deep was the water right here? Could she overcome the current and swim the few yards to shore? She'd always heard that the river's current was awfully strong. She doubted she had the strength to fight the water, even on a good day.

From what seemed like far away, she heard Nigel yell, "No, Bona, stop. Get out of here. Now!" She felt the pier bounce as Bona turned and ran toward the riverbank. She could no longer see him. She doubted he would be back, and she desperately tried to figure out what to do. Maybe she had at least a couple of minutes to figure something out before he came back. But the arm clinging to the pier was rapidly tiring, and her hand slipped farther. She squeezed her eyes shut and held on with what had to be superhuman effort. But to no avail. Her hand continued to slip. She was destined to slide into the river and could already feel the water rushing around the bottom of her sandaled feet.

Suddenly, a hand grasped hers and pulled her up onto one of the few remaining solid boards of the pier, where she lay gasping.

Standing above her was Nigel, with simultaneously sad and frightened eyes. He let go of her hand and left her lying on the pier. She felt the bounce of the boards with each footstep he took. Again she squeezed her eyes shut. Maybe she hadn't been completely wrong all these years. She had been on the edge, and Nigel, once again, had rescued her.

CHAPTER 33

Banteay Srei, Angkor Archaeological Park
Sunday night

Dusk had fallen quickly. The sunset had been fiery, and Heng, beside Jorani, had watched the light slowly disappearing through the window. They hadn't said much. Now they were sitting in the semidark room, tense and awaiting whatever the next step would be. They had been given food a couple of hours previously, but they'd had little appetite. Other than the delivery of their meal and the removal of their trays a short while later, there had been no direct contact with any of the group since Anada had left hours ago. It was clear the guards were listening to everything they were saying, so they had whispered back and forth with ideas about how they might be able to escape. But they both knew it would be impossible. For the past hour, they had sat mostly in silence, not even really looking at one another. Heng had never felt so defeated, and Jorani was wrapped up in her own despair.

"Jorani, how did you know it was Anada?" Heng asked.

"He's brilliant. He needs money. You came back from Bangkok uncommunicative and almost distraught, and that kind of thing only happened once before, long ago, when you thought something was wrong with Anada. The pieces of the puzzle were there. I just put them together. This is not going to end well for him. It may not end well for us either."

Around 10:00 p.m., the door opened, and the two guards pulled them up, tied their hands yet again, and ordered them to follow. One guard led the way, and the second one brought up the rear of their small procession. They were unceremoniously dumped into the back seat of a car and driven a few minutes up the road to the temple site. Through the window, Heng could see Anada directing the men to move tools and trucks into position for the operation.

They were roughly dragged out of the car and brought to sit on a portion of one of the ancient walls of the outer temple precinct. They sat there for a few minutes watching the guards stride over to take up positions overlooking the workers. Anada walked over to them.

"As you can see," he said, gesturing first toward the workers and then the guards, "we are well organized and staffed, and I hope you understand now that we are serious. We are actually going to pull this off."

Heng had to admit that it all looked as if it had the potential for success, but he shook his head. He also said nothing, figuring it was better to let Anada keep talking. The more he talked, the more likely there would be time for someone to show up and help stop the madness.

"Of course," continued Anada, "it's not over until everything is safely on transportation out of the country, but I am confident there will be no problem there, and at any rate, my responsibility ends when the trucks leave the site."

Heng looked away from his friend, again shaking his head and feeling downtrodden. When he turned back to Anada, he glimpsed a smirk that seemed to convey, to the watching guards, that the situation was all under control. But then Anada leaned in to speak softly and directly into Heng's ear.

"Heng, listen to me very carefully, because I have to be quick here. Several months ago, I was approached by the Royal Thai Police and an agent of Homeland Security Investigations, who is based at the US embassy in Phnom Penh but who comes frequently to Bangkok. They told me they knew about the role I have played in Nigel's network, and they offered me a way out. I had been increasingly racked with guilt for the past few years about my role in Nigel's operations, and I wanted to try to make some kind of amends. I realize this doesn't make up for all the problems I have created in the past, but I am doing what I can now to atone. I am deeply ashamed. I know I have lost a great deal of face with people who are very important to me. Like you and Jorani. No one else here knows about this." When Heng started to speak, Anada pretended to cough but held his finger to his lips and whispered into his hand. "Don't say anything, please. Just listen." He met Heng's eyes for confirmation of understanding and then proceeded. "I'm with you and Jorani. I am planning to end this theft before it even starts by paying off the workers and telling them to go and then freeing the heritage protection police on-site, who we have immobilized over on the far side of the temple under the trees. There will be time for questions later. For now, I want you and Jorani to play along with the planned theft. Please do not let on to anyone that I have said anything to you. I have enough information to help you end Nigel's war on the cultural heritage of Southeast Asia. I may end up in prison, but I am willing to do what needs to be done. You, my friend, were very eloquent earlier today, but I want you to know that I am already on your side. Granted, I was forced to your side, but I am here. Now, though, it's time for me, and me alone, to take action. I will free you up and give you a signal. I would like you to run for the truck parked in the woods, just out of sight over there." He pointed to a stand of trees. "Take the truck and drive to the nearest office of the heritage protection police and alert them to the situation."

Heng looked up at Anada with astonishment on his face, nearly smiling.

"No," hissed Anada. "Give me a disgusted look. Show me your fear and loathing. Play it out for the sake of appearances even in this darkness. But tap your foot to assure me you understand and will cooperate."

Heng spat on the ground and said, "Anada, you are dirt and you will pay for what you're doing here." For a long moment, his foot remained inert. But then he tapped it, twice.

Anada stood up and hooked his thumbs in his belt loops. "Yes, you *would* say that. I don't think I will pay. I know that *you* will pay."

He snickered convincingly and then strode off toward the temple and the workers who were starting to prepare the equipment needed to remove some of the smaller sculptures from the lintels of the temple buildings.

Jorani had been sitting on the other side of Heng and had only heard fragments of what had been said. She placed her bound hands on his knee and whispered, "Tell me."

Heng's voice was urgent and low. "Anada just told me he is working with the Royal Thai Police and the Americans on an operation dedicated to stopping Nigel's large trafficking network. He plans to abort this operation tonight. I don't know whether or not to believe him, but I think I may have caught a glimpse of the old Anada when he was whispering in my ear. I want to believe him. And it seems a good choice right now. What more do we have to lose?"

"You mean besides our lives?"

He set his clasped hands over hers. "I do believe him," he said. "He told me that you and I need to play out the operation as if we were on our own. I don't know how he's going to do this, but I have to trust that he knows what he's doing."

Jorani's eyes widened. "Are you delusional? I don't know how you can think there's any good left in him. Very dubious. Where's the proof? Look at all we have been through, thanks to him, just in the past few days." She felt the pressure of Heng's warm hands on hers. "But I'm not sure what other choice we may have."

They sat there for a few more minutes before the guards who had come with Anada returned and ordered them to their feet. Heng and Jorani were marched toward the central area of the temple complex. They stood at the entry to the inner sanctuary, surveying both the temple and the looters at work with their tools of the trade, all they would need to cut the stonework and drag it to the waiting trucks.

"They must be going to take only small sculptures," Heng said, "as I don't see any equipment to take anything larger. They are probably planning to cut off some of the finest remaining pieces." Though not small by the standards of many civilizations, the temple was far more modest in scale than most temples at Angkor. The sculpture was its defining feature. It was no wonder that it was called a "jewel box" by many, and not surprising that it had drawn the attention of members of the French Geographical Service and someone like André Malraux. It was not as grand as the enormous constructions of Suryavarman II and Jayavarman VII in the central part of the Angkor Archaeological Park, but it was certainly one of the most beautiful, perhaps the *most* beautiful, temple in Cambodia.

Heng remembered the first time he and Anada had come here in the 1990s. It had been only a few months since the authorities had finished clearing the mines laid by the Khmer Rouge, and he and Anada were among the first to visit since the 1970s. Both had been overcome by reverent silence as they looked at the delicate undercut sculptures of pink sandstone and the powerful, squat temple guardians. Now, decades later, Heng was still overwhelmed. And he was particularly moved by the reproductions of the guardian figures in the central court of the temple. They were sculpted in the same style as the Uma and Shiva sculpture about which his father had written, and from which Nigel had ripped off the head, so many years ago. This temple was clearly a touchstone in his life. He regretted that he had not been here in years and that these were the circumstances under which he was visiting again.

But for now he needed to fight off the wave of sadness he felt and concentrate on their current situation. Which included the unsettling thought that there was a small possibility he and Jorani might not walk out of here alive.

"Bring them over here," ordered Anada. Jorani and Heng were roughly forced over to one side to sit under one of the remaining temple lintels, where their feet were tied up. "Let them watch before we get too far into the process. They may even learn something." He laughed and stared at the two of them.

The setup progressed, though thus far without any actual sawing of the stone or breakage. Heng was beginning to lose faith, when Anada called a break. The workers stopped and sat down, facing away from Heng and Jorani. It was almost as if they were embarrassed by what they were doing and didn't want to be identified. Anada walked over to them and lowered his face to within inches of Heng's. "I am going to cut the two of you loose now," he whispered, "but you need to pretend you are still bound. Blink your eyes twice if you understand." Heng and Jorani both blinked. "Good. Now, please continue to trust me."

He cut the ties binding their hands and feet.

Anada continued in a low voice. "Now, stay here until I give you a signal, which will be two waves behind my back, and then move toward the small truck that is parked about half a kilometer off in the forest over there. The keys are in the cab. Heng, drive to the office of the heritage protection police and alert them. Return with them when they come to the temple. I will stay here and ensure that nothing disappears from the site and will meet the authorities when they arrive and explain what has happened. By then the workers will be gone. I know that things will go badly for me, but this must end here and now."

Heng and Jorani exchanged the sort of look that two lovers might exchange just before they leaped off a cliff to their mutual doom. Heng was sure Anada caught it, and to Jorani he offered assurances that they would be OK. "Now, back to the plan. I was told by my contacts not to talk to anyone in the heritage protection police about this, prior to today, in case there might be someone there working with Nigel. So I have not told them anything. It may take you a little while to explain the situation. And it may take them a little while to muster their forces, but I will wait here." He placed a gentle hand on Heng's shoulder. "One more thing? A favor, Heng, given our long friendship? Can you do your best to ensure that my mother and my sister are taken care of? I don't think my mother is long for this world, but can you see that she is comfortable and that her funeral is honorable? My sister, as you know, is also very ill and requires a great deal of medical care. I would ask that you do the best you can for her as well. I have failed them, and I will pay for my failure."

Heng whispered hoarsely, "Anada, please do not talk like this. We will find a way out of this for you."

Anada smiled sadly and shook his head. "I am afraid it is too late for me, and we will be apart for a long time now. Oh Heng, please, don't cry. Not now, anyway. We must not give the guards any reason to suspect. Just confirm for me that you understand what to do when I give you my signal."

Heng was paralyzed, trying his best to keep the tears and sobs from escaping. But Jorani, always strong when Heng needed her to be, nodded her understanding to his best friend. As Anada headed back toward his group, he did not turn back to look at them. Jorani leaned into Heng's shoulder and rested her head on him.

They watched as Anada's team resumed working. After about five minutes, they saw his signal—two little waves of his hand behind his back. The workers were concentrating on removing the first works, and the guards were concentrating on the workers. Heng and Jorani crept away quietly, into the woods, where the cover of landscape protected them during their sprint to the truck. It was parked on the access road, right where Anada had said it would be. Heng put the key in the ignition, shifted the truck into gear, and pulled onto the road that led to the main Angkor site. He felt as if he were in a dream, but Jorani seemed to be more fatalistic about their situation. She kept her hand on Heng's arm as he drove. He counted on her strength to keep him steady and get them through the next few hours.

They drove through the darkness and soon began passing houses and small shops on either side of the road. Heng felt as if he had come home, now comfortable in his environment for the first time in days. He had intended to follow Anada's plan but suddenly decided that he would not go directly to the office of the heritage protection police but instead to the house of his friend Seng Arun, one of the heritage protection police officers with whom he had worked for many years. Heng wasn't completely sure who he could trust at this moment, but he trusted Arun completely. They pulled off the main road and up a narrow dirt path that led to Seng Arun's house, where a single light was illuminated in one of the rooms. Heng hoped he still lived there.

Jorani asked what he was doing. "This doesn't look like a police station," she said, her voice accusatory.

"Trust me," he said, and she sighed. "Why don't you stay in the truck? I'd like to have you as little involved in this as possible."

Jorani looked at him in disbelief. "Hell no! In the past few days I have been almost run over by a motorbike and robbed in Phnom Penh, kidnapped, tied up multiple times, hauled around in the back of a van across half of Cambodia like a sack of rice, and held captive in a house outside one of the most beautiful temples in the world. I think I'm about as involved in this as a person can be. I'm coming in with you."

Despite the seriousness of the situation, Heng grinned to himself. Jorani was back.

They climbed out of the truck and strode to the door. He still felt tentative but also more empowered than he had in days. Also, it was clear someone was home, so that was a good sign. Heng knocked.

"That's the first smile I've seen on you in days," Jorani said. She grasped his hand and squeezed.

The door squeaked open, and there stood Arun, beer in hand, wearing boxers and flip flops and no shirt. A TV flickered behind him.

"Arun, I cannot tell you how glad I am to see you!" He felt as if his knees were about to fail him. Thank goodness he had Jorani's hand in his.

"Heng?" A big grin spread across Arun's face. "What are you doing here? I'd heard you had disappeared! Come in, come in, and tell me what's going on. And Jorani, what are you doing here in the far reaches of Angkor with this guy in the middle of the night?"

He gave Heng an enormous bear hug and then hugged Jorani as well with just a little more grace, taking care not to crush the cast. After ushering them into the house, Arun quickly turned off the TV and asked them to sit and relax awhile.

Heng remained standing. "Arun, I'm afraid we don't have a lot of time to catch up, though I promise I will tell you everything when I can. Right now, there is a theft in progress at Banteay Srei, and we need to get officers out there immediately. I'll tell you all about how I know this afterward, but for now, you need to trust me. We need to go."

Arun didn't hesitate. He dashed into his bedroom and hurried back out with his uniform, keys, and phone. He slipped on his shirt, haphazardly buttoning half the buttons, and stepped into his pants.

With shoes still in hand, he followed Heng and Jorani out the door, and as he climbed into the passenger seat of the truck's cab, next to Jorani in the middle, he began to call and text his fellow officers and tell them where to meet up. Once the communications were taken care of, he asked for more details.

"There is one supervisor," Heng said, deciding not to reveal, just yet, that it was Anada. Better to keep Arun focused on the immediacy of what needed to be done. "And I saw at least seven workers and guards, though there may have been more who were out of sight. They hadn't started cutting into the sculpture yet, but I suspect they are planning to hack off some of the smaller pieces. They don't have the equipment to transport anything large, and anyway, I suspect it's the smaller pieces that collectors are looking for these days."

"Did you see any of the heritage protection police at the site?" Arun asked. "There should have been at least two of them."

"Yes, there were at least a couple of guards following the supervisor's orders. I don't know if they were part of the HPP or if they were just hired thugs. Or what the plans are for them. So if you're wondering if you'll be able to count on any help from them, the answer is I don't know."

"Are they armed?" Arun asked.

"Yes."

The night blurred past as the truck raced along the highway. "OK, I think I have a plan," Arun said. "Let's take the most direct route to get us there the fastest." He directed Heng about which turns to take, and soon they approached an intersection where two other trucks were idling. Arun told Heng to pull over, and the three of them hopped out of the truck.

Arun huddled his seven associates together. "OK, listen up, everyone. You all remember Heng, who worked here many years ago with Anada on some of the sculpture and architecture of Banteay Srei?" Heng and Anada both had been popular with the group of heritage protection police officers, as they had taken the time to explain more than most of the other students and scholars had. Plus there was the beer. There were murmurs all around, and most of the officers nodded their heads.

Arun continued. "Heng has information about a theft in progress at Banteay Srei." He paused and looked at Heng. "I can't explain too much about this right now, but we need to move. He isn't sure about the security situation on-site, which could mean that the assigned police are out of commission and we won't be able to count on them. Is everyone ready to go? Do you all have all of your equipment?"

Heng found the resounding chorus of affirmation heartening.

"OK, follow us," Arun said, "and we'll stop short of the site and regroup there." Arun took the wheel and led the convoy down the road toward Banteay Srei. The warm Cambodian night enveloped them in its soft humidity. Here and there, birds chirped in the distance, unaccustomed to nighttime traffic and activity on their isolated country road. The cicadas were also singing, and Heng remembered from his studies that they normally were quiet at night.

He attributed their music to the temperature and nearly full moon.

Arun briefly took his eyes off the road and leaned forward in the cab so that he could see across Jorani to Heng's face. "Just tell me how you wound up here from Phnom Penh. We can leave the rest for later."

Without taking his eyes off the road, Heng replied, "Tied up in the back of a van up the road from Phnom Penh to here. After being kidnapped when I was on my way to participate in a Zoom session at the museum."

Arun chuckled. "I'm sure you've got quite a story to tell." He said no more for the rest of the ride other than to speak briefly by phone with his team in the other trucks and reconfirm the plan of action. Heng thought about Arun's questions about the guards and hoped, silently, that nobody else was armed. He also remembered that Anada had said he would send the workers away before Heng returned with the police, which meant Anada wanted to keep the workers safe. But Heng said nothing. It was better not to set an expectation of safety and to have everyone on their toes.

When they reached the designated rendezvous point, everyone, including Heng and Jorani, got out of the trucks and began to walk toward the temple. As they approached, they all noted the silence.

"I had expected more noise—shouting, saws, the sounds of moving stone. This is very odd," said Arun. And when they reached the temple, and there was absolutely no sign of activity—just Anada sitting on one of the low walls of the outer temple enclosure, looking at them as if he had been waiting for them to arrive—Arun stopped in his tracks, clearly stunned. "What's this? First Heng and now you? What the hell are *you* doing here? And where is everyone else? I was told there was a major operation underway."

Anada came over and stood before Arun, Heng, and the rest of the group. "It's me that you want to take. There is no one else here. I am responsible for what has happened here tonight."

Arun looked at him, then at Heng, and then back at Anada, still confused and astonished. "I don't get it. What's going on here?"

Heng thought it was almost funny, watching Arun's disbelief. But his temptation to laugh might very well have been a desperate need to release all the stress and tension building for all this time. Besides, he was more than happy to let Anada explain everything right now.

"I can explain," Anada said. "Your heritage protection police officers are asleep, knocked out with GHB or some similar drug, under one of the trees on the other side of the temple. They will have fierce headaches tomorrow morning, but they will be fine." Arun motioned for two of his people to go and look for the missing officers. "Please be assured that neither of them was involved in any way with this operation. It was just me."

Heng now knew for sure that what Anada had told him was true, at least in part. After he and Jorani had left in the truck, Anada must have paid off the workers and instructed them to leave the site and get as far away as possible as soon as they could. Anada, his university colleague and his best friend, was going to take complete responsibility. Heng felt so sorry for Anada. And so sick.

Heng had to try to help Anada save himself. "But Anada, can you tell us about how this operation was planned and who was responsible and how you got involved with it? Is there anything you want to tell us about other partners in the theft? Please, Anada."

Anada was clearly not going to say anything more about the situation. He was not going to incriminate Nigel.

As Arun led Anada, in handcuffs, back to the trucks, Jorani pulled Heng aside and told him what she'd been busy doing while he and Arun had been dealing with Anada. "We're going to need to leave the truck with the police as evidence, so I've arranged for Arun's people to take us back to Siem Reap. We can get a little sleep there. I'm sure the heritage protection police, as well as the local police and APSARA, are going to want to talk to us tomorrow morning—and probably for the next few days—and I think the best thing we can do for ourselves, and for Anada, is to be well rested and prepared for that."

She was always so smart, his Jorani. They would need to wait awhile for the remaining heritage protection police officers to look around the temple and protect it as a crime scene, although Heng was sure by now that nothing had been taken, that Anada had stopped the theft in progress.

He turned when he heard the other truck and saw that Arun was about to back out, with Anada in the front seat beside him. Heng ran toward the passenger side of the cab and knocked on the window. "Don't worry, Anada! I'll do everything I can to help you out. I promise! I'll catch up with you in Phnom Penh."

When he climbed into the truck that he and Jorani would be riding in, he found the two heritage protection police officers in the back seat. They had been located just outside the west exit of the temple, and he felt confident that, as Anada had predicted, they would be fine, though they would likely need a few days off work to recover from the drugs. As they all made their way toward Siem Reap, Heng began to feel drowsy as well. After all he had been through, he felt as if he had also been drugged, and he was sure he would need some solid recovery time too.

CHAPTER 34

Bangkok
Sunday night

Sarah rolled over and looked to her right. She saw James lying motionless on the end of the pier closest to the shore. She must have been out of it for no more than a minute. As she rolled to her left, facing out toward the river, she saw Nigel gesticulating wildly at the lights of a motorboat rapidly approaching. Sarah closed her eyes, and then stood, swayed, and grabbed on to the nearest post to help her regain her balance. Her head spun, and she felt nauseated, and pain pierced her back as if someone had twisted her violently in two directions at the same time. Her lower left arm also hung at an odd angle, useless from below her elbow. It didn't hurt, though there was no sensation around her wrist when she squeezed it with her other hand, and she vaguely registered that this probably meant she was in shock. Her left leg, she then realized, was in tremendous pain when she tried to take a step and put weight on it. But she knew she needed to move. So, with heroic effort, she pulled herself up to her full height, and, grabbing the pier pylons one by one, she staggered toward Nigel, who was standing near the edge of the rickety structure.

"Nigel, stop! This is madness. I'll help you. I'll help you. We can figure this out. Just please, no. No. Please, Nigel."

He turned and appraised her sadly. For a second, she thought maybe the old Nigel was back. She felt a glimmer of hope. Then his eyes turned cold. "Sarah, my reputation is shot. No one is going to want to give me the time of day anymore. The world changed. I didn't. There's nothing left for me here. It's time for me to go." His voice was resigned and weary, so weak she could barely hear him. "Take the files and all the written information and books in my library. I was, and still am, fond of you, Sarah, despite what has happened over the past few days. Your—our—exhibition will be memorable. I hope you can remember me well."

He wobbled a bit on the pier. "Or at least not too badly." A grim smile punctuated that last statement.

Sarah looked straight at him, blocking out the glittering world of the Chao Phraya around her. Standing on this decrepit dock, she and Nigel seemed to inhabit the eye of a hurricane swirling around them. The rapidly flowing river, the boats with lights, bright and dim, sailing or motoring chaotically across and up and down the dark waterway, and the dark cloudless sky, with its hopeful moon and array of stars, were all in her peripheral vision as she concentrated on Nigel and the motorboat, which had almost reached the pier.

"Nigel. Please don't do this," she said in a strangled voice, not quite sure what *this* was. "You just saved my life. I can help you save yours. I will."

He slowly shook his head and turned away from her to walk the last few steps to the end of the pier. The motorboat sidled up into position. But Nigel didn't wait for the driver to tie up. He stepped down into the boat with his left foot and started to swing his right foot into the craft. The bag with the head, still strapped around his chest, seemed to interfere with his balance and made him appear unsteady.

As he straddled the water between the pier and the boat, the wake of a large cargo ship heading downstream toward the Gulf of Thailand caught the motorboat and rocked it violently from side to side. The boat tore away from the dock. Nigel teetered off balance for a few ex-cruciating seconds between the motorboat and the pier before falling into the roiling river.

Sarah staggered the few feet to the end of the dock to try to grab him, but in the time it took her to navigate the few steps, Nigel had already been carried several yards away by the river's strong current. He was rapidly disappearing. She could see the straps of the bag across his chest as he struggled against the force of the violent and muddy water. For an instant, she thought about jumping into the river after him and prepared to leap. Then he disappeared from view.

Without waiting for a single beat, the motorboat driver took off upstream and raced out of sight, never looking back at the man whom he had been tasked with collecting.

Sarah slumped down onto the dock. "No, no, no," she quietly said to herself before standing up and screaming. "No!" She fell back to the dock and lay there for a moment, turning her head to look at James at the other end of the pier. It was too dark to see whether he had re-gained consciousness, but what she could discern were silhouettes of other people.

"Royal Thai Police," a voice announced, and a flashlight shone at her. Other flashlight beams bounced around up on the riverbank, and in the commotion, she realized several guns had been drawn and someone was running down the riverside path toward the pier. She attempted to stand up, to run to meet them, but instead she collapsed in a heap on the rotting wood planks.

CHAPTER 35

Bangkok
Tuesday afternoon

Some kind of bird or animal was chirping insistently, slowly bringing Sarah out of a deep sleep. She opened her eyes and looked around at what seemed to be a darkened hotel room with beautiful furnishings and decor. Heavy curtains were drawn across a window, but a ray of light peeked through the crack where the curtains didn't quite meet. She lay there for a few minutes, then sat up with some difficulty. Gingerly, she extended her legs over the edge of the bed, placed her feet on the floor, and wobbled over to the window to open the curtains. The bright sunshine flooded in, along with the awareness that she was in Bangkok, overlooking the river from what she assumed was a room at the Mandarin Oriental Hotel. It was only then that she fully registered her left arm was in a cast and her left leg had been wrapped tightly in bandages from mid-thigh to foot. Her back hurt a great deal. In fact, everything hurt like hell.

The details of how she had come to be where she currently found herself were fuzzy. She slowly lowered herself down into the desk chair, grimacing as the base of her spine touched the seat. A pad of paper confirmed where she was. As memories began to surface and crystallize, some of them faded as quickly as they had come. The chirping began again. Sarah hoisted herself back up and out of the chair and shuffled across the room to her phone, where she noted she had missed three calls, all from James. And now he was calling again. She swiped to answer but was too tired, or too groggy, to even say hello.

After a few seconds, she heard his voice. "Sarah? Sarah? Are you there? My God, how are you feeling?"

"I feel as if I've been hit by a train, but I'm alive and I'm talking to you so I guess things could be worse." She glanced at her phone screen. "Is it really Tuesday afternoon? How did I get to a room in the Oriental? Where are you, and do you have Heng and Jorani? And are they OK?"

"Yes, it's Tuesday afternoon, and Heng and Jorani are fine. Do you feel well enough to talk? I can answer as many of your questions for which I have answers. I'm actually in the hotel lobby. Can you meet me down here in half an hour or so?"

"I'll be down in an hour. I'm moving pretty slowly."

"Perfect. I'll be waiting."

Sarah's muscles relaxed in the blasting hot shower. She had carefully unwrapped the bandages around her leg, which was almost completely black and blue, though apparently nothing was broken, and she took care to ensure that the cast on her arm stayed dry. After carefully drying herself and rewrapping her leg with the supply of clean bandages that someone had left for her on the bathroom vanity, she dressed in the sleeveless Khmer silk blouse that she'd had custom made in Phnom Penh years ago. Her black linen pants, which had been carefully ironed—*how and by whom?*—were waiting for her in the closet. Her black sandals were also there on the floor, and the diary which had caused so much angst had been placed on a shelf in the closet—as had, she noted with relief, her computer. As she dressed, she shrugged off the many questions about what must have happened during the past day and a half, especially as to how the diary had mysteriously moved from the safe at the Shangri-La to this room. Or why. "So much for security," she thought.

She looked at the diary. She felt safer having it with her, so she carefully wrapped it in the hotel laundry-service sack and put the small parcel in her shoulder bag, carefully not slinging it over her shoulder. She was still too sore for that. In the hallway, she called the elevator to take her down to the lobby.

As the elevator door opened, she saw James seated on a sofa. He stood and picked up a pair of metal crutches before hobbling over to her, a friendly smirk on his face. She surprised herself with how concerned she felt for him. "What happened to you?" she asked.

"Nothing much," he said, although it looked like more than nothing much. "I have what the doctor called 'extreme bruising' and 'serious sprains,' and I guess I've also got a couple of broken ribs and a broken bone in my foot. Not to worry. I'm sure I'll be fine in a few months. But, more importantly, what about you? You were pretty battered up night before last, and you're probably wondering how you ended up at Bangkok's most fabulous hotel. You were pretty dazed when the hospital released you and probably don't remember being brought here."

"I'm still trying to figure it all out. I think I'm OK. My leg, arm, and back all hurt, and the memory of being at a hospital, with people working on and around me, is coming back, but I think you had better begin from the moment we got to the rotting pier south of Wat Yannawa. I suspect there's a lot that I either don't remember or am choosing not to."

He agreed to fill her in on everything, but suggested they go outside and sit by the river. "It's such a beautiful day. Let me buy you a drink." The hotel lobby's expansive windows opened onto beautiful gardens, and beyond them was the Riverside Terrace restaurant. They sat down next to each other rather than across from one another, presumably so they could both have a lovely view of the river. James ordered a Singha, and Sarah ordered a sparkling water. They each took sips from their glasses and looked awkwardly at one another before gazing out over the river again.

"Well, I guess I'll begin," James said. "First, and most importantly to you, Heng and Jorani are in a room upstairs, also recovering. I knew that you would want to see them for yourself and pulled some strings with the Cambodian authorities to get them here, at least for a day or two. My understanding is that they're both still exhausted and a little out of it after what they've been through. They were both found at

Banteay Srei, along with a man Nigel had hired to be his chief collaborator on many of his thefts throughout Cambodia.

"Do you recall Nigel saying this was going to be their last theft?
The plan was to frame Heng for the crime, which seems a little crazy
to me given Heng's reputation in the field, but that's certainly something that you know more about. Anyway, I would describe both Heng
and his wife as being freaked out but fine."

She asked more about the man who was helping Nigel and where
he was now.

"About three months ago, the Royal Thai Police confronted him,
saying there was enough information on him and his role in Nigel's
network to send him to prison for many years. I was at that meeting,"
James said. "It was clear to me, during the conversation, that he felt
truly sorry for his role in everything and wanted to find a way out.
But he needed money for his family's medical and life needs. So he
agreed to work with us, and he has been passing information to us ever
since. It's largely due to him that we knew what was happening this
past weekend. He's been a great asset, shouldering the burden because
we couldn't make the heritage police aware of what we were doing in
case there were informers or someone working with Nigel on the inside there. As it turned out, there were not, and they were extremely
efficient and helpful. APSARA and the ministry of culture were, of
course, also aware of what was going on with the investigation. This
really was the last opportunity that we had to catch all of them in the
act."

Sarah opened her mouth but couldn't formulate the questions she
wanted to ask. She indicated he should go on.

"Nigel's assistant ended up freeing Heng and Jorani, who had been
held captive for several days, and setting them up with a truck to go to
the heritage police. When the police arrived at the scene, he surrendered without a fight."

A family walked past their table—a mother, a father, and two
young children—each appearing relaxed and joyful. The parents were
both wearing navy-blue shirts and held hands. The little girl, adorned
in a pink floral dress, was skipping from flagstone to flagstone. The
hooded adolescent boy stared down into his phone, laughing. It was
interesting how two different groups of people could occupy the same

space on the planet but have entirely different experiences and per-spectives. Though at this particular instant, Sarah didn't feel as if she were completely on planet earth.

"And Heng and Jorani?" Sarah asked. "They never were held responsible?"

"No, they weren't. They came here yesterday after preliminary in-terviews with a number of the cultural authorities in Phnom Penh, and they will need to go back later in the week as the investigation progresses. But I think all will turn out fine for them."

"Thank goodness." Sarah reflected back on the short time she and Jorani had spent together the previous week: eating Chinese food while trying to figure out what had happened to Heng, getting chased down by a motorbike, and landing in the same hospital room.

"Despite her not insignificant injuries," James said, "Jorani was desperately worried about you, and it was she who collected your clothes and things from the Shangri-La and got you into bed upstairs. Apparently, you have used the same safe combination forever, and Jorani somehow knew it. Probably not wise. When was the last time you changed your passwords? I also convinced the Thai police to let me retrieve your computer from Nigel's apartment. Just in case you decide that exhibition of yours should go forward."

His grin suggested he wasn't being nearly as critical of her as the question might have otherwise sounded. And he was right: She wasn't that great at taking appropriate security measures. She responded with her own grin but decided not to let the conversation digress in that direction. "So she was able to retrieve the diary from my room at the Shangri-La?"

"Yes, with help from the police and the hotel management."

This was all a lot to digest, and something in Sarah's heart and mind were racing as she remembered her earlier pressing question. "Who did you say Nigel was working with on his looting of temples around the region?"

"I don't think I did. His name was Anada Srisawat. Why?"

Sarah pursed her lips and shook her head. "No! That can't be pos-sible! I know him. He, Heng, and I were a tight little trio at the Ban Chiang excavation site many years ago when we were beginning our careers. He has been our contact at the national museum here in

Bangkok for this exhibition and was a contributor to the catalog. I can't believe he has collaborated with Nigel! I thought he and Heng continued to be very close, and I'm quite sure they saw each other every time Heng came to Bangkok. In fact, I think Heng would have described him as his best friend. If this is true, he must be crushed by this."

"Yes, Heng was devastated. My understanding is that Anada kept sinking deeper and deeper into a financial abyss because of the significant medical care his sister and mother needed. I was told that his father had died in a construction accident, on one of the big high-rise buildings here in Bangkok, years ago, and his remaining family members meant everything to him."

Poor Anada.

"And he was really the perfect addition to Nigel's group," James said, "with his tremendous art knowledge, familiarity to the authorities at Angkor, and apparently friendly relations with the heritage police and the local population. He would have been above suspicion."

"Where is he now?" Sarah asked, trying to figure out if there was anything she could do to help. Doubtful—but she hated to see him in such distress. She'd always liked him.

"He's in custody in Phnom Penh and will undoubtedly be prosecuted. I hope the fact that he has been working with us so intensely, and was instrumental in thwarting this final theft, will be looked upon favorably by the authorities."

"Didn't you promise him some sort of immunity in exchange for helping you?"

"We couldn't do it up front, but I'm hoping that collectively the group can sway the Cambodian government. In my experience, it's hard to predict what will happen. I will certainly be doing everything I can to ensure that he is either freed or serves a short sentence. I will also do what I can to try to protect his reputation in the field. We have documentation confirming that Anada had been working diligently with us before the attempted theft, and I'll share this with the authorities. I hope it'll help. Though he may have a long and difficult road ahead of him. I'm sure any help from you and Heng would be appreciated."

Sarah nodded. "Who else is being prosecuted?" Nigel floated up in her mind, but she didn't want to think of him right now. Her question really revolved around any others on the team who might share the criminal burden with Anada.

"No one. Anada let all the workers who were helping him with this theft flee after he sent Heng and Jorani to notify the heritage protection police. When the police arrived, he was the only one there, so he'll be facing the consequences solo unless they can round up the site workers. Meanwhile, I've already heard that the cultural authorities there are planning to officially thank Homeland Security Investigations for their participation in stopping Nigel. I imagine you'll somehow be recognized for your contribution too."

Their server brought the check, and Sarah reached for her handbag. But she was far too stiff to get to it faster than James could whip out his credit card. "Thank you," she said.

"You're most welcome. And you may also want to thank me for the news that Bona has been picked up by the Thai authorities and is being held in custody. I'm not sure what will happen to him, but I am sure the police will want a statement from you about the encounters you've had with him."

She asked whatever happened to the police who were supposed to be there at the warehouse to serve as their backup. "Why were they a no-show? Did they really get stuck in traffic?" She lifted the arm in the cast, as if showing it to him. "Maybe things would have turned out differently if they'd kept their promise."

"Yeah, I'm sorry about that. But yes, it's true. My HSI colleague and the Royal Thai Police got caught in Bangkok's infamous traffic. At least they got us both to the hospital."

Somehow she couldn't muster much gratitude for that small measure of protection. "What about Ahmi? Is she OK?"

"Ahmi disappeared when she left Nigel's house. We've tracked her down, and she admitted she was afraid, given what she knew, though she resurfaced later when word got out about what happened to Nigel. She is back at home now with her family. Looks like no one is holding her responsible for anything. In fact, the US ambassador's family has offered her a position working at their residence, and she is delighted at this new prospect. I'm guessing that life with Nigel had become quite difficult over the past few years, and she is relieved to be out of that situation and into a safer environment."

The server returned with James's card, and he took the last sip of his beer before checking his watch. But Sarah wasn't quite ready to leave. She needed to ask the big question.

"And Nigel? The last I remember, he had fallen into the river, and the boat which had apparently come to take him away sped off. I remember glancing around for a life preserver. And I think I thought about jumping in after him. Is he . . . ?"

James hung his head and peered up at her. "He's gone, Sarah." His voice was gentle. "The Royal Thai Navy searched for his body yesterday for several hours, but by now it could be anywhere along the length of the Chao Phraya or somewhere in the Gulf of Thailand. He was probably dragged down by the weight of the bag with Uma's head. I remember he had it strapped to his body, and he probably couldn't wrestle himself free."

"That head was his first theft. Back in 1975," Sarah said. "And ironically, it helped to bring him down in the end."

James said he'd been pondering this too. Perhaps Nigel could have survived under normal circumstances, but between the weight of the bag and a freak and unseasonal recent rainstorm that triggered a rise in water level, and a swifter current for a few hours, the odds were against him. "Besides, he was getting up in years," he added.

Sarah hoisted herself out of her chair and shuffled over to the railing. She surveyed the overall view and then watched the water flowing along the river's edge. Poor Nigel. She turned around toward James and said, softly, that he couldn't have survived no matter what the circumstances. "Nigel didn't know how to swim."

His absence was just beginning to make an appearance in her heart. Even after all the bad things he had done and even some of the hurtful things he had said, he was one of the dearest people in her life. She wasn't willing to admit the truth. "I wish I knew where Nigel had been planning to go in that boat. It would have been a long ride to Cambodia or Malaysia. Maybe he was just headed farther south to Hua Hin or somewhere else on the coast. Maybe he just wasn't thinking clearly anymore."

James beckoned her with his hand. "Sarah, please sit down. Nigel is gone. You need to accept that. And I admit I can't say that I can even begin to understand completely what he meant to you, but I will say that I'm sorry. I know you'll need some time to become adjusted to his death and to what he had done in his later life. I will also say, though—and you may not want to hear this—that the cultural heritage world is better off without him, despite his contributions over the years."

Sarah wanted to hate James just then. Or slap him, maybe. How dare he say something so irreverent about this man who had done so much for the Khmer art world! And the man who had been his father's dear friend too. She felt her cheeks reddening and pivoted back to the river so that he couldn't see her anger. Or maybe so he couldn't see her conflicted emotions at the moment.

"Lastly," James said, after walking over to the railing and standing beside her, "I want to let you know that you have been better in the field over the past week than many of the agents I've worked with in the past—smart, knowledgeable, cool under tough conditions, and willing to follow my lead, even though I realize I probably didn't do much to deserve the support. I'm not suggesting you make a career change"—he laughed—"but I did want to make sure you knew how I felt."

Sarah glanced around to see if the restaurant was crowded. She wasn't ready to leave but knew they couldn't commandeer a table if there were other customers waiting. Fortunately, there were several vacant tables, including the one where that adorable family had been seated. How long had she and James been sitting there reliving everything?

She returned to her chair, and he followed her lead, returning to his. Suddenly, she felt much older than her years and not a lot wiser. "I know, I know. I'm reconciling myself to what happened with Nigel, and I'll do my best to move on. The years I spent with him feel like many life experiences. I'll never forget, but I'll try to favor the good and minimize the bad." She shuddered as she said those last words. "It's funny. Nigel was once probably the most important person in my life, and now when I close my eyes and try to picture him, I get nothing. My brain seems to have blanked him out. He'd just always seemed so . . . bulletproof to me."

She closed her eyes and continued, "I also am pretty desperately wondering what is going to happen with me and my exhibition, which was the reason I was here to begin with. This kind of stuff just doesn't happen in conjunction with major art exhibitions. Is the museum even going to continue to support it after what has happened? These days, even a whiff of scandal is enough to tank a project. Crap, do I even still have a job? I haven't looked at my email for days. And I'm definitely not looking forward to some of the conversations I'll need to have when I get home. Damn."

She paused, then again said, "Damn."

She opened her eyes and looked at James. "And what about you? As long as I'm baring my soul here, what about you and me? Any chance we could keep in touch? We've been through a lot in the past couple of days, and we both have a lot of thinking to do. Might it be useful to think things through together? I'd sure like some help here."

James grinned at her and took both of her hands. She tried not to flinch when he moved the arm in the cast.

"Sounds like a plan to me, Sarah Burroughs."

She took a deep breath, relaxed her shoulders, and felt her first authentic smile in days. "Well, OK then. Let's figure it out."

James leaned forward, and she was almost sure he was going to kiss her, until he was interrupted by a subtle cough. They both looked up to find Heng and Jorani, standing a few yards away and holding hands. A cormorant flapped its powerful black wings overhead, and a fish splashed out of the water and then back in.

Her dear friends were both beaming, and Sarah got up from her chair as quickly as she could to embrace the two of them together and then each of them separately. Her body wasn't thrilled with her movements, but she didn't care. As she wiped tears of joy from her cheeks with the back of her good hand, Jorani pulled a packet of tissues from her bag and handed it around.

Sarah's face was growing tired from so much smiling. There would be plenty of time later to hear their version of what had happened to them, filling in the details beyond the bones of the story recited by James. She was more interested in seeing the two of them standing before her, alive and mostly well, though they also both looked exhausted, with dark circles under their eyes. Jorani's arm was still in a cast, which Sarah thought must have been awfully awkward and painful during those hours she was tied in restraints. Jorani moved slowly, like an old woman, and Heng looked as if he had aged ten years. Despite their smiles, they also looked sad.

James had warned Sarah that Heng had seemingly been in denial about Nigel's and Anada's involvement in so many thefts, but the sorrow on his face suggested that he was beginning to come to terms with the full truth.

Heng broke through the joyful moment first. "Sarah, I don't know what to say about our friends Anada and Nigel. You know, Anada was my best friend. I have shared more with him than almost anyone else on the planet, even Jorani. I am heartbroken at what has happened, and I don't fully understand it, though I will try to do all I can to ensure he is set free. I know a little of the story, including that he began to work with the Royal Thai Police and US HSI, but I am going to need someone to explain the whole thing to me.

"And I don't know where to begin to talk about Nigel. The authorities in Phnom Penh told us what happened on Sunday night and that Nigel's body hadn't been recovered. I don't know what to say. I believed in him, and though I knew his faults and flaws, I thought I understood him. Clearly, I was wrong. Maybe it was because I was so wrapped up in my own work that I didn't notice any small changes that came over him over the years. I think I just attributed them to aging rather than anything more nefarious. I am so very sorry for both of us, and I am sorry for Nigel. He was a lion in the field. The art world is such a changed place now, and there will probably never be anyone again who can play the kind of role with the introduction of the art of a relatively unknown culture to the world. I know I'm going to miss him terribly."

"Me too," Sarah said. "A lot."

"But," Heng said, "I also have to say that, on some level, I am incredibly angry with both of them for having deceived me—Nigel for a long time, and Anada for the past many years. I may have been naive, but they betrayed me, and it will take a while for me to get over that."

Jorani gently said, "Not now. That conversation is for later, Heng."

Heng continued in a calmer tone. "I am also beginning to wonder if Nigel's rescue of me from the camp in Thailand so many years ago wasn't just happenstance. He may have known who I was and who my parents were and may have decided that it was a way in which he could atone a little for what he had done, and more importantly what he had not done, in Phnom Penh in 1975. I am haunted by wondering if he could have saved my parents. I have a lot to think about."

Sarah shook her head and blew her nose. "Don't be so hard on yourself, Heng. We both failed to notice any signs of a change of that magnitude. Maybe there was nothing to notice and all the change was on the inside? Early dementia, maybe? Or immense guilt and shame? I wonder if Nigel ever tried to ask for help or tried to talk to us about what he was doing or how he was feeling. What if he did and we missed it? I don't know. I do know that despite the anger I feel right now for what he did to me, I still inexplicably admire and respect his memory on some level. How do you measure the great good that someone does during their life against the major missteps they've made? How does it all balance out? We can both grieve, but then we need to move on. And the sooner we start, the better."

Jorani reached out for Sarah's hand—the one not holding a tissue. "Sarah, I want to apologize for leaving the hospital that night without waking you. I've been thinking about this over and over and feeling like I abandoned you. But I couldn't take the chance you would try to stop me. You must have been frantic with worry, but I didn't know what else to do. I was desperate."

"You're right. I was frantic. James can attest to that." She nodded toward him. "And I understand why you did what you did, though I still wish that you had shaken me awake to talk about it. I'm honestly not sure if I would have tried to keep you there. I probably would have let you go and then incessantly worried about you anyway. I am just glad you two are OK." She laughed. "And please, let's promise to not ever do this again."

Sarah reached down to her bag, drew out a small parcel, and handed it to Heng. "Here is your father's diary. I have been its keeper ever since Jorani and I locked it into the safe in my room at Le Royal, which seems like a lifetime ago. Since then, it's been in a series of five-star hotel-room safes as well as in my checked luggage on a flight from Phnom Penh to Bangkok, and it has survived all that in addition to everything it survived before you discovered it. I'm guessing Nigel kidnapped the two of you in large part so that the contents of this diary were never made public. It wasn't just about Banteay Srei; he needed to get his hands on this notebook. But of course it really belongs to you and to Cambodia's heritage and history, and I am grateful to no longer be responsible for it. I'd sure appreciate, though, having the opportunity to see a translation of the entries at some point in the future, if they aren't too personal and painful for you to share. We might even be able to incorporate passages in the exhibition. I can already envision it displayed in the gallery devoted to the history of the Angkor site after the fall of the empire. But honestly, Heng, it's your call. If you don't want to share it, I understand."

Heng gripped the diary tightly with both hands as if weighing not just Sarah's request but everything it represented. The notebook was a lifeline for him to understand more of his own life story, much of which had been upended in the past two weeks.

After a respectful moment of silence, James extended a hand out toward Heng while remaining balanced on his crutches. "I suppose it's time for a proper introduction, Heng. I am James Carlyle, Homeland Security Investigations agent attached to the US embassy in Phnom Penh. I am the one with whom Anada has been working, and I will do everything I can to ensure he is treated fairly. He did really good work for us. And so did Sarah in these past few days. I feel like I know you incredibly well by your reputation and especially through everything Sarah has told me. I am sincerely impressed with your calm and levelheadedness in this difficult situation and thank you for everything you did."

Then he repositioned his crutches and held his hand out to Jorani. "Jorani, I saw you briefly in the hospital in Phnom Penh, but you were pretty sedated, and we didn't speak. I also know your reputation as a sculptor, and I was very impressed with the work I saw at your show at the Three Rivers Gallery in Phnom Penh last year. But more importantly, I know that you and Heng mean a tremendous amount to Sarah. I just can't tell you how very pleased I am to finally meet both of you."

For the first time in days, Heng fully grinned his sly grin. "I have the feeling we may be seeing each other more in the future."

Jorani nodded vigorously, giggling. James laughed. It almost seemed everyone except Sarah was in on a secret, or maybe on a joke where she didn't understand the punch line. She acknowledged them with a cautious smile.

The four of them stood looking at one another. Sarah couldn't decide if it was an awkward silence or the kind where you were so comfortable with the people around you that you didn't feel the need to fill the space with words. She also didn't know enough about James to know if this was a typical or unusual week in his life, but she was sure that it had been a most extraordinary week for Heng and Jorani. And it certainly had been for her as well. Had it really just been a week since she'd gone to Nigel's for the Zoom meeting and Heng had disappeared?

Finally, Jorani interrupted the lull. "Has enough time passed since your first round of drinks, Sarah? I think it's time for another round . . . to talk about anything but the last week."

Laughing, they walked and shuffled and hobbled to a larger table and sat down, overlooking the dynamic life on the River of Kings.

CHAPTER 36

San Diego
Five months later

From the balcony overlooking the gallery, Sarah watched Heng and Jorani escort the Cambodian ambassador to the US, along with his family, around the opening installations of the exhibition. They were accompanied by the museum's director and board president, both of whom had wisely let Heng take the lead with his fellow countryman. Heng, decked out in a tuxedo that was perfectly crafted by one of Bangkok's foremost tailors, had been delighted to learn that this particular form of dress was at times called a "penguin suit" in English. In her long, brightly colored Cambodian silk dress, Jorani looked like a tropical bird and clearly caught the gaze of many guests as she moved gracefully through a sea of black formal wear. She pointed out important objects to the dignitaries, and Heng joked with them that he was known as "Heng the Penguin." Neither showed any effects of their experiences five months ago, though Sarah knew they were both still recovering, more mentally than physically. They were changed, as was she. They were all figuring out how to deal with their new reality.

Heng had finally translated all the entries in his father's diary and in the process had discovered that Nigel had urged Sokha to leave Phnom Penh with Bopha and had offered to facilitate their departure. Sokha had declined the offer with tragic consequences. It had been one more devastation for Heng, but it had affirmed for him that Nigel had had the best of intentions toward his family.

The exhibition was poised to be a resounding success with both the critics and the general public—something, Sarah thought wryly, that was not at all common these days. To the contrary, exhibitions of Hollywood art and other populist topics ruled. Maybe the art of the Khmer Empire would one day become as popular as Egyptian antiquities, impressionist paintings, and gold artifacts, three surefire winners from around the world—though probably not. The art was artistically superb, and the history was poignant and fascinating both in terms of ancient mythologies and relatively recent political turmoil. But it remained a little inaccessible to most Western audiences. The sheer logistic and financial challenges of mounting this exhibition, filled with stone sculptures weighing tons, had been daunting, and she doubted there would be another exhibition of Khmer art of this scope and scale anytime soon. Still, she was pleased to note there were a lot of important, influential, and smart people here at the opening, and she knew they had come from all over North America and western Europe to be here tonight.

She heard the soft tap of a cane, accompanied by the steady click of men's leather-soled dress shoes, behind her. She knew it would be James, also attired in a Bangkok-tailored tuxedo.

"It's time to go down and meet your admiring public," he said, lightly settling his hand on the back of the Cambodian silk jacket she wore over her long black silk dress. Sarah flinched, drew away, and yelped quietly. The broken bones in her arm, and the contusions and deep bruises on her leg, had healed over the past few months. But her back was still recovering. Her doctor had assured her that soreness and pain would eventually disappear, but she might have some significant aches and pains for a while. When she had groaned at that news, he had sternly told her that she was lucky to be alive. At least she didn't need to walk with a cane, like James, whose broken foot hadn't healed as quickly as he'd hoped.

"Oh my God, I am so sorry," James said, withdrawing his hand as if he had touched a hot pan on the stove. "You look extraordinary tonight, not at all like someone who went through what you did, and I just wasn't thinking. My deepest apologies." He kissed her softly on the back of her neck, sending pleasant shivers down her spine. "Is that better?" he asked, turning her toward him as he tucked a strand of errant hair behind her ear.

As it had turned out, the mental and psychological damage she had incurred over the past few months was more problematic than the physical travails. She couldn't shake the vision of Nigel's body as he was carried away from her, swept by the chocolate-brown waters of the Chao Phraya out to the Gulf of Thailand. His body had eventually been recovered and cremated in Bangkok. Sarah had not gone to the ceremony, nor had any of the dealers, collectors, or wealthy patrons of the arts whom he had served during his life. The tote bag with the head of the goddess Uma had not been strapped around his body when he was found and was probably at the bottom of the river or the Gulf of Thailand.

It was an indicator of his continuing hold on her life and work that she had wondered, more than once, what he would think of this exhibition, which was the culmination of all their work—the exhibition that, it was already clear, had cemented her reputation in the museum world. Given everything that had come out recently about his activities of the past decades, his role and contribution to the exhibition had been downplayed in the final installation, though he had been given credit where it was specifically due. She had also modified and amended the interpretation and information in the galleries to ensure that the section of the exhibition about Banteay Srei was the highlight. Somehow, perhaps irrationally, she felt she owed that to Nigel and to everyone else who had been so affected by those events of five months ago. So it wasn't so much the physical pain when James had touched her that had triggered that reaction. It was everything else that accompanied the pain.

She sighed and summoned a smile. "It's OK. I'll be all right. We will both be all right, though who knows how long it will take."

James lightened her mood by tapping his cane on the floor. "Yes, you're right, though the sooner I can lose this cane, the happier I will be. The doctor told me this morning that I should be able to stop using it in a couple of weeks if I feel stable enough on my feet." He offered his arm. She slid hers around his and mentally prepared herself to smile at all the attendees.

The life in which she had been so comfortable and content just a few months ago seemed like the life of a person she no longer knew. Had this all been worth it? There were moments when she wondered if she had risked her life, and another person had lost his, for something as trivial as an art exhibition, even though she knew the exhibition was not responsible for what had happened and the stakes of the events of five months ago were far higher, and the consequences further reaching, than an art show. Nigel's smuggling ring had been broken, and with its end, the governments and ministries of culture of many of the nations of Southeast Asia had breathed a sigh of relief.

His collection was now in the process of being dispersed back to the countries of origin, according to the plan Nigel had set into place. She had been advising the various parties involved with as much information as she had. Soon there might be no evidence that all this had actually happened, though she was sure there was documentation of it in his files, which were locked up in Thai police custody. She hoped that someday they would be available to scholars, or at least, she thought with an internal smile, to her.

They all—Sarah, James, Heng, Jorani—had done as much as they could with the Thai and Cambodian authorities to try to ensure that Anada was treated as fairly as was possible under the circumstances. There was no question he had made a huge mistake in working with Nigel. But because he had thwarted the theft at Banteay Srei and given other pertinent information to the authorities, the Cambodian government declined to prosecute him. Unfortunately, Anada had lost his position at the national museum in Bangkok. Sarah had not spoken to him since she had left Thailand, but Heng had been in contact and was trying to help his friend put the pieces of his shattered life back together. It was probably the best that could have been expected under the circumstances.

And James? She still hadn't fully absorbed the significance of this person beside her who had become such an integral part of her life in such a short time. Was this a direct result of what they had been through? Would a relationship that had been born in crisis and chaos survive the normal day-to-day of a routine? And could they sustain it across a separation of fifteen time zones? Or *should* it even survive? He had talked about his mandatory retirement in the next few years. They could wait and see. She didn't know what the future had in store, but tonight she wasn't going to let it intrude on what had been accomplished and was on exhibit on the floor below.

"Earth to Sarah," James said as he pressed the button on the wall. "It's time to go downstairs. We're taking the elevator, if you don't mind. No stairs tonight."

They rode down in companionable silence, still arm in arm. As the elevator doors opened on the main level, Sarah and James strolled slowly together through the murmuring penguins and colorful birds in attendance, all of whom congratulated and applauded Sarah as the couple made their entrance into her exhibition and were swallowed by the crowd.

AFTERWORD

Uma's Head is a work of fiction. Although the main characters—Sarah, Nigel, James, Heng, and Jorani—may resemble actual players in the world of Southeast Asian art, they are all products of the author's imagination. Any similarities between them and actual people are strictly coincidental.

There is no San Diego Museum of Asian Art, though the Asian collection at the San Diego Museum of Art and the exhibitions of objects from Asia at the Mingei International Museum are excellent and worth a visit.

Historical events and the actions of real people have been mentioned in the narrative at several points, including the 1914 relocation of the sculpture of Uma and Shiva from the tenth-century temple at Banteay Srei, to what became the National Museum of Cambodia in Phnom Penh, by an officer of the Geographical Service of the French Army. Another well-documented event was the attempted theft of sculptures from Banteay Srei in 1923 by André and Clara Malraux and a friend. They were arrested by the French colonial police on Christmas Eve of that year, though none served any time. André Malraux was appointed to the post of French minister of cultural affairs in 1959 by Charles de Gaulle.

Historians estimate that during the period from 1975 to 1979, 25 percent of Cambodia's population died in the Khmer Rouge's attempt to return the country to Year Zero. Most of the population of Phnom Penh was forced into the countryside during the first weeks of Khmer Rouge control in April of 1975. Some residents of the city were killed on the grounds of the Cercle Sportif, now the site of the United States embassy.

Sources vary as to whether the National Museum of Cambodia remained open during that period. The Khmer Rouge apparently used the building for housing and offices for the regime and allowed important foreign visitors to tour the galleries. As of 1978, the national museum seems to have been relatively intact. But by 1979, it had been ransacked.

The head of the goddess Uma from the sculpture of Shiva and Uma taken from Banteay Srei, which is still in the collection of the National Museum of Cambodia, did disappear from the museum under unknown circumstances, though it was probably at some point in 1973. The author has taken liberty with that date for the storyline.

Foreigners have removed sculptures from Angkor since the middle of the nineteenth century, when French naturalist Henri Mouhot "rediscovered" the site for the West. (It should be noted that the Cambodians always knew the site was there.) Many of the objects taken out of the country during the time the French colonized Indochina found a home in the Musée Guimet in Paris, the largest and most important collection of Khmer art outside Cambodia. Other prominent collections of Khmer art can be found in museums and in the hands of private collectors.

Angkor was a source of great pride to the Khmer Rouge, though they neglected it and fast-growing vegetation took over. Major looting of it and other archaeological sites of Cambodia did not actually become rampant until the decade of the Vietnamese occupation of the country from 1979 to 1989.

In more recent years, the looting of the main Angkor site has slowed significantly due to the diligent work of APSARA, the authority for the protection and management of Angkor and the region of Siem Reap. However, outlying Khmer temples have remained targets for thieves over the past few decades.

The Ministry of Culture and Fine Arts, which oversees the National Museum of Cambodia, also plays a critical role in the preservation and interpretation of Khmer art.

As a part of its work, Homeland Security Investigations, a division of US Immigration and Customs Enforcement (ICE), investigates and combats the illicit trafficking of cultural property, art, and antiquities into, out of, or through the United States. The agency has a special focus on the criminal networks involved.

Museums, galleries, auction houses, and private collectors around the world have slowly begun to return works of Khmer art to their homeland. Thus far these recoveries represent a fraction of the art that has disappeared from the sites of what was once an incomparable empire.

The Kingdom of Cambodia continues to request the repatriation of its material cultural heritage.

Uma's head is still missing.

ACKNOWLEDGMENTS

For early readings, valuable critiques, wise advice, and general encouragement, I am indebted to Linda Shaw, Anne Spackman, Joanne Niedzwicki, Debra Wells Thayer, Joyce Motylewski Hansen, Davies Stamm, Marcy Kaplan, Marianne Pantano Rutter, Barbara Whitney, and Carolyn Kelly.

Margaret MacLean's expertise in issues related to the trafficking of cultural property saved me from major errors, and her adroit use of the word *lame* saved me from heading in the wrong direction with at least one plot line.

My thanks to Joanna Rom for the introduction to John Burgess, who was very generous in sharing his expertise on the archaeological site at Angkor and its history after the decline of the Khmer Empire as well as his broad knowledge of Cambodia.

I am very grateful to John McDermott, who supplied the photograph of the sculpture of Shiva and Uma, which appears at the front of the book.

Tammy Greenwood's online novel-writing course through San Diego Writers, Ink during the COVID-19 pandemic gave me the impetus to dig out the files and research and begin writing.

Thanks to the writers, editors, and critics at *The Economist*, whose review, "Gods on Display" (in the June 7, 2007, edition, page 98), of Angkor: Sacred Heritage of Cambodia, an exhibition held at the Martin-Gropius-Bau in Berlin, wisely confirmed my suspicion that wondering about the location of Uma's head was worthwhile.

My heartfelt thanks to all those at Girl Friday Productions—Christina Henry de Tessan, Kristin Duran, Gail Kretchmer, Adria Batt, David Fassett, Paul Barrett, and Kylee Hayes, who are the ones who skillfully guided me through the process of creating a book I'd been thinking about since my first visit to Cambodia in 1994.

Lastly, I owe an enormous debt to all the guides, tuk-tuk drivers, and conservators at the Angkor Archaeological Park and to all those obsessed with the Khmer Empire who have shared their expertise and enthusiasm with me over the past thirty-plus years. Your world is extraordinary. I hope this book helps bring that to life.

Mistakes, errors, stretches of authenticity, and flights of fancy are solely my responsibility. Some events depicted in the book would not have played out the same way in reality. Such is fiction.

ABOUT THE AUTHOR

Kristin Kelly is an art historian and former museum professional who
first fell in love with Southeast Asia on a trip to Vietnam in 1993. She
has authored two nonfiction books on Southeast Asian cultural heritage and lectured for Bryn Mawr College's Alumnae Association travel
program. A longtime Californian, her thirty-five-year career in museums and cultural heritage included significant time with the Getty
Trust. She holds an AB in history of art from Bryn Mawr College and a
PhD in art history and archaeology from Columbia University.

www.ingramcontent.com/pod-product-compliance
Lightning Source LLC
Chambersburg PA
CBHW020134120726
47903CB00007B/2254